Special thanks to Jenny Walters
Thanks also to Richard Jones M.R.C.V.S., for reviewing the
veterinary material contained in this book.

Copyright © 1999 Working Partners Limited
Created by Working Partners Limited, London W12 7QY
Text copyright © Working Partners Limited
Illustrations copyright © Ann Gowland

First published in hardback in Great Britain in 1999
by Hodder Children's Books

A Catalogue record for this book is available
from the British Library

ISBN 0 340 73622 4

Typeset by Avon Dataset Ltd, Bidford-on-Avon, Warks

Printed and bound in Great Britain by
Clays Ltd, St Ives plc

Hodder Children's Books
A Division of Hodder Headline plc
338 Euston Road
London NW1 3BH

LUCY DANIELS
Perfect Ponies

Keeping Faith
Last Hope
Sweet Charity

Illustrated by Ann Gowland

Hodder
Children's
Books

a division of Hodder Headline plc

To Eva Mein – a perfect friend

Keeping Faith

One

Josie Grace jumped down the last step from the bus to the pavement and stood there for a moment, hesitating.

'Come on, Josie!' said her friend Anna Marshall, following on behind and jostling her out of the way. 'There's going to be a pile up if you don't get a move on.'

Anna's twin brother, Ben, was close on her heels, swinging a huge rucksack stuffed full of school books and his football boots. 'Are you OK, Josie?' he asked quietly as the bus drew away. 'You've hardly said a word all the way back from school. Is anything wrong?'

'No, not really,' Josie muttered. 'It's just that – oh, it doesn't matter.'

'Of course! How could I have forgotten?' Anna groaned, hitting herself on the forehead with the palm of her hand. 'Oh, Josie, I'm sorry. Some friend I am. The local paper comes out today, doesn't it?'

'So what?' said Ben, looking puzzled. 'Why's that such a big deal?'

'I'll explain in a minute,' said his sister, hustling him off towards the village of Northgate, where they lived. 'I'll come up and see you later,' she called back to Josie. 'Promise me you won't get depressed!'

'I promise,' Josie said with a wave and an attempt at a smile.

Josie and Anna had been close friends for three years now, since they'd first met at the age of nine. The twins' parents had separated, so Ben, Anna and their mother had moved into a little terraced house in the village. Josie had been put in charge of looking after Anna on her first day as a new girl at school, and they had hit it off straight away. The very next weekend, Ben and Anna had turned up to help at the riding stables Josie's mother ran, and before long it had become their second home.

Josie watched as the Marshall twins made their way down the road, Anna talking ten to the dozen as usual and Ben bouncing a tennis ball, not paying her much attention. You could tell they were brother and sister: they both had the same olive skin and black hair, though Ben's was curly while Anna's hung in a straight, shining curtain.

'It's not fair,' Josie often grumbled as she dragged a brush through her own untidy auburn waves. 'How come your hair always looks so perfect?'

'Well, how come you have blue eyes and I've got boring brown ones?' Anna would retort, and that always shut Josie up.

With a sigh, Josie hitched her bag more comfortably over her shoulder and started walking in the opposite direction to Anna and Ben, towards Grace's Riding Stables. Usually she couldn't wait to get back home from school, change into some jeans and then rush outside to help her mother with the ponies. Today, though, was different. There was something waiting for her at home she'd rather not see.

When she reached the drive, she could hear her mother's encouraging voice floating across from the outdoor schooling ring. 'That's it, Michael! Up, down, up, down, up, down. You know, I think you've got the hang of rising trot now!'

Well, you have been coming here for a year, Michael Lee, Josie thought grumpily to herself, stopping for a second to lean on the gate and watch. *If you don't get the hang of it soon, you never will.* She was in no mood to be kind to anyone, which was unlike her.

Returning her mother's wave, Josie went on past the duckpond and up a narrow path to School Farm, the low thatched cottage in which the Graces lived. She stepped over a pair of riding boots in the porch and pushed open the heavy front door.

'Calm down, Basil,' she murmured, as the family's mongrel terrier threw himself at her, wagging his tail and licking her hand enthusiastically. She gave him an absent-minded pat and he followed her down a short hallway into the comfortably shabby kitchen, his claws clicking on the wooden floorboards.

And there was the newspaper, lying on the kitchen table. Heart thumping, Josie let her schoolbag drop to the ground and began to turn the pages until she reached the classified ads section. She scanned the columns quickly, hardly daring to look too closely, until her eyes came to rest on a short, advertisement.

Good Home Wanted For Elderly Mare
Bay Welsh cob, 14.2hh, perfect temperament,
22 years old, but sound, requires loving home.
Ideal for beginners and good with other horses.
Price negotiable
Ring Grace's Riding Stables, Northgate ***763529***

Josie let out another long sigh and read the

advertisement once more before closing the paper. So there it was, in black and white. She still found it hard to believe that they really had to part with Faith, who had been around ever since Josie could remember. Faith was the first pony she'd ever ridden, as a small girl of three. The mare was always patient and calm, and Josie's confidence had grown from the first day she'd been placed on Faith's broad, comfortable back.

Josie went over to the big wooden dresser and picked up a framed photograph from one of the shelves. She smiled as she looked at herself: a solemn little girl with curly reddish-brown hair, on top of a steady bay pony. She was clutching a handful of mane and holding on for dear life, her plump little legs stuck straight out on either side.

Suddenly the door swung open and Mary Grace came rushing into the kitchen. 'Hello, love,' she said, giving her daughter a hug. 'What did you think of Michael today? He's coming on, isn't he?' And then she noticed the photo Josie was looking at, and her face became more serious. 'Are you feeling all right?' she asked sympathetically.

'Would it make any difference if I wasn't?' Josie replied grumpily.

'Oh, don't be like that,' her mother said, sighing heavily. She sat down at the table, glancing at the newspaper before pushing it quickly to one side. 'I don't want to lose Faith any more than you do. She was my first pony here, remember? You know there's nothing we can do about it. The stables have got to close, and we've got to find new homes for all the ponies, starting with her. We've been over all this a hundred times – there's no alternative.'

'Oh, why did Mrs Wetherall have to die?' Josie groaned, pulling out a chair opposite her mother and slumping into it. 'And why did her horrible nephew have to go and inherit everything?'

Mrs Wetherall was the old lady who'd owned School Farm, the stables and the fields in which the horses grazed. She'd lived on her own in a large house in the village, and had been happy for the Graces to rent the property from her very cheaply. 'I just want the place to be put to good use,' she'd said.

But then, out of the blue, Mrs Wetherall had had a stroke and died a few days later. After a couple of weeks of uncertainty, the Graces had received a letter from her nephew's solicitors, telling them that he was the new owner and that they had three months to find 'other accommodation' and leave the house and the stables.

'Well, we always knew it couldn't go on forever,' said Mrs Grace, 'leasing the house and stables from her at such a low rent. We just didn't expect it to end quite so suddenly. But it's not really fair to expect her nephew to carry on the arrangement. He'll get five times the money if he sells the site to a developer.'

'Are you sure we can't afford to buy it ourselves?' Josie asked desperately.

'On your father's salary?' answered her mother, smiling ruefully. 'I'm afraid not, love. Teachers don't get paid that much, and we only make enough out of the stables to cover our costs.'

'Couldn't we find some other premises to rent, though?' Josie asked, jumping up impatiently from her chair and pacing around the kitchen. 'Then we could just move the ponies there and carry on as we are now.'

'No, that's just not an option,' her mother replied. 'For one thing, we'd never find anywhere with such a low rent, and for so few ponies. All the other stables around here are for fifteen or twenty horses at least. We couldn't possibly afford to expand so suddenly.'

'We could if we got a bank loan,' Josie said stubbornly, leaning against the dresser and folding her arms.

'But bank loans have to be paid back, Josie,' said Mrs Grace. 'Oh, come on, love, we've talked all this over. You know what the plan is. Hope and Charity will stay with us for as long as possible, so we can carry on using them for teaching. And we've started looking for Faith's new home now, so that we've got ample time to make sure she'll be really happy wherever she goes.' Josie's mother sighed again. 'That's the least we can do for old

Faith, after all the years of willing service she's given us.'

Mrs Grace got up and went to fill the kettle. She put it on the stove and then stood staring out of the kitchen window. Josie watched her, realising how unusual it was to see her mother stay still for any length of time. She was always on the go, full of ideas and energy. Josie noticed her mother's faraway expression and the worry lines that creased her forehead and felt a sudden pang of guilt. She'd been so wrapped up in herself, she hadn't spared much time to think about how anyone else might be feeling. And her mum loved Faith just as much as she did. Josie walked over and, putting an arm round her mother's neck, rested her head on her shoulder for a minute.

Mrs Grace patted her hand. 'You're getting to be as tall as I am,' she said.

'What are you thinking about, Mum?' Josie asked gently.

'About the day I found Faith,' she answered, smiling. 'At the gymkhana. Come on, I've told you the story a dozen times.'

'Tell me again,' said Josie. She never tired of hearing how the first pony had come to Grace's Riding Stables.

'Well, your dad and I had just moved to School Farm. It was like a dream come true when we found this place and it looked like I could open my own stables at last,'

Mrs Grace said, tearing her gaze away from the window and reaching for the tea caddy. She threw some tea bags into the shiny brown tea pot. 'There were six loose boxes, and I planned on keeping three or four horses at livery, with perhaps a couple of ponies at some stage in the future for riding lessons. You weren't born then, but we wanted to have a family and it was the ideal way for me to work and look after a child.' The kettle began to whistle, so she took it off the hob and filled up the pot. Josie unhooked a couple of mugs from the dresser and took a flowery china milk jug out of the fridge.

'Well,' Mrs Grace went on as she poured the tea, 'I wanted to get to know some horsey people, so I went along to the gymkhana to put some feelers out. And then I saw Faith, in the bending race. I couldn't take my eyes off her!' She passed a steaming mug to Josie and then blew on the other one, smiling at the memory. 'She was trying so hard, though the boy who was riding her was much too big and heavy. I got talking to his mother and she said they had just decided to sell Faith and buy a new horse. Faith was the ideal first pony, so she said, very good with beginners. She seemed perfect, and I loved her name – so quiet and trusting, somehow. It really suited her.'

Mrs Grace reached across for the biscuit tin before continuing. 'Anyway, then I found out how much money the owners wanted for her,' she said, offering the tin to

Josie. 'We had nowhere near enough, and it made me think I'd have to shelve the whole idea for a while. I was going home afterwards, feeling flat and miserable, when there she was, stuck in traffic in the trailer in front of my car! She was poking her head out of the back and looking at me as if to say, 'Well, here I am. What are you going to do about it?' We looked at each other for five minutes and then I got out of the car and offered her owner most of our savings, plus so much a month for the rest of the year. And, amazingly enough, she agreed!'

'And Dad was furious at first but he forgave you as soon as he set eyes on her,' Josie finished off, munching on her biscuit, 'and Faith was your anniversary, birthday and Christmas present all in one.'

'That's right,' laughed her mother. 'But I hid her in the stables for a whole day and a half before I plucked up the courage to tell your father. She soon began to earn her keep, though. There must be hundreds of children round here who've learned to ride on Faith . . .' She paused. 'Anyway, love, that's all in the past, now. I'm afraid it's time to look to the future.'

She lapsed into an unhappy silence. Basil sat against her leg, looking up at her with adoring brown eyes, and she gently stroked one of his soft ears.

'You have another cup of tea, Mum,' Josie said. 'I'll turn Faith out into the field.'

'Thanks, love,' her mother said gratefully. 'I've untacked her, so you just need to pick out her feet.'

'OK, Mum,' Josie replied, running up to her room to change into jeans and a sweatshirt.

Across the yard was a row of six roomy loose boxes, and Faith was waiting patiently in the first one. As the weather was getting milder, the horses were left out overnight and the Graces' other two ponies, Hope and Charity, were already in the field. The three horses kept at livery were grazing in the other paddock: Captain, a chestnut hunter, Tubber, a skewbald belonging to another teacher at Mr Grace's school, and Connie, a beautiful black mare who was Mary Grace's own particular favourite.

'Hello there, old girl,' Josie called softly as she let herself into Faith's loose box. There was an answering whinny as Faith came to greet her, nuzzling against Josie's shoulder. She had a dark bay coat, with a white stripe on her face and four white socks. Josie reached into her jeans pocket and pulled out a peppermint. She held the mint out on the flat of her palm and Faith crunched it happily, tossing her head up and down a few times in appreciation. Josie took a hoofpick out of the grooming kit that was kept handy in the loose box. Bending over, she slid her hand down one of Faith's legs, picked up her foot and ran the hoofpick around it to clean out the sand and dirt.

It was peaceful, working quietly away in the sweet-smelling stable, and Josie decided to give Faith a quick going over with the body brush. Drifts of loose hair came away with each stroke. Faith was losing her rough winter coat now spring had arrived.

'That'll make you more comfortable, old girl,' Josie said as she dealt with the matted clumps on the mare's chest and belly. She loved spending time with the ponies, and she knew how much they enjoyed being groomed. Having something practical to do took her mind off all the anxiety, too, and made her feel calmer about what the future might bring.

'You're not worried, are you, Faith?' she muttered as she brushed with steady strokes. 'You'll just accept whatever happens and deal with it in your own way, won't you? Well, I'm going to try and do the same.'

By the time she had finished with Faith and was leading her out of the stable, dusk was falling. A pair of headlights lit up the shadows as a car came slowly up the drive and parked in the yard. Josie's father got out of the driving seat and gave her a wave.

'Hi, Dad,' she called. 'How was your day?'

'So so,' he replied, walking over. 'Year Ten are finding *Romeo and Juliet* a struggle, and I've got a pile of marking to do.' Robert Grace had never taught at any of the schools Josie attended, much to her relief. She liked to keep her home life quite separate. 'How are you?' he added, taking a look at his daughter's solemn face.

'Not great,' Josie replied. 'Faith's advert went in the paper today. It's on the kitchen table, if you want to see it. Somehow, it makes the whole thing seem real. I always thought something would crop up at the last minute and we wouldn't have to move, but it's not going to, is it?'

'I'm afraid not, sweetheart,' said Mr Grace sadly. 'But I bought a lottery ticket today – after all, miracles can sometimes happen!' He scratched Faith's white stripe and she blew down her nose at him in her usual friendly way. 'Dear old Faith,' he said. 'It'll be strange without her.'

For a while the three of them stood quietly together in the gloom, and then Mr Grace said, 'Look, Josie, I understand how difficult this is for you and your mother. If there was anything I could do to change things, I would.'

'I know, Dad,' Josie said. 'But I've been thinking it all over, and I'm going to try and make the best of things – just like Faith does. I think she knows we won't let her down. And anyway, we'll probably still be able to see her in her new home, won't we?

'I'm sure we will,' said Mr Grace, ruffling her hair. 'Somewhere, there's bound to be someone who'll care for her and love her just as much as we do. Don't worry – we'll find them!'

Two

Josie led Faith across the yard and towards one of the fields beyond the outdoor schooling ring. 'Shoo, there!' she said, as a couple of ducks waddled in front of her on their way back from the small pond that lay between the fields. She opened the gate and walked the pony through, closing it securely behind her. Then she took off Faith's head collar, knowing she would have no problem catching her again. 'Off you go!' she said, giving her a farewell pat on the shoulder.

Faith stretched out her neck and shook her mane, then ambled around the paddock for a while before lying down to roll in a patch of bare earth by the water trough. She waved all four legs in the air with the sheer joy of being out in the open, then trotted off to join Hope and Charity.

Josie smiled as she saw the three ponies greet each other, and sat on the gate to watch them for a while. They sniffed noses and exchanged a few playful nibbles, then Faith led the other two in a sweeping circle round the paddock. Hope's light grey coat shone out in the dusk, with the larger shadow of Charity beside her. Even Josie had to admit that Hope was not the most beautiful pony in the world. She had a long, straight face with rather small eyes, and an especially broad back. Those shortcomings were more than made up for by her sweet nature, though. She was as calm, gentle and affectionate a pony as you could ever hope to meet. Her daughter Charity had a slightly darker coat and a more attractive face, with intelligent, expressive eyes. Every visitor to Grace's Stables fell in love with her instantly, and she was always in great demand for lessons.

Josie sighed as she looked at the ponies together. They would miss each other just as much as she was going to miss them. Then suddenly, she felt two hands come around her waist from behind and squeeze, digging in just below her ribs. 'Hey!' she cried, laughing and nearly falling off the gate. 'Anna!'

Turning round, she saw her friend's smiling face and

immediately felt better. Anna had such an infectious grin, it was hard to feel sad when it beamed your way.

'I've come to cheer you up,' Anna announced, digging into her jacket pocket and pulling out a packet of prawn cocktail flavour crisps. 'Your mum told us you were out here.'

'Oh thanks, Anna, you're a star,' Josie said, helping herself to the open packet which Anna was waving in front of her nose. 'Is Ben here too, then?'

'Yes, he's saying hello to Tubber,' Anna replied, pointing towards the other field. Her brother was just opening the gate while Tubber trotted across the grass to meet him, whinnying in greeting. Josie watched as he made a big fuss of the friendly skewbald. The other two horses kept at livery, Captain and Connie, raised their heads for a moment to watch, and then carried on grazing.

'Ben just loves that horse,' Josie commented as she munched her way through a handful of crisps. 'I hope Mrs Collins can find somewhere close by to keep him.'

Tubber was one of the first horses to be boarded at the stables, fourteen years before. His owner, Sue Collins, was a busy teacher at the school where Josie's father worked. She only had time to ride him at weekends, so Ben had begun to help Mrs Grace exercise Tubber after he and Anna had learned to ride. Mrs Grace had given them free lessons in return for their help around the stables at weekends. Most of the children she taught had their lessons on Saturday or Sunday, apart from a few who came after school in the week, so there was always plenty to be done.

'Oh, I think Ben would cycle for miles to ride Tubber,' Anna said, smiling. 'Now, come on, tell me all about it.'

'Well, the advert for Faith is in today's paper,' Josie replied, 'but no one's rung yet. And Mum's told a few people whose children come for lessons that we're selling her.'

'I bet you'll get loads of offers,' Anna said, watching Faith as she grazed contentedly. 'She's such a sweetheart.'

'I know, but she's quite old,' Josie said seriously. 'We need to find someone who understands the kind of care she needs and won't expect her to go hacking for miles every day. It's not going to be easy.'

Anna nodded in agreement. 'I don't know how you're going to be able to say goodbye to Faith. You've known her all your life, after all. It'll be like losing one of the family! Oh, sorry,' she said, catching sight of Josie's stricken expression. 'I'm not doing a very good job of cheering you up, am I? What I was really coming over to say was that Ben and I are going to Dad's this weekend, but we're not leaving till Saturday. So, why don't the three of us take the ponies for a hack after school on Friday? Go on, Josie – it'll be fun! After all, it might be our last chance, you know. The three of them aren't going to be together for very much longer.'

'Anna! Stop going on about it, for goodness' sake!' Josie exclaimed. 'I'm going to throttle you in a minute!'

She jumped off the gate and started chasing her friend round the pond. Within a few minutes they were both giggling as Anna gasped, 'Sorry, sorry, sorry! I'm trying to be tactful, honest!'

'Well, you'd better try a bit harder,' Josie replied, flopping down on the grass. 'It's difficult enough putting on a brave face, without you reminding me how awful everything is the whole time.'

'OK, point taken,' Anna said, sitting beside her. 'Put it down to stress. We're meeting Dad's new girlfriend this weekend, and I'm not exactly looking forward to it.'

'No, I bet you're not,' Josie said sympathetically. She knew how difficult Ben and Anna found the weekends away at their father's. Mike Marshall had stayed in the city when he and his wife had separated, buying a flat near the centre, and Ben and Anna went to spend the weekend with him once a month. The visits were not always happy ones, though their father tried his best to make them a success.

'It's just that we don't really know anyone there any more,' Anna said, watching a bossy coot chase a mallard duck across the water. 'We'd sooner be hanging out with our friends or helping you here than watching videos in Dad's flat all day.'

'Come on,' Josie replied, scrambling to her feet and holding out a hand to pull Anna up. 'I think a ride on Friday is just what we all need. Let's do it! And can you and Ben stay for supper tonight?'

'Yes, please,' said Ben, looming up out of the shadows beside them. 'We left Mum a note, just in case you invited us.'

'Great,' Josie smiled. It was funny how often Ben and Anna appeared at mealtimes, but the Graces were always happy to feed them.

'It's no trouble – Rob always cooks too much anyway,' Mrs Grace would say, laying a couple more places at the table. Josie's father liked to relax after a hard day at school by trying out some new recipe – the more complicated, the better. He was happy to spend hours chopping up vast quantities of vegetables, while the kitchen windows clouded over with steam from the various pots bubbling away on the stove. This evening, an enticing smell was wafting out from the house.

'Mmm, get a load of that garlic,' Ben said, wrinkling his nose in appreciation. 'Your dad's a great cook, Josie – you are lucky.'

'I know,' Josie replied, looking at the peaceful scene as they walked back towards the house. The last few chickens and ducks were making their way to the hen house for the night, and she made a quick detour to close the door behind them, safe from the foxes. Across the yard, their two black-and-white cats, Millie and Rascal, were playing in the straw by the open barn doors, and Basil was snuffling around one of the empty loose boxes. Josie had lived here all her life, with animals everywhere and ponies in the field below her bedroom window. How could she possibly move anywhere else?

'I bet you feel really awful about having to leave the cottage, as well as the stables closing down,' Anna said, as though she could read Josie's mind.

'Anna!' Ben exclaimed, glaring at his sister.

'Oh, it's OK, Ben,' Josie told him. 'I'm getting used to her by now. It's kind of like shock therapy, having your nose rubbed in how awful everything is.'

'All right, all right!' Anna said, holding up her hands in surrender. 'I won't mention it again, I promise.'

'Hello there,' Mr Grace said to Ben and Anna as they trooped into the kitchen. 'Mary told me you were around, so I've counted you in for supper. OK?'

'Yes, please,' Anna replied.

'Something smells great!' Ben added. 'What is it?'

'Spaghetti with an amazing sauce of my own invention,' Mr Grace replied. 'We're nearly ready – I just need someone to make a salad and someone to lay the table.'

Five minutes later, Josie had laid the table with five places and put in the middle a rather odd-looking salad that Ben and Anna had cobbled together from all sorts of leftovers in the fridge. Thick chunks of cucumber, cold peas and some mandarin orange segments were scattered over the lettuce leaves, and they had garnished the whole thing with slices of salami. 'Very artistic,' Mr Grace said with a smile as he dished up the spaghetti. 'Give your mother a shout, could you, Josie?'

Mrs Grace came in from the study. 'One day I'm going to disappear and you'll eventually find me under a huge pile of paperwork,' she said, pulling out a chair and sitting down. 'So, you two, how's your mother? I haven't seen her for ages.'

'She's really busy on this decorating job,' Anna said, passing down a plateful of pasta. 'It was nearly finished, and then the woman didn't like the wallpaper in the hall, so Mum had to strip it off and start all over again.'

Lynne Marshall really wanted to be a full-time artist, but that didn't bring in enough money, so she worked as a painter and decorator to keep the family going. She and Mary Grace were nearly as close as Josie and Anna. 'Lynne doesn't have an easy time of it,' Josie had heard her mother say in private only the other day. 'It makes me realise how lucky I am, in spite of everything.'

'Oh no,' Mr Grace groaned as the phone rang just when they were all about to start eating. 'Let's ignore it – it'll stop eventually.'

'We can't, Rob,' his wife reminded him, getting up. 'It might be someone calling about Faith.' Josie put down her fork, her stomach sinking and her mouthful of food suddenly hard to swallow. She strained to hear what her mother was saying in the hall outside, and caught the words, '. . . good with children . . . yes, very placid . . .'

Anna opened her mouth to say something, then shut it again quickly as she caught Josie's eye. They carried on eating – or trying to – in silence, until Mrs Grace had said goodbye to whoever was on the other end of the phone and replaced the receiver with a final click. After a short pause, in which you could have heard a pin drop, she came back into the kitchen.

'Well?' Josie said, unable to restrain herself. 'Who was that? It was about Faith, wasn't it?'

'Yes, it was,' her mother replied, with an expression that was hard to read on her face. 'That was Juliet Henderson. You know, Jerry's mother.'

'The red-haired boy?' Anna said. 'With about fifty little brothers and sisters?'

'That's the one,' Mrs Grace said. 'Though, there's only three of them, I think. It just seems like more because they're all so—' She let the sentence hang, searching for the right word to describe the Henderson children.

'—so naughty,' Josie finished off, looking appalled. 'Mum, we couldn't let Faith go to the Hendersons, surely? Do you really think they'd look after her?'

'Well, I couldn't just say no outright,' Mrs Grace said. 'We've got to investigate every possibility, and the Hendersons have got a field, apparently, and some kind of a stable. Mrs Henderson's very keen on us going to have a look at it, and I couldn't really refuse. We ought to give them a chance, at least. If the place isn't suitable, we can put them off and, if it is, we can have a good chat with them about looking after Faith. They seem very determined – Mrs Henderson told me to name the price.'

'It seems strange to be thinking about money in exchange for Faith,' Mr Grace commented. 'Like selling one of the family. I wonder how much Josie would fetch?'

'Thanks very much, Dad!' Josie said, flicking a pea at him.

'Don't worry, love,' Mrs Grace told her, 'I'll advertise your father first, though I don't know how many offers we'd get.'

'Oh, we'll have him,' Anna said. 'He can be our housekeeper, and cook us for us every day. We'll keep him in the living room and let him sleep on the sofa.'

The shrill ring of the phone cut short their laughter, and Mr Grace sighed. 'I think I'd better put your plate in the oven, Mary,' he said. 'It looks like we're in for a busy evening.'

Three

It was a busy evening, and by the end of it, there had been seven phone calls from people interested in looking at Faith. Some of them were parents of children who were taught at the riding stables and one girl, Emma Price, was due to ride Faith the next day.

By the time Emma's lesson was under way, Josie was sitting upstairs in her bedroom after another long day at school. She was trying to concentrate on her homework and resist the temptation to look out of the window.

'Now, Emma, I want you to change the rein,' she

could hear her mother say. 'When you get to the letter H, go left across the arena to F, and turn right. Shorten your reins a little now, to get a better contact.'

Josie had been hearing phrases like that all her life – she often thought she could take a riding lesson in her sleep, though she knew she wouldn't be as patient as her mother.

'Prepare to turn now,' Mrs Grace was saying. 'Shorten your left rein and squeeze with your right leg. *Right* leg, Emma, the one next to the fence. Get Faith to move her whole body when she turns, not just her head.'

Josie couldn't bear it any longer. She put down her pen and leaned on the windowsill to watch what was going on, resting her chin on her hands. Her mother was in the middle of the ring, dressed in her usual uniform of dark polo neck and stretch jodhpurs. From a distance, she looked almost as young as Josie, with her curly brown hair and slim figure. Emma was having a lesson on her own and, from the look of it, her mind was on other things. She guided Faith along a meandering line to the letter F on the other side of the arena fence. Once there, though, she left it too late to ask the pony to turn right, so they had a very sharp corner to negotiate.

'Can't we do some cantering now?' Josie heard her ask. 'This is boring!'

'Look, Emma, there's more to riding than cantering,'

Mrs Grace replied. 'You've got to control Faith, get her listening to what you're saying. She's drifting about all over the place because you're not giving her clear instructions. Just trot a twenty-metre circle for me on the right rein and really try to remember everything I've been telling you. Then we can finish off with a quick canter, if you like.'

'Great!' said Emma, brightening up. 'That's more like it.'

'Shorten those reins and prepare to trot,' said Mrs Grace resignedly. 'Now, trot on!'

Josie watched as Emma eventually managed to get Faith into a half-hearted trot, leaning forwards with her reins flapping over the pony's neck. She was unbalanced and her weight was all at Faith's front end, so that the pony's hind legs were not moving as actively as they should.

'Sit tall!' said Mrs Grace. 'Take up your reins and keep your legs long. That's better!' Gradually, with lots of patient encouragement, Emma got herself together into a more balanced position, and she and Faith began to move together in harmony.

'Look, you're even on the right diagonal,' said Mrs Grace. 'See? You're sitting down in the saddle as Faith's right leg goes forward. Well done! That looks so much better.'

'I'm doing it!' Emma cried. 'This is great!'

'Faith will do whatever you ask her,' Mrs Grace said. 'You're just got to make sure you're giving her the right signals. Now, she's trotting well and you're in a good position to move to a canter. At the next corner, take up contact, sit down in the saddle and squeeze with your legs. Outside leg behind the girth, remember.'

Josie walked over to the schooling ring just as Emma was finishing her promised canter, her eyes shining and her cheeks pink with effort. She said hello to Mr Price, who was sitting on a tree stump watching his daughter's progress, then opened the gate and walked alongside Faith as Emma rode her back into the yard.

'Good lesson?' she asked, though the answer was obvious.

'It was wonderful!' Emma replied. 'Faith's the best pony ever. I think I could canter on her for ever!'

'Well, she's due for a rest now,' Mrs Grace replied. 'Hop down and hold her for a minute while Josie takes off her saddle. I'll go and book you in for the same time next week.'

Josie ran up the stirrup leathers and unbuckled Faith's girth, heaved off the saddle and took it to the tack room. She came back with a rug that she threw over Faith. Emma stood holding the pony's reins, telling her father just how wonderful she was.

'I'm really making progress, Dad,' she said excitedly. 'If Faith was my own pony I could ride her every day, and canter for miles. We could enter Pony Club shows – maybe even go hunting!'

Josie looked up in alarm, uncertain whether to interrupt. Luckily, her mother was walking back from the office and had overheard what Emma was saying. 'Now, hold on a minute,' she told the Prices good-naturedly. 'I don't want to bring you down to earth with a bump, but I'm afraid Faith's hunting days are over. She's quite an old lady now, you know – she just can't handle too much exercise.'

'But if Emma's happy on her,' said Mr Price, 'that's the main thing, isn't it? We want to find a pony we can trust, and Faith seems to fit the bill perfectly. We could keep her at livery over in Littlehaven, and Emma could ride her every day after school. Then she could canter to her heart's content! Just tell us what kind of sum you're looking for and I'm sure we can match it.'

Josie took the reins from Emma, seething inwardly. *Of course Emma being happy isn't the main thing!* she felt like saying. *It's whether Faith is being well cared for that matters.*

'I'm sorry, Mr Price,' her mother said firmly, 'but I think Faith is really too old for the kind of riding Emma has in mind. She's nearly ready to retire now.'

'Well, what if I doubled the highest bid you've had so far?' Mr Price said, with a wink. 'I bet that would make you change your mind!'

Josie was taken aback and, for a moment, her mother seemed lost for words. 'Look, Mr Price,' Mrs Grace said eventually, 'our main priority is finding Faith a home where she'll be happy and looked after in the right way. It's time for her to start taking things easy and I don't think she's the right pony for Emma. Really, it wouldn't be right for either of them.'

'What a strange man,' Mrs Grace said to Josie as they led Faith back to her loose box. 'Thinking it was all a question of money. Surely he could see the sense of what I was saying to him? Faith's a wonderful pony to learn on, but we couldn't let her go to some keen young girl who'd want to ride her all day, every day. Emma's really coming on now, and she's quite impatient. I'm sure she wouldn't be happy with Faith for long.'

'We won't let Emma get hold of you, don't worry,' Josie told Faith, opening the loose box door and leading her inside. Mrs Grace shut the lower half of the door behind them and Josie began to unbuckle her bridle.

'There is another possibility, though,' Mrs Grace said carefully, leaning over the door. 'I had a phone call today from Jane Randall, Isobel's mother. You remember Isobel, don't you? She had lessons here for a while a few years ago.'

'Oh, yes, I do,' Josie said, hanging the bridle over her arm. 'She was nice, wasn't she? A bit older than me.'

'That's right,' said her mother. 'Well, the family's moving up to Scotland, apparently. Mr Randall's been offered this wonderful job and they've found a big house near Glasgow – with stables and a paddock.'

Josie looked at her mother, horrified. 'And?' she said. 'Surely they're not thinking of taking Faith all the way to Scotland?'

'Well, yes, they are,' said Mrs Grace, not wanting to meet her daughter's eye. 'They're going to get a horse for Isobel's brother, and they thought Faith would be perfect for Isobel. She's a bit nervous, but she learnt to ride on Faith and she trusts her completely. She's a sensible girl, and I know she'd look after Faith properly. And her parents think it would help Isobel settle in if she had a pony to look after.'

'But what about Faith, going miles from home?' Josie burst out. 'How would she feel about it? And how could we possibly keep in touch with her, so far away? We'd never see her again!' She was dangerously close to crying.

'I understand, love, honestly I do,' Mrs Grace said soothingly. 'It's only an idea at this stage. But it might turn out to be the best thing for Faith, and I don't think we should dismiss the offer without considering it very carefully. Now, I need a cup of tea – it's been hard work this afternoon. Are you coming back to the house?'

'No, I'll stay here for a while,' Josie said. After Mrs

Grace had gone, Josie leant her head against Faith's smooth neck and closed her eyes as she breathed in the warm horsey smell. 'You can't go up to Scotland, I won't let them take you!' she muttered despairingly, but Faith just turned away and ambled over to the haynet.

Letting herself back out of the loose box, Josie was startled to hear the impatient beep of a car horn. An immaculate, shining estate car was parked in the middle of the yard. Standing beside it was an equally immaculate sandy-haired man in a tweed jacket and neatly pressed trousers.

'I'd like to see whoever's in charge, please,' he announced smartly when he saw Josie appear.

'Um, OK,' said Josie, slightly startled. 'That'll be my mother, Mary Grace. I'll fetch her for you. Can I tell her what it's about?'

'I think I'm the best person to do that, wouldn't you say?' the man replied. He looked coldly at Josie with pale blue eyes underneath bushy eyebrows. 'You run along and get her for me, and I'll take over from there.'

Josie felt the colour rise in her cheeks. The man hadn't exactly been rude, but he'd put her very firmly in her place. It was clear he thought explaining anything to her would be a complete waste of breath. 'I won't be a minute,' she said, walking off towards the house. When she came back to the yard with her mother, the man was pacing up and down beside the car, looking at his watch.

'There you are at last,' he said when he saw Mrs Grace. 'I don't have very much time to spare this afternoon.'

'And you are?' Mrs Grace asked, raising her eyebrows.

'The name's Philip Hyde-White,' the man replied. 'Won't beat about the bush. Saw your advertisement in the paper – elderly mare, needing a good home. Well, if she's what I'm looking for, I can give her the best home she'll find around here. You can be sure of that.' And he smiled – a very self-satisfied smile, Josie thought. She turned his name over in her mind; it sounded vaguely familiar, though she couldn't quite work out why.

'And what are you looking for?' Mrs Grace said.

'A good companion for my other horses,' Mr Hyde-White said. 'Got a pair of two-year-olds I'm bringing on. Lots of potential, but they need a mature animal around to show them how to behave, and my old hunter died last month. Damn shame. We do have a couple of older horses as well, but they're not much use. My daughter, Hatty, has got a temperamental gelding, and my wife's dressage horse is an anti-social creature. Your mare might be just the job. You say she's got no vices?'

'Absolutely none,' Mrs Grace replied. 'She's very

good-tempered, easy to catch and to shoe, and quiet to handle.'

'And how's her health?' he asked sharply. 'Does she suffer from arthritis?'

'We haven't seen any signs so far,' said Mrs Grace. 'She's stumbling a little, but the vet's checked her over and says she's basically fine.'

'I'll take a look at her, then,' said Mr Hyde-White. 'Where is she?'

'She's in her stable at the moment,' said Mrs Grace calmly, but Josie could tell by the way her mother had drawn herself up to her full height and squared her shoulders that she was beginning to find Philip Hyde-White rather irritating.

'Well, why don't you get your girl to ride her round the arena?' he said. 'I don't have much time, as I said, but I'll be able to tell very quickly if it's worth taking this any further.'

'I'd be happy for my daughter to trot Faith round the yard on the leading rein, but I'm not going to saddle her up again,' said Mrs Grace firmly. 'She's been working hard today, and she needs a rest.'

'But I wanted to see her put through her paces!' said Mr Hyde-White indignantly.

'Then you should have rung up first and made an appointment,' said Mrs Grace, returning his gaze with an equally steely one of her own. 'If you'd like to come back at another time which is convenient for both of us,' and she emphasised the 'both', 'then we can certainly let you have as much time as you want with Faith.'

There was a short silence as Mr Hyde-White stared at the determined woman in front of him. Mary Grace was quite small, but she had a natural air of authority about her that worked as well on people as it did on horses. She didn't need to raise her voice; one look from those clear grey eyes was just as effective.

'All right,' he said abruptly. 'Just bring her out here and I'll see whether I need to come back again. Take your point. Don't want to overtire her.'

Round one to you, Mum, Josie thought to herself as she took a headcollar and lead rope from the tack room and went to fetch Faith.

'Here she is,' said Mrs Grace proudly when they appeared. 'This is Faith. I bought her locally at the age of eight, and she's been with us for fourteen years. She's absolutely bombproof, as steady a pony as you'll find.'

Josie looked at Mr Hyde-White, ready to jump to Faith's defence if he began to criticise her. She couldn't bear the thought of anyone not liking their beloved pony. True, Faith was getting on a bit, but surely it was obvious what a darling she was, standing so patiently there in the yard. She carried her head proudly, and she had an alert, intelligent expression in her shining brown eyes.

Luckily for him, Mr Hyde-White seemed to appreciate Faith's finer points. 'Holds her head nicely,' he said approvingly. He went up to the mare and patted her

quietly, taking a look at her teeth with a practised eye. All the bluster seemed to have gone out of him as he concentrated on the pony in front of him, and it was clear he was enjoying getting to know her. He ran his hands down each of Faith's legs and checked one of her hooves.

'I should imagine the pony's not going to need too much exercising?' he said, watching closely while Josie walked her up and down the yard.

'No, we're cutting down on the amount of work she does,' Mrs Grace agreed. 'That's why we don't want her to go to someone who'll want to ride her into the ground.'

Of course! Josie said to herself as she led Faith smartly along. *I know who his daughter is – Harriet Hyde-White! No wonder the name sounded familiar. And she looks just like him.*

'Mum,' Josie said as they watched Mr Hyde-White pull out of the yard in his big shiny car, 'I know his daughter, Harriet! She used to come to the Pony Club dos when Anna and I were going. Remember?'

'That would be about a couple of years ago now,' Mrs Grace said. 'What was she like? Can she ride?'

'Oh, perfectly,' Josie groaned. 'She had this lovely little bay pony and they used to win all the competitions hands down. She always looked immaculate, too.' She cast her mind back and pictured Harriet Hyde-White cantering round the ring, her strawberry-blonde hair in a thick plait and her shirt a dazzling white. 'She was a bit stuck up, though,' she added. 'She never talked to anyone and she was really horrible to Anna once.'

'Well, maybe she's like her father,' Mrs Grace said. 'I think he finds animals easier to deal with than people. He really warmed up once he'd met Faith, though, didn't he? I was ready to swing for him until then, but maybe he's not so bad. And he certainly knows his stuff.'

'Huh!' said Josie. 'I'm not convinced. "Get your girl to ride her round the arena." Charming, I must say!'

'I know, I know,' said her mother, chuckling. 'I had to swallow hard a few times, I can tell you. But the important thing is whether Faith would be happy with the Hyde-Whites. And if the set-up's anything like he says, I think we should give him the benefit of the doubt. Anyway, we'll soon have a chance to find out. He's invited us round next Monday afternoon – they're away over the weekend, apparently. Harriet won't be there, but we can see the stables.'

'Well, I suppose there's no harm in looking,' said Josie, relieved to hear that at least Harriet wouldn't be around to inspect them at the same time.

'No,' agreed her mother. 'Besides, they live at Littlehaven Hall. I've always wanted to have a look at that house. They opened the gardens to the public once but I couldn't go. Everyone said it looked like a palace.'

'Oh,' said Josie, her heart sinking again. Faith in a palace? Somehow, she couldn't quite picture it.

Four

On Friday afternoon, the three ponies and their riders clattered out of Grace's Riding Stables into the clear spring sunshine. They turned left on to the road, away from Northgate village and towards the open countryside. Josie breathed in the fresh air, smelling a faint trace of blossom on the breeze.

'Oh, it's good to be off for a hack on a day like this,' she said, her eyes sparkling. 'I was beginning to think it would stay grey and rainy for ever.'

On either side of them a patchwork of fields stretched out for miles, bright emerald with the young spring grass or chocolatey brown where the tractor had been ploughing. Every so often, a powder puff of pink or white blossom burst out against the blue sky and dark green hedgerow. Everything looked bright and fresh, as though it had been washed clean. Faith was walking along with a spring in her step, her ears flicking back and forth alertly. It was the end of a long week and Josie was determined to put all her problems behind her, for a few hours at least. She was off for a ride with her friends, and she was going to enjoy it.

'I think Hope feels the same way,' Anna said, turning round to look back at Josie. 'She's dancing along like a two-year-old.' Often, Hope would lag behind when she had the chance, but today she was eager to be off.

Hope pricked up her ears in response to this familiar voice, and Anna patted the grey pony's neck affectionately. Mrs Grace had taught Anna to ride on Hope when she and Ben had first turned up at the stables, three years before, and the plain, homely pony was still her favourite.

'She may not look like a million dollars, but I trust her,' Anna always said. 'And I know all her little ways. I know how she likes to be ridden, and she knows what I like. Not too fast and furious.'

Although Anna was much more bubbly and outgoing than Josie, she wasn't quite so confident on horseback. She'd fallen off a jumpy pony on a trekking holiday a couple of years before, and she still hadn't completely got her nerve back.

Josie usually rode Charity when the three of them went out hacking, but today she'd chosen to take Faith. While she would never have put it as bluntly as Anna, she knew there probably wouldn't be many more opportunities to ride the old pony and she wanted to grab every chance she could.

'Where shall we go?' Ben called from the front, on Charity. 'Usual place? Do you think Faith could manage a canter?'

'She's only been out for a couple of lessons today, so she's quite fresh,' Josie replied. 'I think she'll be fine. Mum said they're ploughing up the twenty-acre field, but if we keep to the edge we should be all right.'

'Sounds good to me,' Ben said, turning back again.

Josie smiled as she saw Charity take a crafty snatch at the hedgerow along the side of the road. You could tell Ben was used to riding Faith and Tubber, who were usually much better behaved. Charity would get away with as much as you'd let her.

A car whizzed quickly past them and Josie saw Anna tense up. 'Nearly off the road now,' she called, to reassure her. There was a fairly constant stream of traffic going by, but the ponies were so well-schooled they didn't pay it much attention. Fast cars and heavy lorries made Anna nervous, though, and Hope would be able to sense her anxiety.

'Good!' Anna replied. 'Can't come too soon for me.'
Josie watched her hold up a hand to thank an estate car
that was now edging slowly past. Luckily, most of the
drivers they met on the road were country people, who
knew to overtake horses cautiously and give them plenty
of room. And Mrs Grace always insisted that Josie, Anna
and Ben wore fluorescent belts and armbands, so they
could be clearly seen.

A few minutes later, they came to the field where
they usually left the road to ride cross-country.

'I'll get the gate,' Josie called, and Ben and Anna
reined their ponies back on the verge whilst they waited
for her to open it. Josie leaned down from the saddle
and grasped the gate firmly in one hand, while Faith
walked slowly forward so that she could push it open.
The bay pony was gate-opening champion at the riding
school: she hardly needed any instructions from Josie
to wheel her hindquarters round gracefully while the
gate was held open.

'Faith makes it look so easy!' Anna said as she
and Hope followed Ben through. Charity had started
fidgeting and stamping at the edge of the field, eager
to be off.

'You go on,' Josie called, seeing Ben was having
trouble holding her back. 'I'll catch you up.'

Carefully, Faith walked forward so that Josie could
close the gate. Hope and Charity were already off,

galloping along the edge of the big empty field. There was no one else in sight except a solitary tractor, turning over neat stripes of soil.

'Come on, then, girl!' Josie whispered, turning her round and giving the lightest squeeze of her legs against Faith's sides. With a snort of delight, the pony took off. She had a wonderful canter, smooth and balanced, and Josie felt as though she was sitting in a comfortable old rocking chair. She watched Faith's shoulder muscles ripple under her glossy coat, then held her face up to enjoy the sunshine and their graceful, leisurely pace.

Ben and Anna were standing waiting for them near the little spinney at the top of the field.

'Faith's on great form!' Anna exclaimed as she watched Josie ride up. 'She doesn't act her age, that's for sure.'

'I know,' Josie laughed, patting the pony's sweating neck. 'Not quite ready for the retirement home, is she?'

They trotted along a quiet lane at the top of the field, then cantered along a bridleway that led down to the river.

'I can't help worrying about Faith, though,' Josie confided as they splashed along the shallow riverbed. 'I can't bear the thought of her going somewhere she might not be happy.'

'But your mother would never let that happen,' Ben said, waving away an early bumble bee that was humming around Charity's withers. 'She'll make sure Faith has the best home she can find.'

'I know,' Josie said uncomfortably, 'but it may not be easy to tell which the best home is.' She drew Faith to a halt and they stood for a moment so that the ponies could enjoy the cool water rippling over their fetlocks.

'How do you mean?' Anna said, squinting at her in the bright sunshine that bounced off the water.

'Well, a Mr Hyde-White came to look at Faith the other day,' Josie began, looking cautiously at her friend to see how this news would go down. She still hadn't quite worked out how she felt about the Hyde-White option for Faith. 'You know, Harriet Hyde-White's father.'

'What?!' Anna cried out so loudly that Charity shot out of the water and up the riverbank like a rocket. 'You can't be thinking of letting Faith go to Horrible Harriet!'

'Careful, you great nellie!' Ben grumbled from the top of the bank, after he'd managed to get himself together and calm the pony down. 'At least give us some warning if you're going to start shouting your head off!'

'Look, her father wasn't as bad as all that,' Josie said. 'He knows a lot about horses, and he's got a groom and fantastic stables. They wouldn't ride Faith very hard, and there would be other horses to keep her company. And they're local, so I'd still be able to visit her. There

are some other people interested – but they want to take her up to Scotland and I'd probably never see her again! Nothing's been decided yet, though,' she added hastily, as she noticed Anna's glowering expression. 'We're going round to look at the Hendersons' place tomorrow evening, and the Hyde-Whites' on Monday,' she added, urging Faith up the riverbank to join Ben.

'But why do they want Faith in the first place?' Anna asked, looking up at them both. 'She's not nearly posh enough for precious Harriet, is she?'

'Oh, come on, Anna! Are you and Hope going to stand in that river all day, or can we get going?' Ben called, as he and Charity began walking off.

'Apparently they need an older pony to show the young ones how to behave,' Josie called back, following him along the top of the bank.

'Huh!' Anna snorted indignantly. 'If you ask me, it's Harriet who needs teaching how to behave!' She and Hope scrambled up the bank and trotted to catch up with the other two. 'I've never told you what she actually said to me at the gymkhana, have I?' she said, slightly out of breath.

'No,' Josie said. 'I only knew she'd been really nasty.'

'I didn't want you to hear exactly how nasty!' Anna told her. 'It was when Hope and I were the last ones left in that knockout jumping competition. Oh, what's it called again?'

'Chase Me Charlie,' Ben said automatically.

'Yes, that's it. Well, it was down to the two of us – me on Hope and Harriet on that nice little bay she had. She went past us with her nose stuck up in the air and said–' and here Anna lowered her voice, as though she didn't want Hope to overhear the hurtful remark, ' "It'll take more than a plaited mane to make the creature you're on look halfway decent." I could have thumped her!'

'How could she!' Josie gasped. She looked at Hope's

honest, plain face. How could anyone be so unpleasant about such a sweet-natured animal? And what would Harriet find to say about Faith? That she needed to go to the knacker's yard, probably.

'All that was a couple of years ago now, though,' Ben said. 'Maybe she's grown up a bit since then.'

'Oh, don't be so nice about everybody!' Anna snapped. 'Once a stuck-up cow, always a stuck-up cow. I wouldn't let Faith anywhere near her if I were you!'

Five

'Listen, Josie,' said Mary Grace. 'I don't care what Harriet said to Anna two years ago at a gymkhana. The Hyde-Whites know all about looking after a pony like Faith. If the home they're offering is the best one for her, we should accept it – and gratefully, too.'

It was early Saturday evening and, after a busy day at the stables, she and Josie were on their way to the Hendersons' house to see exactly what was on offer.

'I suppose we don't have to decide straight away,' Josie said, staring out of the car window as she thought it over. 'Something else will probably turn up. Perhaps we'll see the Hendersons' place and think it'll be just perfect for Faith.'

'I wouldn't hold out too much hope of that,' said Mrs Grace sceptically. 'Still, I suppose you never know. Maybe we're being a bit hard on Jerry and his family. They might give Faith loads of love and attention.' She yawned. 'After a day like today, I'd sooner be relaxing at home than flogging out to see them, all the same.'

'I know what you mean,' Josie said. 'Saturdays seem to get busier and busier, don't they?'

'Not for much longer, though,' Mrs Grace replied. 'We'll have to get used to a whole new kind of weekend soon. Just think, we may be able to have a lie-in once in a while. Here, pass me that piece of paper, could you? I think we're nearly there.'

'What will you do, Mum?' Josie said, as Mrs Grace quickly consulted the scribbled directions she'd taken down over the phone. 'You couldn't bear to give up horses altogether, could you?'

'I wouldn't mind a rest from teaching,' Mrs Grace admitted. 'I think I'm getting a bit stale now. I'll carry on riding Connie, though.' Connie was the black mare who'd been kept at full livery in the stables for the past eight years. Her owner had quickly become a good friend of Mary Grace's, and Mary had been riding Connie nearly every day for all that time. 'Jane's going to move her to another livery stables near by quite soon,' she went on, 'but she's asked me to keep on exercising her. I'm sure there'll be lots of opportunities like that for you, too – if you want them.'

'Hmm,' Josie said, frowning. She couldn't imagine riding someone else's pony, and she didn't want to think about a future without the three they had. It was too painful. She had come to realise that the only way she could get through the next few weeks would be to take them one step at a time. Concentrate on Faith first, she told herself, and don't look too far ahead.

'Here we are,' said Mrs Grace, turning into a narrow driveway. 'Now, brace yourself for the Hendersons!'

The car crunched over the gravel and drew to a halt outside a large, rather dilapidated house. Josie caught sight of a couple of faces at the window, and soon two red-headed boys and a little girl with carroty ringlets had spilled out of the front door and surrounded the car, all chattering at the same time. They wore strangely old-fashioned clothes: the boys were both dressed in corduroy knee britches and the girl in a pinafore of the same material, with a round-collared shirt beneath.

'Where's the pony? Why haven't you brought her with you? Come and see our stable! What's your name? How old are you?' they clamoured, tugging at Josie's arm as she opened the passenger door.

'Now, children,' came a slower, deeper voice behind them. 'One at a time, remember?' A tall woman with long red hair came sailing towards the Graces, smiling serenely. Josie had seen her a few times, picking Jerry up from his riding lesson.

'Hello, Martha,' she said to Mrs Grace, and Josie had to bite her lip to stop herself from giggling. Mrs Henderson obviously wasn't very good at remembering names. 'The children have been simply dying for you to get here,' she went on. 'Do come in, and bring . . .' Her eyes focused on Josie, and she waved her hand vaguely in the air to include her in the invitation.

'Josie, my daughter,' Mrs Grace added helpfully, as Josie was carried off towards the house by the tide of children.

'And what's your name?' Josie asked the little girl, who was clinging on to her arm with a grip of steel and hustling her through the front door.

'I'm Jemima,' came the piping reply. 'And my one brother is Joshua and my other brother is Jerry. And our cat is called Chlöe and she's had kittens. Look, there's one!'

By now, they'd reached the kitchen and, following Jemima's pointing finger, Josie saw that one of the faded flowery curtains seemed to be bulging and writhing, as though it were alive. Dragging a chair over to the windowsill, Jemima climbed up on it and began wildly tugging the curtain to and fro with a look of fierce concentration on her face.

'No, stop! I'll get it!' Josie cried, rushing up to the curtain and gently disentangling a tiny ginger kitten who was clinging desperately to the other side. She put the little creature down on the floor and it immediately took refuge under an armchair covered in threadbare red velvet, peeping out with big saucerlike eyes.

'And here's my guinea pig!' said Joshua, pushing a large wooden train along the floor. In the front sat a bemused-looking white guinea pig with pink eyes. 'She's an albino and she's called Snowy.'

'Animals and children, that's what we go in for,' announced Mrs Henderson, sweeping in with Mrs Grace and scattering children and pets before her. 'The more, the merrier! That's why we could give your dear old pony such a lovely happy home.'

'That's my train!' came an angry cry from Jerry, as he jumped on his brother and began punching him. 'Give it back!'

'No! Snowy likes it!' shouted Joshna defiantly, defending himself with clenched fists.

'I think Snowy might like to go back in her cage now, don't you?' Josie suggested quietly to Jemima, pushing the train with its guinea-pig driver safely out of reach of flailing arms and legs.

'Snowy doesn't have a cage,' Jemima announced loudly.

'No,' said Mrs Henderson, somehow overhearing

above the din. 'Lucky Snowy has a lovely cosy cardboard box. Now, come on, Miriam. Let's leave the children playing and go out to the meadow.' And, ignoring the chaos, she swept a speechless Mrs Grace out through the back door.

'Why don't we put Snowy in her lovely cardboard box for the moment, then,' Josie said. 'D'you know, I think we've got an old rabbit hutch in the barn. I could dig it out and Snowy could have that. What do you think?'

'What's wrong with her box?' Jemima said suspiciously. 'I've drawed all over the side. Look!' And she proudly pointed to a large brown box covered in wax crayon scribbles in a corner of the kitchen.

'Those are lovely drawings,' Josie said carefully, 'but poor Snowy can't look out of her box and see what's going on, and it's not very strong. I think she might like the hutch better.' She took Snowy out of the train and popped the poor bewildered creature into her box as a temporary shelter. At least it was clean, and there was a margarine tub of water and some wilting lettuce leaves on a sheet of newspaper at the bottom.

'Now, come on, you two,' she said cheerfully to the boys, who by now had stopped fighting and were both crying bitterly. 'Are you going to show me the field?'

And so, along with cries of 'I will! I will! No, she's my friend! But I have riding lessons and you don't! Well, I said it first!' she was borne out of the back door.

At the bottom of the overgrown garden was a small field, surrounded by a sagging barbed wire fence. The two women were standing in the long grass, talking earnestly together. As Josie approached with the children, she heard her mother say, '– a lot of work to make this field suitable for keeping a pony in, unfortunately. You've got ragwort everywhere.'

'Yes, I'm so looking forward to seeing its pretty yellow flowers,' said Mrs Henderson. 'We cut armfuls and make posies for the house – don't we, children?' But Jerry, Joshua and Jemima had already rushed off shrieking, to climb through the window of what looked like a tumbledown garden shed.

'Ragwort's poisonous to horses, though,' Josie put in anxiously. 'You'd have to dig up every last scrap.'

'That's right,' said her mother. 'And there's a yew tree at the bottom of your garden, there, overhanging the fence. That would have to be cut right back – it's even more lethal. You'd need to repair the fence, too, or a pony would try to scratch on the barbed wire and could cut herself quite badly. And I'm afraid if that's the stable, it really won't give enough shelter.'

'Oh, I'm sure any pony would love the stable!' cried Mrs Henderson dramatically, shading her eyes to watch the children wriggling in and out of the gaping holes in its rotten sides. 'It's so old. Quaint and picturesque, just how we like things to be!'

'Yes, but it doesn't have a roof,' said Mrs Grace. 'That's quite a drawback.'

'Well, there's obviously more to this pony-keeping business than I thought,' Mrs Henderson said, tossing her long red hair and preparing to sweep back to the house. 'Perhaps Jeremiah would be better simply carrying on with lessons for the time being.'

'I think that might be best,' Mrs Grace agreed, adding tactfully, 'He has the makings of a very good rider. I was going to try him over the trotting poles in the lesson tomorrow.'

'And you could pick up the hutch then,' Josie offered. Seeing Mrs Henderson's blank look, she explained, 'I was just telling Jemima, we've got an old rabbit hutch in the barn that would be perfect for Snowy. You'd be welcome to it, if you'd like.'

'An *old* hutch, you say?' Mrs Henderson asked, raising an eyebrow.

'Oh, very old,' said Josie. 'Practically an antique, and very picturesque.' She coughed loudly, to cover up the strange snorting noise that her mother was making.

'Why, thank you, Janie dear,' said Mrs Henderson loftily. 'What a kind thought. I think that would suit Snowy very well.'

Six

'I'm still booking people in for lessons on Faith next week,' said Mary Grace, up to her wrists in soapy water the next evening, 'but we've got to face the fact that she might not be around for much longer.'

'It'll take a little while to sort everything out, though, won't it?' Josie asked, her heart sinking. She was standing next to her mother, drying the pots and pans and vainly trying to keep up with the breakneck speed at which they were being washed. Because there were riding lessons throughout the day on a Sunday, the Graces tended to have their main meal in the early evening. Mr Grace cooked, and Josie and her mother dealt with the washing up.

'Well, once we've decided which is the best home for her, there's no reason why things shouldn't move quite quickly,' her mother replied. 'I know the Randalls are on a tight schedule with their move, and I shouldn't think the Hyde-Whites would want to drag the whole process out either.' She pulled out the plug and let the dirty dishwater drain away.

Josie wiped away furiously at the saucepan in her hand, avoiding her mother's anxious glance. It was just about manageable to think of losing Faith at some vague time in the future, but not immediately.

'So how's it going so far?' Mr Grace said, looking up from the Sunday papers that were spread all over the kitchen table. 'Still a choice between the Hyde-Whites and the Randalls?'

Mary Grace nodded, sitting down at the table opposite him. 'I've had a few more offers from families of some of the children I teach,' she said, 'but none really suitable. I'm beginning to realise it's not a question of money – talking to Emma's father made me see that.'

'Oh, he was awful!' Josie said, trying to force a saucepan into the crowded cupboard. 'As if doubling what we'd been offered for Faith would make any difference.'

'Exactly! We've got to concentrate on getting the right

home for her, not on what we can gain financially from the sale,' said Mrs Grace. 'We have to find somewhere she can spend the rest of her days quietly and peacefully, with people who really know how to look after an elderly pony.'

At that moment, there was a loud knock on the door. Basil leapt up from his basket under the kitchen table and burst into a volley of barking, leaping around in excitement.

'I wonder who that is?' Josie said in surprise. 'It can't be Anna and Ben – they're not back till late tonight.'

'Oh, did I forget to tell you?' said her mother, getting up to answer the door. 'The Randalls are coming round to talk things over. Maybe they'll be the answer to our prayers.' She went off down the hall, Basil at her heels.

'Yes, you did forget to tell me,' Josie muttered, throwing down her tea towel. 'Still, I don't suppose it makes much difference.'

'Now come on, love,' said her father, putting his arm round her shoulder. 'Remember what you said about making the best of things?'

'Josie, why don't you and Isobel go and see Faith while it's still light enough?' Mrs Grace said, after she'd introduced the Randalls. Josie had recognised Isobel at once from her time at the stables – she had fair skin with a dusting of freckles and kind blue eyes.

'Great!' Isobel said at once. 'I can't wait to see Faith again – I used to love riding her.'

'Then let's go,' Josie said, encouraged by the enthusiasm in Isobel's voice.

'Here! You might want to take these with you,' said Mrs Grace, throwing across a tube of peppermints, which Josie caught neatly. 'We'll be out in a minute, after we've had a chat.'

'Follow me,' Josie said. 'The ponies are in the front field.'

'How's Charity getting on?' Isobel asked. 'I remember when your mother was schooling her.'

'Oh, she's wonderful,' said Josie, her face lighting up as they walked over to the field. 'She can be a bit cheeky sometimes, but she's really steady. All three of them are special, in their own way. Look, there they are!'

Hope and Charity were standing together in the middle of the field, Hope nibbling at her daughter's withers. Faith was grazing, a little way apart from them.

'Oh, Hope's doing her grooming routine again,' Josie smiled. 'She's such a fusspot, but I think the others like it really.'

'Faith's going to miss the other two,' Isobel said, leaning on the fence and looking over at the peaceful group.

'I know,' Josie sighed. 'It's a funny thing, though – recently I've noticed she's been going off on her own a little more. I suppose it's because she's getting older. She seems to want some time to herself. Come on, take a few mints and let's go and say hello.'

The two girls climbed over the fence and made their way across to the ponies. Faith trotted up, giving a neigh and shaking her mane. Isobel patted her affectionately and, in return, Faith nudged her nose into Isobel's shoulder.

'I think she remembers you,' Josie smiled. 'She doesn't do that with everyone she meets.'

Isobel laughed as the pony nuzzled her pocket. 'Or maybe it's just that she can smell these,' she said, holding a peppermint out on the palm of her hand. 'Oh, Faith, you haven't changed a bit – you're just as lovely as you always were. And you don't look a day older.'

'She is getting on a bit, though,' Josie said, watching as Faith crunched up the mint, tossing her head so that her mane rippled. 'She's not picking her feet up quite as well as she used to, and she does get tired. Would you be wanting to ride her much?'

'No,' Isobel replied thoughtfully, stroking Faith's soft nose. 'I think we'd really be looking on her more as a pet. I'd ride her sometimes, of course, but nothing too hard or competitive. My brother's mad about horses and Mum and Dad have promised him a hunter, but that doesn't appeal to me. They don't want me to feel left out, though, and I suppose riding is a good way of meeting people.'

Something in the tone of her voice made Josie look at Isobel more closely. 'How do you feel about moving?' she asked, interested to find out more but not wanting to seem nosey.

'To be honest, I'm dreading it,' Isobel sighed. 'A new school as well as GCSEs coming up, new friends to make, new house – new everything! I wish things could just stay the way they are.'

'I know exactly how you feel,' Josie said. She held out a mint for Charity, who was pushing her way forward to have a share in the attention. 'We won't be moving as far away as you, but it still feels like my whole life's going to be turned upside down.'

'Yes, I bet it does,' Isobel said sympathetically. 'I suppose taking Faith off to Scotland wouldn't be so good from your point of view, would it?'

'No, not really,' Josie admitted. 'But at the end of the day, I just want her to be happy. I'd sooner she was with nice people up in Scotland than miserable down here.' And she gave Isobel a half-hearted smile to show there were no hard feelings.

'Have you had any other offers?' Isobel asked, watching Faith trot off round the field.

'Yes, plenty,' Josie replied, 'though none of them have seemed quite right so far. But listen, here's me wittering on and I haven't even offered to tack Faith up so you can ride her. Do you want to?'

'Oh, don't worry,' Isobel replied, her eyes still fixed on Faith. 'I've ridden her plenty of times in the past, and seeing her again is enough to remind me what a star she is.'

'Would you like to have her, if you could?' Josie asked. 'I mean, if your parents and mine agree and the price is OK?'

'Yes,' said Isobel slowly, 'I would. I'd feel awful about taking her so far away from you, Josie, but if she's got to go somewhere, I think she'd be as happy with us in Scotland as anywhere else.'

Josie nodded. Maybe she would, she thought to herself. And maybe I'll just have to get used to it.

'Hi there, stranger!' Anna said, plonking her tray down next to where Josie was sitting on her own, in the school cafeteria. 'Didn't you wash this morning or are you just feeling antisocial?'

'Oh, Anna, it's great to see you!' Josie replied, beaming. 'Seems like you've been away for a month. How was the weekend?'

Josie and Anna were in different classes, so this was the first chance they'd had to talk.

'How was the girlfriend, you mean,' Anna said, unloading a plate piled high with sausages, beans and chips. 'She wasn't as bad as I thought, as a matter of fact. It was a bit weird at first, seeing her with Dad, and I think he felt nervous too. She's quite trendy. She took me and Ben shopping and bought us some cool clothes, which was nice of her, but Mum wasn't too pleased about it.'

'Why not?' Josie asked, mashing cheese and butter into her baked potato.

'You know – "I'm the one who ends up buying the school shoes, why should they have all the fun?" etcetera, etcetera, etcetera. Oh, it's too boring to talk about,' Anna said, with a bright tone in her voice that didn't fool Josie for one second. 'How about you? What's happening with Faith? Has Harriet got hold of her yet?'

'Well, Mum and I are going round to their place tonight,' Josie said, starting to eat. 'Harriet won't be there – she's a weekly boarder at some private school or other – but we can have a look at the stables. We did see the Randalls, though. They're the people who are moving up to Scotland. D'you remember Isobel? She used to come to the stables a couple of years ago. Long hair, pretty.'

'Oh yes,' Anna replied, chewing slowly and thinking it over. 'She used to ride Faith, didn't she?'

Josie, her mouth full, nodded.

'So, do they want to have her?' Anna asked.

'I think they do,' Josie said. 'Isobel seemed keen, and

you can tell she's really fond of Faith. They said they'd talk it over and give us a ring as soon as possible.' She pushed some salad around her plate, not feeling quite so hungry all of a sudden.

'And how do you feel about it all?' Anna asked through a mouthful of sausage. 'Would they give her a good home? Better than the Hyde-Whites?'

'They showed us pictures of the stables and field at their new house,' Josie said. 'It looks fantastic, and Isobel's brother's getting a horse too – so Faith wouldn't be lonely. And Mum likes them, and I'm sure they'd look after her really well. It's just . . .' Her voice trailed away.

'It's just they're moving up to Scotland,' Anna finished the sentence for her. 'And you'd probably never see Faith again, and you couldn't ride Hope or Charity round to visit her – while you've still got them, of course.'

'Oh, Anna,' Josie said, uncertain whether to laugh or cry, 'how do you manage it?

'Manage what?' Anna asked innocently.

'Manage to put your finger on everything I don't want to think about and remind me of it,' said Josie, pushing away her plate.

'Well, you've got to face up to things,' Anna said briskly. 'And I'm not going to let you mope around on your own. We're going to get through this together, the two of us, and Ben's going to help too. That's what friends are for, after all.' She gave Josie one of her dazzling smiles. 'Can I have the rest of your potato if you don't want it?' she asked. 'These chips are gross.'

Seven

Josie and her mother stared at each other for a moment without saying a word as they pulled up in the car outside Littlehaven Hall. Mrs Grace switched off the engine and they took another look at the imposing building before them.

'What an amazing place!' Josie said, after a pause. 'It looks like something out of a film. I never thought it would be as grand as this!'

'Nor me,' said her mother. 'You'd never guess it was here, tucked away down the drive like this, would you?'

They had turned off a main road between Northgate and the small market town of Littlehaven to find the house. It was built out of grey stone, and roofed in thick slates of the same colour. Circular columns supported a grand porch over the front door. Tall, rectangular windows looked out over a velvety lawn that was enclosed by the sweeping drive. It had recently been mowed in neat stripes. There was one flower bed in the middle of this green sea, spiked with roses, and the stone statue of a galloping horse nestled among trees at the far end.

There was something about the house that Josie didn't like. It's too perfect, and it's got a haughty air about it, she thought, as she gazed up at its gracious walls. Just like the Hyde-Whites.

'Come on,' said Mrs Grace, picking up her shoulder bag, 'let's ring on the bell before I lose my nerve.'

A middle-aged woman in an overall answered the door and said she would fetch Mr Hyde-White for them. She walked softly away and left Josie and Mrs Grace standing in the empty hall. Josie stared nervously at the gloomy oil paintings hung all around it, not feeling much like talking in that large, echoing space. It wasn't exactly welcoming.

'Hello, there. Jolly good,' said a brisk voice, and Mr Hyde-White appeared from one of the doors that led off the hall. He looked exactly the same as when he'd appeared at the stables – identical tweed jacket and sharply creased trousers. Josie tried to imagine him dressed in the jeans and sloppy jumpers her father wore at weekends, but she couldn't quite picture it.

'Glad you could make it,' he went on. 'Shall we go out to the stables straight away? No point in wasting time.'

He led them down a corridor and out through the back door, into a walled garden. Josie and her mother exchanged a quick smile as they followed behind him. It was obvious Mr Hyde-White didn't believe in chatting for the sake of it. Still, at least that gave them the chance to look around, Josie thought. She noticed how neat and tidy everything was, from the stone urns precisely arranged on the terrace, to the straight, regimented rows of plants in the vegetable patch.

They carried on down the path until Mr Hyde-White stopped at a door in the far wall. 'This is where we keep the horses,' he said, throwing it open and standing aside to let them go past.

Josie walked through first. 'Oh, what lovely stables!' she said in delight.

A cobbled yard lay in front of them, with two sets of loose boxes opposite each other on either side. Two horses were peering out of the left hand row inquisitively. Across the yard, a handsome dun was tied with a rope from his headcollar to a ring on the wall, while a young man in jodhpurs and a sweatshirt groomed him vigorously. The tidy muck-heap was walled off in the far corner, and what looked like the storerooms for hay, feed and bedding stood opposite. Beyond the courtyard, Josie could see an outdoor schooling ring, a paddock with a number of jumps in it, and then a sweeping view of fields and open countryside. She caught a quick glimpse of a woman on an iron-grey horse, moving slowly round the ring at a sitting trot.

'This all looks very well organised,' Mrs Grace said, sounding impressed.

'Yes, we run a tight ship,' said Mr Hyde-White proudly, squaring his shoulders. 'Come on, I'll take you round. Introduce you to the residents.'

Josie and her mother smiled uncertainly, not quite sure whether this was meant to be a joke. They followed Mr Hyde-White over to where the dun horse was standing. The groom was just giving his beautiful glossy coat a final wipe over with the stable cloth.

'This is Milo, Hatty's gelding,' said Mr Hyde-White. 'Stand back, David, so we can see him properly.'

Without a word, the young man stood to one side at Milo's head. He didn't acknowledge the Graces or look at Mr Hyde-White.

'She used to have a bay pony, didn't she?' Josie asked, walking up to the horse and cautiously giving him her hand to sniff.

'That's right,' said Mr Hyde-White. 'Useful little thing, but Hatty grew out of her very quickly. She's on a different level with this fellow.'

'He's got a lovely deep chest,' Josie said, gently stretching out her hand. Milo shied away, laying his ears back against his head and rolling his eyes.

'He doesn't like strangers,' Mr Hyde-White replied. 'Takes a lot of getting to know, but he's a super jumper – simply flies over the fences. Mind you, so he should. Cost me a small fortune.' He gave a short laugh, without much humour in it. 'Right, you can put him back in his box, David. Let's carry on with the tour.'

Briskly, he took Josie and her mother over to the other loose boxes and showed them the two-year-olds he was schooling: Jack, a chestnut stallion with a white star between his eyes, and Clementine, a Palomino mare.

'We're working Jack every day on the lunge rein,' he told Mrs Grace. 'He's got the makings of an excellent hunter, but he's a bit jumpy at the moment. That's why he needs a good role model to calm him down. A mother figure, you might say.'

'And that's a nice-looking mare you've got,' said Mrs Grace, as Clementine stretched her neck over the stable door. 'Doesn't she have a pretty head?'

'We're going to keep her as a brood mare,' Mr Hyde-White said matter-of-factly. 'She has a great pedigree, but she's a devil to catch.'

'She's gorgeous!' Josie exclaimed. She couldn't resist

stroking the horse's soft nose, enjoying its whiskery tickle against her fingers, and patting her gleaming golden coat. Clementine drew her head back warily, but she didn't shy away completely.

'That's enough fussing, don't you think?' Mr Hyde-White said sharply. 'Now, come this way and we might be able to catch my wife before she finishes her dressage session.'

Josie was taken aback. She'd never thought of stroking a horse as fussing – she knew how much they enjoyed being touched. Mr Hyde-White obviously had a very different attitude. He marched off towards the arena and they had to hurry to keep up with him. As she went, Josie caught sight of the groom watching them go. She smiled, but he turned away.

The dark grey horse was going through its paces in the ring. His rider, a whippet-thin woman with short blonde hair, sat deep in the saddle with a ramrod-straight back. She kept her eyes fixed ahead and didn't look once in their direction.

'Shouldn't think you see this kind of thing very often in your neck of the woods,' said Mr Hyde-White, with a superior smile. 'None of your pupils are up to dressage, I'd imagine.'

'Oh, some of the adults are,' Mrs Grace replied. 'One of our livery horses regularly competes in dressage events and I give his owner lessons.'

'Probably not at my wife's level, though,' Mr Hyde-White said, looking rather put out that they should even consider such an idea.

'She certainly has a marvellous seat,' said Mrs Grace politely.

Mrs Hyde-White hardly seemed to be moving at all, but she obviously had complete control over her horse. His every movement was smooth and graceful, and he seemed simply to flow from one gait into another. Josie sometimes found watching dressage exercises rather boring, but she had to admit that there was something very beautiful about this perfectly balanced partnership of horse and rider.

'Look at that wonderful extended canter, Josie,' said her mother, as the horse threw out his legs and lengthened his stride. 'She's really got him moving his hindquarters so he doesn't overbalance. We ought to get Emma Price over to have a look at this!'

'We don't encourage spectators,' said Mr Hyde-White stiffly.

'Oh no, of course not,' said Mrs Grace hurriedly, quite flustered. 'I was only joking. Oh, I think they've finished.'

Mrs Hyde-White had slowed her horse directly from a canter to a walk. She let her reins flap loosely so that he could give his neck a good stretch as they came out of the arena.

'This is Mary Grace, darling,' said Mr Hyde-White as she approached. He obviously didn't think Josie was worth mentioning. 'You remember, she's looking for a home for her old mare. I think the pony'll help settle my young ones.'

'Oh yes,' said Mrs Hyde-White, languidly reaching down a hand so that Mrs Grace could shake it. 'Had a look round, have you?'

'Yes, we have,' said Mrs Grace, forced to squint into the sun as she looked up at her. 'The yard looks great. Tell me,' she added, turning back to Mr Hyde-White, 'would you be thinking of putting Faith out to grass straight away?'

Josie looked round at the lush green fields. She had to admit, it was nice to imagine Faith spending the rest of her days grazing quietly in such peaceful surroundings.

'Oh, I think we could ride her every so often,' Mr Hyde-White replied. 'David or Hatty can hack her out and we'll see how she goes.'

'Is she regularly shod at the moment?' Mrs Hyde-White put in, flicking a blade of grass off one shining riding boot with the end of her whip.

Mrs Grace nodded. 'Every six weeks or so.'

'Well, if her feet are in good condition and she's still wearing shoes, there's no reason why she shouldn't have some light work for a few years,' Mrs Hyde-White continued. 'When we can fit her in.'

'I could come and take her out if you didn't have the time,' Josie offered, feeling she'd been left out of the conversation for long enough. Mrs Hyde-White stared down at her as though she'd just noticed an unpleasant smell and wanted to see exactly where it was coming from. 'Oh no, dear, I don't think that will be necessary,' she said.

'It might unsettle her,' Mr Hyde-White added. 'Once the pony's here, better for her to be in our sole charge, wouldn't you say?'

That wasn't what Josie would have said at all, but the tone of Mr Hyde-White's voice was final. She glanced across at her mother with a look that said, 'We need to talk about this later.'

'Well, you can work out the details,' said Mrs Hyde-White brusquely. 'I need a hot bath and something to drink. Walk on, Jasper.' And with that, she and her horse made their stately way back to the yard. Josie watched them go and saw Mrs Hyde-White spring lightly to the ground, hand the horse's reins over to the groom, and walk towards the house without a backward glance. She didn't bother to give Jasper a pat of thanks or praise.

'Of course, before we give you the final decision about whether we'll take the pony,' Mr Hyde-White said, 'we'll have to let Hatty have a look at her. She's away at school in the week, as I said, but we could make it on Friday evening. Then if she gives the go-ahead, we can arrange a time to pick the animal up. We'll pay your asking price. No point haggling. And I take it that covers her tack as well?'

'It would be fine for you and your daughter to come on Friday evening,' Mrs Grace said, 'but I ought to mention that there is another family interested in Faith. They're thinking it over at the moment. We may decide that, for one reason or another, she might be happier with them in the long run.'

Mr Hyde-White stared at her. 'I can't imagine for a moment why you would,' he said. 'You've seen our facilities. We have a very able groom, plenty of land and a great deal of expertise. If I were you, I'd think very hard before turning this opportunity down.'

Josie and her mother sat in the car without speaking as they drove away from Littlehaven Hall. Eventually, Mrs Grace shot Josie a sidelong glance. 'Well?' she said.

'Oh, Mum!' Josie replied. There was no need to say any more. She could tell her mother knew exactly how she felt.

Mrs Grace sighed. 'The thing is, he's right,' she said. 'We can't just dismiss their offer out of hand. Those are fantastic stables, and the fields look great, and there are other horses for company. And I'm sure the Hyde-

Whites would look after Faith very well.'

'But they're so cold!' Josie blurted out, clenching her hands so tightly that her fingernails dug into her palms. 'Did you notice, Mum, he didn't call Faith by her name once! It was always "the mare" or "the pony" or "the animal". And he's not exactly affectionate with his horses, is he? I don't think he touched one of them the whole time we were there.'

'Of course, he doesn't look after them on a day-to-day basis,' Mrs Grace reflected. 'I should imagine it's the groom who'd be doing that. And according to Mr Hyde-White, he really knows his stuff.'

'Well, I didn't take to him either,' Josie said. 'He didn't say hello to us, or smile, and he didn't seem to like Mr Hyde-White much. Come on, Mum – didn't you think there was something rather odd about that whole set-up? I know it's an amazing place and everything, but can you really imagine Faith there?'

'Actually, I can,' Mrs Grace said slowly. 'I think you're projecting your own feelings on to Faith, Josie. Just because you don't like the Hyde-Whites, you think she won't be happy living with them. Well, I'm not sure you're right. I can see her keeping those young horses in order and grazing on their land quite happily. And I can see the Hyde-Whites taking care of her as she gets older, too.'

'Well, I can't,' Josie said gloomily. 'And once she goes

there, that's it. We're not going to be invited back for a visit, you can count on that. Did you notice how horrified they looked when I offered to come and ride her out?'

'Yes, they didn't exactly jump at the prospect, did they?' her mother smiled. She took one hand off the steering wheel and put it over Josie's. 'Look, I can't deny that I liked the Randalls a hundred times better. They're much more friendly and on our wavelength. But Faith is the one we have to think about here, not ourselves. We've got to keep her best interests in mind. Let's wait and see what the Randalls say, and then we can decide.'

Soon they were pulling into their driveway and past the field full of brightly-coloured fences and poles. 'The Hyde-Whites had some marvellous jumps. Did you see?' Mrs Grace asked Josie absent-mindedly. 'Like a proper show-jumping course. I must try a new layout for ours.'

'There's not much point, is there?' Josie replied. 'We're going to have to get rid of them all soon.'

'Perhaps you're right,' Mrs Grace said reluctantly. Then she spotted her husband's red car in the yard and her face brightened. 'Oh look, Dad's home early. That's nice!'

'Is it?' Josie said grumpily. She got out of the car and stomped up the path to School Farm, flinging open the front door with a crash.

Her father came out of the kitchen, alerted by the noise. 'What's up with you?' he said, looking at Josie's cross face.

'Everything,' Josie muttered, taking off her jacket and jamming it on the post at the bottom of the stairs. 'We've just been to see a wonderful new home for Faith, that's all. Can't wait to pack her off there.'

'Now come on,' Mr Grace said, putting his hands on Josie's shoulders for a moment and looking her straight in the eyes. 'Don't think you're the only one who's finding this difficult.'

'Finding what difficult?' asked Mrs Grace, coming through the door. She gave her husband a kiss and added, 'Hello, love. Good to see you home early for a change.'

'Nothing in particular,' Mr Grace replied, with a last warning look at Josie. 'Oh, before I forget, Mary, there were a couple of messages on the answer phone. The Randalls want you to call them back, and someone else I hadn't heard of. Atter-something, I think.'

The Randalls! Josie felt her heart leap. Had they rung to say they wanted to buy Faith? And what would her mother decide, if they had?

'Thanks, love. I'll ring from in here,' her mother said, taking off her coat and going into the study. She closed the door behind her.

'Why don't you and I go into the kitchen, Josie,' said

her father. 'I could do with a willing assistant, and I'm sure Mum doesn't want you hanging on her every word. Come on.' And he walked her down the corridor, a gentle hand on her back.

'I know it's not easy for Mum, either,' Josie said as they went into the kitchen, 'but at least she gets to decide where Faith ends up.'

'Well, your opinion counts too,' Mr Grace said, fetching a handful of carrots from the vegetable rack. 'You know your mother always listens to what you say. But someone has to make the final decision, and it stands to reason that person should be her. And anyway, she'd never let Faith go to anyone who wasn't going to treat her properly.'

'You're right,' Josie admitted, rooting in a drawer for the vegetable peeler. 'Maybe it's just the idea of Faith going away from us at all that's so hard to take. But if you'd seen the Hyde-Whites, Dad, you'd understand. They're so rich and stuck-up.' She began to peel the carrots. 'Still, perhaps the Randalls were ringing to say they want Faith, and Mum will sell her to them, and then I'll have something else to worry about.'

'No, that's one worry you can cross off your list, Josie,' said her mother, coming into the kitchen. 'The Randalls aren't going up to Scotland after all. Mr Randall was offered a fantastic deal today by his present company so he'd stay with them, and that's what he's decided to do.

They said the only thing they really regretted was that now they wouldn't be able to have Faith.'

'Oh,' said Josie, pausing with the peeler in mid-air. 'I don't know whether to be disappointed or relieved.'

'I know exactly how you feel,' said her mother, sitting at the table and running a hand through her hair. 'It's great that Faith isn't going up to Scotland, but it's a pity the Randalls can't have her. I'm afraid this leaves the way clear for the Hyde-Whites, Josie.'

'What about the other people who left a message?' asked Mr Grace.

'I couldn't get hold of them,' Mrs Grace replied, 'though I'll keep trying. But unless an ideal offer comes along before Friday, I simply can't see a better alternative for Faith than going to Littlehaven Hall. That's all there is to it.'

Eight

Josie gave one last look for Anna and Ben as the bus that would get them to school on time drew up at the stop. They always seemed to leave it till the very last minute. The double doors were just swishing shut as she caught a glimpse of two figures hurtling up the road from the village.

'Hang on – they're just coming!' she said to the bus driver, relieved.

He sighed, shaking his head. 'One day, I won't wait,' he said, pressing a button to reopen the doors. 'That'll teach them a lesson.'

'Sorry! Thanks!' panted Anna as she threw herself up

the steps next to Josie and slapped down the money for her fare.

'Ought to get yourself an alarm clock,' the driver said grumpily to Ben as he followed his sister.

'Come on, it's the first time we've been late this week,' Ben replied, tearing his ticket out of the machine.

'Well done! It's only Tuesday,' the driver called after him as the three of them went down the gangway to their usual seats near the back.

'Well?' Anna said, as soon as she'd got her breath again. 'How did it go yesterday, with the Hyde-Whites?'

'Oh, you can imagine,' Josie said. 'They've got this amazing house, and wonderful stables with a groom and everything. They're keen to have Faith, but they don't want to be bothered with us coming to visit her. We're not on their level – they made that very clear.'

'So did you decide anything?' Ben asked. 'You've still got that other lot interested, haven't you? The ones who are going up to Scotland?'

'No, that's the other thing,' Josie said. 'They rang up yesterday to say that they're not moving after all, so they won't be able to have Faith. At the moment, it's the Hyde-Whites or nothing – apart from some people Mum hasn't been able to speak to who left a message on the machine. Harriet just has to give her gracious approval, and then Faith will be all theirs. She's coming to check her over on Friday evening.'

'You can't let Faith go to the Hyde-Whites,' Anna said. 'It would be all wrong! How can your mother even consider it?'

'Because they've got stables and a groom, and plenty of land, and they know all about horses,' Josie said. 'Anyway, there doesn't seem to be any other option at the moment. What else can we do?'

'I've been thinking this over,' Anna said, as the bus rumbled on its way through the winding country roads. 'Just tell me – do you agree, the main thing is to get the Hyde-Whites out of the picture?'

'I'm not sure,' Josie said doubtfully. Then she thought back to the huge cold house, and the unsmiling groom, and the sharp woman on her dressage horse, and came to a decision. 'Yes!' she said firmly. 'You're right. Down with the Hyde-Whites, and we can take it from there!'

'Good,' Anna said. 'Then you leave it to Ben and me. It might be better if you didn't know too much about the plan so that you won't get into trouble with your mother. She might not be so hard on us. Besides, you're so hopeless at keeping secrets, you'd be bound to give the game away.'

'What plan is this?' Ben asked. 'Is it going to end up with us both getting into trouble, as usual?'

'Look, Ben, do you want to help Josie or not?' Anna demanded. 'If you don't then, fine – leave it up to me. But I've thought of something that might do the trick,

89

and it'll be easier if you're in on it too. If it works, no one needs to know we were involved at all.'

'And what if it doesn't work?' Ben asked, giving his sister a sharp look. 'Your amazing schemes have been known to fail in the past.'

'Yes,' Josie chimed in. 'Remember the catching-a-bus-on-the-cross-country-run idea, and the just-nipping out-of-school-to-buy-an-icecream one? They weren't huge successes, were they?'

'Well, at least we'll know we've tried, rather than just sitting here doing nothing,' Anna said firmly, rooting among the exercise books in her bag. 'Anyway, this plan's foolproof. Now, I s'pose I'd better look at those History dates I should have learnt last night. Ben, I'll fill you in later about what we're going to do.'

Ben looked at Josie and she raised her eyebrows. What on earth was Anna dreaming up?

Over the next few days, no matter how hard she tried, Josie couldn't get Anna or Ben to spill any information about their plan. So she tried to put the Hyde-Whites' visit out of her mind and spent as much time with Faith as she could. The days came and went, filled with schoolwork and stable chores and riding. Now the evenings were getting lighter, she had more time to take Faith out after school, and they went for a couple of lovely long hacks through the fields. It was soothing to groom her too, and Josie took pride in making sure Faith's bay coat was shining and her hooves were oiled.

'That pony looks immaculate,' her mother smiled, coming into the loose box early on Friday morning. 'They're not coming till this evening, you know.' It was the first time she'd spoken about the Hyde-Whites since their visit to Littlehaven Hall.

'Mum, do we really have no other choice?' Josie asked, giving Faith a firm stroke with the plaited hay wisp, to tone up her muscles.

'There just isn't anyone else on the scene that can match their set-up,' her mother said decisively. 'I did manage to get hold of the Atterburys – you know, the people who left a phone message – but I had to tell them we had another offer on the table.'

'And who are the Atterburys?' Josie asked. 'Are they local? Do you know them?'

'Yes and no,' her mother replied, taking a body brush and starting to work on Faith's tail. 'They moved to Littlehaven a little while ago, but I've never met them. It's quite a sad story, actually. Their daughter, Jill, had her own pony, but she was involved in a car accident last year. She dislocated and fractured her hip very badly, and the doctors told her it would be a long time before she could ride again – if ever.'

'Oh, how awful!' Josie exclaimed, letting the wisp fall to the ground.

'I know,' said her mother, nodding. 'Just imagine that. It puts our problems into perspective, doesn't it? Anyway, they sold her pony and all the tack, but apparently Jill's been beside herself without him. They thought getting an older pony that she could look after, even if she couldn't ride it, might make things a bit easier.'

'Well, couldn't we let them have Faith?' Josie asked eagerly. 'Doesn't that sound like a good idea?'

'I don't know, love,' her mother replied. 'I'm really not sure it would be so good from Faith's point of view. They don't have any other horses, for one thing, and she'd hate to be on her own after living here. And she's going to need some exercising, too.' She put down the brush and, giving Faith a farewell pat, took Josie's arm. 'Now, come on time for breakfast, or you'll miss the bus.'

The day flew by. Even double French – usually an endurance test for Josie – didn't seem to last as long as she'd have liked. Before she knew it, Anna was waving goodbye to her at the bus-stop.

'See you later – we'll come round about six,' she said. 'We'll need a little bit of time alone with Faith and Harriet, but that shouldn't be too difficult to manage.

Whatever happens, don't look surprised, OK? Just go with the flow.'

Josie made one final appeal. 'Ben, are you sure you know what you're doing?' she asked. 'No one's going to get hurt, are they?'

'Well, not exactly,' he replied with a smile. 'Look, this might be a crazy idea, but I think it's worth a try – Anna's convinced me. Just trust us!'

'Why do you both have to be so secretive?' Josie grumbled, a couple of hours later, as she and Anna and Ben hung around the yard waiting for the Hyde-Whites to arrive. They still wouldn't give her any clues about what they were planning, and it was driving her mad. 'I just wish you'd tell me what you've got in mind!' she said, for the twentieth time.

'Believe me,' Anna said, 'the less you know the better.'

'I know, why don't we go and clean some tack?' Ben suggested. 'That'll help pass the time, if there's nothing else we can be doing.'

They were sitting quietly working away in the tack room when the Hyde-Whites' car drew up.

'Are you lot up to something?' Mrs Grace asked, stopping for a moment as she walked past the open tack-room door, on her way to greet them. 'You don't usually go in there unless I've bribed you with a ride first.'

'Come on, you two,' Anna said, jumping to her feet. 'Let's go and make friends with Harriet.' Mrs Grace looked even more suspicious as the three of them trooped out after her.

Mr Hyde-White and his daughter were just getting out of the car. Harriet was exactly as Josie had remembered: thick, strawberry-blonde hair and a tanned, thin face that, she now realised, was the image of her mother's. She was wearing a spotless pale-blue cotton jumper and a pair of jodhpurs that looked brand new.

'Hello, Harriet,' Josie said, feeling as though she ought to make an effort.

'Yes, hi,' said Anna, flashing her a big smile. 'It's great to see you again.'

Looking slightly surprised, Harriet gave them a cool nod in return.

'We meet again,' said Mr Hyde-White. 'We are seeing a lot of each other, aren't we?' And he gave his short, barking laugh.

'Faith's waiting for you in the loose box,' Mrs Grace said. She led the way over, with the Hyde-Whites following on behind and Ben, Josie and Anna bringing up the rear. Harriet obviously didn't want to talk to them, and stuck close to her father's side.

Faith was standing with her head over the stable door, watching them approach. Hope looked the visitors over, too, but Charity stayed somewhere in the depths of her stable. Mrs Grace brought Faith out into the sunshine, and Josie watched as Harriet examined her closely from head to foot. There was a slightly awkward atmosphere, as though no one knew quite what to say. Mrs Grace seemed to sense it too, and after a while she handed the lead rope to Ben, who happened to be standing next to her, and said, 'Why don't you saddle Faith up so Harriet can have a ride on her? I'll take Mr Hyde-White to the office for a chat while you lot spend some time on your own.'

'Good idea,' Mr Hyde-White said. 'We can talk business while the youngsters talk ponies, eh? See you later, Hatty.'

Harriet looked a little alarmed at being left on her own with the other three but Anna immediately went into her most charming mode. 'Josie's told us all about your wonderful stables,' she said, with a warm smile. 'Faith would be so lucky to have a home with you.'

'Well, I'm sure she's had enough of beginners thumping about on her like sacks of potatoes,' Harriet replied, with a thin smile. 'She'll think she's died and gone to heaven if she comes to us.'

Anna carried on chatting in such an easy, friendly way that anyone would have thought she wanted to be Harriet's best friend. She flattered her so cleverly that frosty Harriet began to thaw in spite of herself. Then,

95

very subtly, Anna led the conversation so that it left Josie out in the cold. It soon began to sound as though she had never liked Josie much in the first place, and only came to the stables because she wanted a chance to ride. Harriet sensed what was happening and was quite happy to add her own snide remarks. Soon she and Anna were clearly on one side of the fence with Josie on the other. No one bothered much about Ben, who ended up fetching Faith's tack and saddling her up while the three girls talked.

Although she knew Anna was up to something, Josie couldn't help feeling a little bit hurt by the way she was being treated.

'Why don't you run along to your bedroom and find those photos of you and Faith when you were a little girl?' Anna said to her eventually. 'I'm sure Harriet would like to see them, and I want to talk to her without you hanging round all the time like our shadow. Go on, we'll see you later. Ben's going to take Faith to the arena for us.'

'Take as long as you like – we won't mind,' added Harriet with a sneer. Picking on somebody else seemed to have brought her to life: there was a glint in her eye and she looked like she was really enjoying herself.

'OK,' said Josie, beginning to understand what Anna was working towards. She'd said she needed some time on her own with Harriet, and shutting Josie out was one way to get it. 'I won't be too long,' she added, but Anna had already taken Harriet's arm, and was whispering into her ear.

Josie walked off to the house, so that the next stage of the mysterious plan – whatever it was – could be put into effect. Up in her room, she lay on the bed and waited.

Five minutes later, everything started happening. Josie heard a sudden shout from Ben and a neigh from Faith. Rushing out of her room, she went to the landing window and looked down at the yard.

Faith was tossing up her head and dancing backwards, plainly upset about something. Ben had dropped her reins and was bending over, clutching his arm. Josie saw Anna and Harriet came running up to him from a little way behind, and then all three of them stood clustered together for a moment. Next, Harriet broke away from the group and stormed over to the office, flinging open the door.

Josie had seen enough. She rushed down the stairs and through the front door, then along the path and out into the yard. 'What's going on?' she cried, rushing up to Ben and Anna.

'I'm not sure,' Anna replied. 'Wait and see.' She had taken Faith's reins and, giving the pony a gentle pat, talked quietly to calm her down. Faith's ears were back and she was showing the whites of her eyes.

'Are you OK?' Josie asked Ben. 'Has something happened to Faith?'

'Oh, I'm fine,' he said, still holding his arm. 'Faith's just a bit startled, that's all. Sorry, old girl,' he added, 'but we had to do it. It's for your own good.'

'What's for her own good?' Josie asked frantically. 'What have you done?'

'Tell you later – they're coming out,' Anna hissed. 'Stand away from me, Josie!'

Mr Hyde-White and Harriet came out of the office on the opposite side of the yard, followed by Mrs Grace.

'I don't understand,' Josie's mum was saying. 'I just can't believe what you're saying. It's completely untrue!'

'You would say that, wouldn't you?' Harriet replied nastily, as she opened the car door.

'It's quite clear you haven't been straight with us,' Mr Hyde-White said angrily, getting into the driver's seat. He wound down the window and continued, 'I consider our business here finished. You have behaved in a most underhand way and completely wasted my valuable time. Then again, I never rated your shabby little stables very highly. Should have guessed something like this would happen.' With that, the engine roared into life, and the large shiny car shot out of the yard.

Mrs Grace looked across to where Ben, Anna and Josie were standing with Faith. 'You three!' she shouted. 'I want a word with you!'

'Now who's going to tell me what on earth's going on?' Mrs Grace said angrily, staring at Josie and Anna as they stood in front of her desk in the crowded little office. 'And where's Ben?'

'He's putting Faith back in her loose box,' Anna said.

'So who is going to tell me where this ridiculous story about Faith being vicious has come from?' Mrs Grace demanded.

'What?' said Josie, horrified. 'I don't know what you mean!'

'No, I can see you don't,' said her mother, looking at her face. 'Well, Anna?'

'It was my idea,' Anna said resolutely. 'Josie didn't know anything about it.' She took a deep breath. 'We felt that it would be awful for Faith to go to the Hyde-Whites – none of us would be able to see her again. So I thought, if we couldn't put you off the idea, we'd have to put them off her instead.'

'Go on,' said Mrs Grace in an icy voice, as Anna seemed to have dried up.

Anna cleared her throat. 'Well, I sucked up to Harriet, and then when we were on our own I told her that Faith had this terrible habit of savagely biting other horses, and people as well. And that was why you wanted to sell her.'

Josie stared at Anna. She didn't know what to think. Part of her thought it was a brilliant idea, and part of her wanted to laugh at the very thought of Faith biting anyone. Most of all, though, Josie was terrified of how her mother would react, as she sat there with a face like thunder.

'And she believed you, just like that?' Mrs Grace

asked. 'She even swallowed some story you'd made up about Ben having been bitten?'

'Well, there was a bit more to it than that,' Ben said, coming through the door and standing next to his sister. 'I'd better show you this.' And he rolled up one shirt sleeve and held out his arm.

Josie couldn't stop herself from gasping at the sight. A deep open wound, the edges raw and gaping, stretched its ugly way along Ben's right forearm.

Nine

'Oh my goodness!' exclaimed Mrs Grace, clutching the edge of the table in shock.

'Ben!' Josie cried. 'What happened to you?' She didn't understand how he could stand there so calmly when he must be in agony.

'Oh, it's all right,' he replied. 'Watch!' And he began to peel the wound away from his arm with his left hand, leaving smooth tanned skin behind.

'It's plastic,' Anna explained. 'Ben was given this pack of stage make-up for his birthday last year – which is what gave me the whole idea! These wounds are so realistic. We put one of them on his arm at home, under his shirt. When he was leading Faith over to the ring in front of Harriet and me, he kind of jerked her head up and pretended that she'd bitten him. You'd never have guessed it was fake, would you?'

'No, I wouldn't!' Mrs Grace said, letting out her breath in a rush. 'You nearly gave me a heart attack. Still, that's the least of it.' She got up from her chair and, folding her arms, stared at Ben and Anna for a moment before speaking.

'Did you think for one second about the consequences of what you were doing?' she said. 'Did you not stop to consider where your crazy scheme would leave Faith? That it would take away her chance of going to a good home?'

'But we didn't think it *was* a good home, Mrs Grace,' Anna said. 'Harriet's not a kind person, and we didn't think that anybody there would love Faith like they ought to have done. Like we do.'

'I know the Hyde-Whites have got all the right facilities, Mum, but they're so unfeeling,' Josie added. 'Faith needs someone who'll give her lots of affection, you know she does!'

Her mother sighed. 'We've had this conversation before,' she said. 'You're perfectly well aware of what I think. That's partly why I'm so cross,' she went on, turning to Anna. 'I know you only did what you thought was best to help Josie, but you undermined me completely. You made me look like an idiot – and worse, a liar – in front of that man.'

'I'm sorry, Mrs Grace,' Anna said, beginning to look shamefaced and staring at her shoes. 'I didn't really think about that.'

'Well, you should have done,' she replied. 'I'm beginning to think none of you understand what's at stake here. We have to find somewhere else for Faith to live. We can't keep her, however much we'd all like to – me more than anyone. And what am I supposed to do now?' She looked at the three of them despairingly.

'Ring the Atterburys?' Josie suggested hopefully.

'I suppose I'll have to,' her mother said. 'Though who knows whether they're really interested. In the meantime, Ben and Anna, you are banned from coming here until I give permission. And none of you are ever to pull a stunt like that again. Do you understand me? If you really disagree with something, come and talk to me about it. Don't just take the law into your own hands. OK?'

'OK,' the three of them replied together. Then, with muttered goodbyes and sorrys and a quick wave to Josie, Ben and Anna shuffled out of the office.

Mrs Grace shook her head and looked at Josie. 'At least they had the sense to keep you out of this,' she said. 'That girl! What will she think of next?'

'Sorry, Mum,' Josie said. 'I'm sure she didn't mean to land you in it.'

'Well, she did, whether she meant to or not,' Mrs Grace said, reaching for the phone book. 'And she certainly got rid of the Hyde-Whites pretty sharpish. I've never seen anyone move so fast! Now, I'm going to ring up the Atterburys and have a talk to them – in private. Understand? This time, you leave things to me.'

'OK, Mum,' Josie replied. 'Message understood.' She shot out of the office, feeling she'd got off lightly.

Josie didn't hurry over the evening chores. She groomed the ponies carefully and turned them out, one by one. Sue Collins was out for a ride on Tubber, and her mother had already taken care of Captain and Connie. By the time Josie had come back into the house, her parents were sitting talking quietly together at the kitchen table over an open bottle of wine. Good! she thought to herself, Mum's probably calmed down by now. She snatched a quick look at her mother's face, just to make sure.

Mrs Grace noticed her glance. 'There's no need to tiptoe round me like I'm going to explode,' she said. 'I've stopped seething now. You can understand how I felt, though, can't you?'

'I certainly can,' said Mr Grace. 'I'm not going to go on and on about this, Josie, but remember what I said about things being hard for other people, not just you? Well, I expect you to be helping your mother, not going behind her back.'

'To be fair, Rob, I don't think Josie knew much about it,' said her mother, putting a hand over her husband's.

'I knew something was going on, but I wasn't sure exactly what,' Josie said, pulling up a chair and sitting down at the table. 'We were all so certain that Littlehaven Hall wasn't the right place for Faith, Mum, and nothing I said to you seemed to make any difference.'

Mrs Grace took a sip of wine and stared at Josie thoughtfully. 'I can see that must have been frustrating,' she said eventually. 'Perhaps we should have spent more time talking it over. I really felt Faith would be well looked after there, that's all. I know the Hyde-Whites aren't particularly friendly, but I thought maybe that wouldn't matter to Faith. I was sure they'd never have mistreated her.'

'But how would we have known, Mum?' Josie asked. 'They'd never have let us back into their precious stately home to visit her, would they?'

'No, they wouldn't,' Mrs Grace agreed. She leant back in her chair and stretched her arms up above her head. 'Well, we'll never know now. I don't think Mr Hyde-White will come back to our "shabby little stables" in a hurry!'

'Is that what he called them?' Mr Grace said

indignantly. 'What a nerve! Well, if he does come back, I'll set him straight.' He waved a tea towel in the air. 'Teach him a lesson! Littlehaven Hall or no Littlehaven Hall.'

'Groom or no groom!' Josie said, smiling. 'You go for it, Dad!'

'Dressage horse or no dressage horse!' added Mrs Grace, getting into the spirit of things.

Josie gave her mother a hug. 'I'm sorry, Mum,' she said. 'I'm sorry you had to stand there while he talked to you like that.'

'Oh well,' said her mother, stroking Josie's auburn hair, 'I expect I'll survive. I've heard worse than that before. And while I'm not quite ready to forgive Anna completely for what she's done, things sometimes have a funny habit of working out in the end.'

'How do you mean?' Josie asked, drawing back to look at her mother's face.

'Well, I got hold of the Atterburys,' she said, 'and they are definitely still interested, though they don't want to get Jill's hopes up at this stage. They'd like to come round on their own early tomorrow morning, and take a first look at Faith. I'll talk to them and you can hover around in the background. Understood? This time, we'll play everything by the book.'

'OK, Mum,' Josie said, just happy that everything was back to normal. 'Whatever you say.'

'Josie? Is that you?' hissed an urgent voice on the other end of the phone, the next afternoon.

'Anna?' Josie replied. 'Yes, it's me – Mum's out teaching a lesson, luckily for you. How are you two? Does your mum know about everything?'

'Yes, we told her,' Anna said. 'We reckoned it would come out sooner or later. She's made us write letters of apology and she's going to bring them round tonight and take your mum out for a drink. Don't say anything, though – it's meant to be a surprise. How is she? Still in a mood?'

'She's getting over it,' Josie replied. 'You're mad, Anna, you know that? How on earth did you think you'd get away with that?'

'I never thought Harriet would make such a fuss,' Anna said. 'I thought they'd just leave and then she'd say something to her dad when they were on their own. Oh, I don't know – I suppose I didn't really think that part of it through. Still, you've got to admit the plan worked. We got rid of the Hyde-Whites, didn't we?'

'You certainly did,' Josie said. 'Look, I can't speak too long. The lesson's nearly over and then Mum and I are going to see some other people who might have Faith.'

'Who are they?' Anna asked. 'Are they nice? Where do they live?'

'The Atterburys live in Littlehaven,' Josie said, 'and I don't know what they're like. After your performance yesterday I decided to keep out of the way when they came over this morning. Mum spoke to them and she hasn't told me anything yet. They came and looked at Faith without Jill, their daughter. She's had this accident and she can't ride.'

'Well then, why does she want a pony?' Anna asked. 'Is she crazy or something?'

'Look, I'll explain it later,' Josie said. 'There really isn't time to go into everything now. We can talk it all over on Monday. Oh, and by the way, Anna – thanks. Thanks for everything you did, and Ben, too. Just don't do it again, OK?'

'Charming,' Anna retorted. 'And there was me thinking we'd done you a huge favour.'

'You did, you did!' Josie replied. 'I owe you one. It was a bit dramatic, that's all. Hang on, I can hear Mum calling. Got to go. See you soon!'

She replaced the receiver and hurried out of the house. The lesson was over and Mrs Grace was helping a pupil dismount from Hope.

'Can you help Sally, please?' she called when she saw Josie. 'If you could take Faith from her, I'll follow you up to the loose boxes with Hope, and then we can be off. OK?'

'You're selling Faith, aren't you?' Sally asked, taking her feet out of the stirrups, then swinging her leg over Faith's back and slithering to the ground. 'Have you found someone to buy her yet?'

'Not yet,' Josie replied, looping the reins over Faith's head and handing them back to Sally so she could hold her while the saddle was heaved off. 'Still, I'm sure it won't take us too long. Mum and I are going to look at another place in a minute. Don't you worry, old girl,' she added, giving Faith a pat before she ran up the stirrup leathers and unbuckled the girth. 'We'll come up with the perfect home, just you wait and see.'

But she couldn't help listening to a little voice that kept niggling away in the back of her mind. 'What if nothing turns up?' it said. 'What will we do then? Was turning the Hyde-Whites away a big mistake after all?'

'So,' Josie said to her mother, as she fastened her seat belt twenty minutes later, 'tell me what you think about the Atterburys. I kept out of the way this morning, didn't I?'

Josie had brought Faith in from the field first thing and given her a thorough grooming so she looked her best. When the Atterburys arrived, she made herself busy catching Hope and Charity. Apart from a quick hello, she hadn't talked to them at all.

'Yes, you did,' her mother smiled, as she reversed their car out of the yard. 'You were very discreet. Well, I liked them. They've had such a worrying time with Jill

– it must have been awful! She was out for the day with a friend and some lunatic went straight into the car they were in. Anyway, they sold her pony on the doctor's advice.'

'Poor girl,' Josie said, shaking her head. 'I can't imagine how I'd cope with the prospect of not being able to ride.'

Her mother nodded. 'Apparently Jill misses the pony desperately,' she said. 'Not just for riding, but all the time she spent grooming and feeding, even mucking out! Just having one around the place again would mean such a lot to her.'

'And did her parents like Faith?' Josie asked.

'What do you think?' Mrs Grace replied. 'Everybody likes her, that's the trouble! They thought she was lovely – that's why they wanted us to come round as soon as possible to see their place and talk it over.'

'So is this it, Mum?' Josie asked, as they approached the outskirts of Littlehaven. 'Do you think they're the right family for Faith?'

'I'm not sure,' Mrs Grace said thoughtfully. 'There are a few things to sort out. I don't know whether Faith's ready to retire completely, for one thing. She'll need some exercise for a while. And she might get a bit lonely, all on her own. I think we must be really careful not to get Jill's hopes up, just in case it doesn't work out.'

Ten minutes later, they were drawing up outside a modern detached house near the edge of town. Josie caught sight of a face at the window, which instantly vanished. Seconds later, the front door opened and Mrs Atterbury was smiling at them, her arm round the shoulder of a thin, pale girl with shoulder-length brown hair. 'Jill's been waiting for you to arrive all afternoon,' she said, as Mrs Grace and Josie got out of the car. 'I thought she was going to burn a hole looking through that window!'

'Hi, Jill,' Josie said as she walked up the path. 'I'm Josie. Hello, Mrs Atterbury.'

'Thanks for coming,' Jill said shyly, standing back. She was probably about ten or eleven, Josie thought, with a serious face and big dark eyes that seemed to take everything in.

They all stood about for a little while in the hall, and then Mrs Atterbury said to her daughter, 'Why don't you take Josie to your room, Jill? You could show her your pictures of Marmalade.'

'OK. It's just down here,' Jill said to Josie, pointing along the passageway.

'Do you need this?' Mrs Atterbury said, holding out a walking stick that was propped against the wall.

Jill shook her head. 'I can manage,' she said abruptly.

Josie followed her down the passage, trying not to take any notice of Jill dragging one leg along awkwardly as she walked. 'I had crutches for three months,' Jill said, glancing back. 'I'm trying to do without anything now so that my leg will get stronger.'

'It must be a real pain,' Josie commented, wishing she could think of something more original to say.

'Certainly is,' Jill replied. 'But it's a great excuse for getting out of games.'

They both laughed, and Josie felt a huge sense of relief that the ice was broken. Jill had obviously got used to making people feel comfortable about what had happened to her.

'This is my room,' she said, throwing open the door. 'It used to be the study, but Mum and Dad fixed it up as a bedroom for me so I didn't have to keep climbing the stairs.'

'It looks brilliant!' Josie said, staring around at the hundreds of horse and pony pictures covering every inch of the walls. 'I've never seen so many posters. I've got that one, too – the grey galloping along the beach. He's beautiful, isn't he?'

'That's my favourite,' Jill said. 'I lie in bed sometimes looking at it and imagining I'm on his back, riding off into the sunset.'

'Does that make you feel worse?' Josie asked sympathetically, sitting down on a chair by the desk. Although she'd only just met Jill, she felt as though she could talk to her about anything.

'Not really,' Jill replied. 'I know I'm going to be riding again some day. I've made my mind up that I will.' She reached up for a photo album on the bookshelf and flicked open the pages. 'Look, this is me on Marmalade,' she said, showing Josie some pictures of herself sitting proudly on a beautifully turned-out light chestnut pony.

'Oh, he's lovely!' Josie exclaimed, putting the album down on the desk top to look more closely at the photograph. 'Do you have any other photos of him?'

'Loads,' Jill said, coming to stand next to her and turning over the pages in the album. 'See, there we are jumping – we'd just started together. This is us in the bending race. We came second, you know. I've got the rosette up on my pinboard. Oh, I do miss him,' she added with a sigh, staring out of the window. 'I wish we hadn't sold him so quickly. It's just not the same without a pony around.'

'I can imagine,' Josie said, thinking of all the time she spent looking after their three. She followed Jill's gaze and saw her mother with Mrs Atterbury at the end of the garden, looking out over the field that lay beyond. 'Is that your field?' she said. 'Where you kept Marmalade?'

'That's right,' Jill said. 'You'd never have thought there was all this land here, would you? It's perfect for horses – there's a little stream at the bottom, and a shelter too.' She turned to Josie with an eager expression. 'Now, come on – tell me all about Faith. From what Mum and Dad have said, she sounds lovely.'

She grasped the arm of Josie's chair and used it to lower herself awkwardly into a sitting position on the edge of the bed, her leg stuck out straight in front of her. 'Where did she come from? What does she like doing? I want to know everything!' she demanded.

Josie wasn't quite sure what to say. She remembered what her mother had told her about not raising Jill's hopes. She liked Jill a lot, but would she really be able to cope with another pony just yet? And would Faith be happy, all by herself in that big field?

'Look, Jill,' she began, 'before I start boring you to death, maybe there are a few things we ought to talk about. We think Faith's going to need riding for a while. And she's used to being with other animals – I just don't know if she'd be happy on her own the whole time.'

Josie's voice trailed away, as she tried to think of a tactful way of saying what was on her mind. Then she decided just to be honest about it. 'Look, Jill, I'd love you to have Faith – more than anyone else we've seen so far – but do you really think this is the right place for her?'

Ten

'Oh, you don't need to worry about any of that,' Jill said, waving her hand dismissively. 'It's all sorted! Faith wouldn't be on her own, for one thing. And the riding's taken care of, too.'

'How do you mean?' Josie asked, looking at her curiously. Had Jill understood what she was trying to say?

Jill leant forward from her seat on the bed. 'Listen, as soon as Mum and Dad told me about your pony, we rang up my friend Bev. She's been renting the field from us for her gelding, Midnight. He's sixteen hands, but he's gentle as a lamb – Faith would just love him.

Bev's taken him out for a ride this afternoon, or you could have met him and you'd see what I mean. Anyway, there's plenty of room for both of them in the field and the shelter, too! Bev thinks he's lonely at the moment, so she'd like him to have some company.'

Josie felt a tingle begin to creep its way up her spine. There was something about the way everything was falling into place that made her feel this new home was meant to be. 'That sounds great!' she said. 'Provided they get on, of course.'

'Midnight gets on with everyone,' Jill said. 'He's a big soppy marshmallow. Plus, Bev and her sister would love to take Faith out sometimes – if you agree, that is. They're horse mad and they've been riding for years, so they'd take care of her.'

'Oh, Jill, you really have thought it all through,' said Josie, delighted. 'I think that sounds perfect! You'd look after Faith – she'd be your pony, but other people would exercise her sometimes for you.'

'There is someone else I probably ought to let ride her,' Jill said seriously.

'Oh? Who?' Josie asked, wondering what was coming.

'You, of course!' Jill said, laughing at her bewildered expression. 'You could come and take Faith out whenever you felt like it. I know you'll be moving out of the stables, but you probably won't end up that far away from us.'

'Jill, that would be wonderful!' Josie said, unable to stop the tears coming to her eyes. 'You don't know how much that would mean to me.'

'Well, maybe we shouldn't get carried away,' Jill said, embarrassed. 'Perhaps we should go and see what our mothers have decided first.'

'I just want to say one thing,' Josie said, blowing her nose on a scrap of tissue she found in her pocket. 'If you do take Faith, she'll be your pony, not ours any more. I don't want you to feel that I'd be hanging around all the time. If Mum decides that this is the right place for her too, then I couldn't be happier handing her over to you.'

'If you carry on like this I'll have to use that snotty tissue after you,' said Jill gruffly. 'Come on, give me a hand up and let's go down to the field. You can tell me more about Faith on the way.'

Josie and her mother hardly said a word on the way back to Grace's Stables. It was obvious to them both that, as they couldn't keep Faith any more, the next best home she could possibly find was with the Atterburys. When Josie had gone out into the garden with Jill, she had known from her mother's face that she had made up her mind.

'We'd better not keep you in suspense any longer,' Mrs Grace had said, smiling at Jill's anxious expression.

'Come and have a look at Faith tomorrow. If you like her as much as your parents did – and if Josie agrees – she's yours.'

'I've already decided that Faith would love it here,' Josie said, beaming at her mum.

'And you're bound to love Faith, Jill,' Mrs Atterbury said. 'She's gorgeous – just wait till you see her.'

'Oh, I can't wait!' Jill cried, throwing her arms round her mother and nearly falling over in excitement. 'I'll take such good care of her, Josie, I promise you! And you must come and see her whenever you want. Thank you, Mum! Thank you, everybody!'

They arranged for Jill to come round the next evening, after lessons were over but before the Graces' big Sunday supper. Then Josie and her mother started out on the drive home, both obviously feeling rather quiet and sad. This is it, Josie thought to herself. Faith is really leaving. Even if they had found a wonderful home for her, it was somebody else's and not theirs.

'All right, sweetie?' asked Mrs Grace.

Josie nodded, feeling too choked up to speak.

'It's so strange, to think of Faith going away,' her mother said. 'But I just keep remembering the way Jill looked, when she realised she might be able to have her. She's had to give up so much. She deserves some happiness now, don't you think?'

Josie cleared her throat. 'Yes, she does,' she said.

'She's going to love Faith and look after her, and Faith will love her back. I know this is for the best, Mum – it's just a bit hard, that's all.'

'I know,' said her mother. 'Believe me, I feel it too.'

It was quiet in the yard by the time they got back. Basil must have been inside the house, and the birds were all safely shut up in their hen house for the evening.

'Oh, Lynne's here!' said Mrs Grace, spotting her friend's blue van in the yard. 'Great! I could do with some cheering up. She'd better not have brought Ben and Anna, though.'

'No, I shouldn't think she has,' Josie said. 'See you later, Mum. I'll take care of the ponies.'

'OK,' said her mother. 'Don't stay out here moping, though, will you?'

Josie shook her head and walked over to the loose boxes. Faith was dozing quietly with her lower lip drooping and her long mane falling over her eyes. Josie walked up and rested her head against the pony's smooth, steady neck. 'Oh, Faith,' she said, her tears beginning to fall. 'What are we going to do without you?'

Faith nuzzled Josie's hair gently. Josie looked up into her big brown eyes that had such a wise, intelligent look about them. 'I'm making a fuss, aren't I?' she said, wiping her nose with the back of her hand. She thought about Jill, sitting in her room with all the posters and not knowing whether she'd ever be able to ride again. She must have been one of the bravest people Josie had ever met.

'You're going to have a new home and a new owner, Faith,' she said. 'But I know you'll love her – she's just as special as you are. I think you're going to be really happy together.'

Sunday passed in a blur. The Graces tried to carry on with their normal weekend routine, but Josie could only think about what would happen that evening. She knew her parents were just waiting for the time to pass, too.

'Oh, thank goodness that's over,' Mrs Grace said as she waved goodbye to her last pupil. 'It seems to have been such hard work today!'

Josie looked at her watch yet again. Half past four. One hour to go, and then the Atterburys would be here.

Faith hadn't been ridden since the morning, and was looking out of her loose box at the comings and goings in the yard. 'You've got no idea what's going to happen, have you?' Josie murmured, stopping to give her a quick stroke as she passed by with Charity. 'Well, don't you worry – everything'll work out just fine.' She was trying to be brave, but she couldn't stop the butterflies from dancing around in her stomach.

At five, Josie was hanging around the kitchen, getting in her father's way, when she heard a knock on the front door. Mrs Grace came out of the study to open it, and moments later, Josie heard familiar voices.

'Visitors for you!' her mother announced, as she came through the kitchen door with Ben and Anna. 'Thought you might like some moral support.'

'Oh, great, Mum!' said Josie with a broad smile for her friends. 'I feel better already.'

'Hi, Josie! We've been forgiven,' said Anna, coming to stand next to her. 'Your mum told ours last night we're allowed back, so we thought we'd surprise you.'

'I really appreciated those letters you both wrote,' said Mrs Grace. 'And after all, if it hadn't been for you, Faith would probably have ended up with the Hyde-Whites. Not that I'm saying you were right to do what you did,' she added hastily.

'It'll never happen again, I promise,' Ben said seriously. 'Mum made me throw the make-up away.'

'Oh, shame,' said Mr Grace. 'I was thinking of borrowing it.'

'Just you try!' said his wife, but at that moment there was another loud knock on the front door. Everyone fell silent and looked at each other. 'They're early,' Mrs Grace said, as she went back down the hall.

'I'm sorry, we just couldn't wait any longer,' said Mr Atterbury as he came into the kitchen with his wife and daughter. There was a flurry of smiling and nodding and hand-shaking as Ben, Anna and Mr Grace were introduced. Then, after some half-hearted conversation, Mrs Grace said, 'Well, what are we waiting for? Faith's all ready to meet you, Jill. Why don't you go with Josie and Anna and Ben? We'll join you later.'

The four of them walked slowly down the path and across the yard. Why am I so nervous? Josie thought to herself. She looked at Jill's intent, white face and realised she was feeling exactly the same. Linking an arm through hers, she said, 'Don't worry – I'm sure this is going to work out.'

Jill gave her a smile in return, then tightened her grip as she caught her first glimpse of Faith, looking out of the loose box. She stopped and stared for a moment in silence. Faith gave a neigh and shook her mane, as though she was calling. Jill dropped Josie's arm and began to walk as quickly as she could towards the bay pony.

Anna started to go with her, but Josie shook her head. 'Let her go alone,' she said quietly.

They watched together as Jill went over to where Faith was standing, waiting. She held out her hand, then stroked Faith's white stripe, patted her neck and tickled her nose. Talking gently all the time, she reached into her pocket and brought out a packet of peppermints. Soon Faith was crunching happily,

tossing her head up and down so that her mane shook. Suddenly she lowered her head and, very gently, nuzzled Jill's forehead with her lips.

'Oh, look!' said Josie delightedly. 'She's giving her a kiss! She usually only does that to me and Mum!'

In return, Jill threw her arms round Faith's neck and gave her a huge hug. For a second, she stayed with her face buried in Faith's mane, not moving. Josie felt the tears come to her eyes. Anna grabbed her hand and gave it a squeeze as they looked on silently.

Then Jill turned back to them, grinning from ear to ear. 'She's perfect!' she cried. 'I love her already. Oh, thank you, Josie!'

After that, it was only a question of working out the arrangements after everyone had gathered together round Faith's loose box. It was decided that Mrs Grace would take Faith over to the Atterburys in the trailer the next day, with her tack and anything else that she might need. 'No sense in putting it off, once the decision's been made,' she said.

Jill smiled gratefully. 'That would be wonderful,' she said. 'I just can't wait for Faith to come.' Then she gave Josie an anxious look. 'If you're sure that'll give you enough time to say your goodbyes,' she added.

Josie nodded. 'Faith and I have had a chat already,' she said. 'I've told her all about you. Besides, it's not goodbye for ever, is it? More like *au revoir*. I'm sure we'll be seeing each other again soon.'

'Come on,' suggested Anna. 'Why don't we go and turn Faith out in the field. She's had enough excitement for one day. Do you want to take her, Jill?'

Jill clipped the lead rein to Faith's head collar and brought her proudly out of the loose box. Aware of everyone's watching eyes, she started to make her way rather nervously over towards the field. Faith stayed close by her shoulder, walking slowly and quietly as though she realised she should match her pace to Jill's.

'They look good together, don't you think?' murmured Mrs Grace, putting a comforting arm around Josie's shoulders.

And, smiling through her tears, Josie had to agree that they did. 'Perfect!' she said.

Last Hope

One

Josie Grace shaded her eyes from the bright sunlight as she looked over at the blue car parked in the far corner of the yard at Grace's Riding Stables. 'Are you sure that's Sarah's car, Mum?' she asked. 'Why isn't she getting out?'

'I've got no idea,' said Mary Grace, coming to stand beside her daughter, 'but it's definitely the Butlers' car. I wish they'd get a move on! Hope's all tacked up in her loose box, and Kirsty's ready and waiting on Charity. Could you do me a big favour and find out what the problem is while we get started in the ring? We're going to be behind if I don't begin the lesson soon, and Tom's coming to shoe them all in an hour's time.'

'I'll do my best,' said Josie.

'Thanks, love! See you in a minute,' her mother replied. She turned back to a blonde girl, who was busy trying to stop the grey pony she was riding from taking a crafty nibble at one of the hanging baskets by the office door.

'I hope so,' Josie called, beginning to walk towards the Butlers' car. She could hear the sound of voices as she approached: Sarah's high and determined, and her mother's lower, pleading murmur. What was going on? Sarah had been coming regularly to the stables for the last year, but she'd now missed four lessons in a row. Each week, her mother had rung to say that she was very busy at school and couldn't make her usual Tuesday afternoon lessons. Even though she was here now, it looked as though Sarah still wasn't very keen.

When Josie reached the car, Mrs Butler wound down her window. 'Hello, Josie,' she said apologetically, with a harassed expression on her face. 'I'm sorry about this. Sarah's just coming—'

'No, I'm *not* coming!' Sarah said furiously from the passenger seat.

Tucking her dark auburn hair behind one ear, Josie crouched down by the car and looked across at the sulky nine-year-old. 'Why not, Sarah?' she asked. 'I thought you enjoyed your riding lessons. We've got

Hope saddled up and waiting for you.'

'I don't want to ride Hope!' Sarah burst out. 'If I can't have Faith, I don't want to ride at all.'

'Sarah!' her mother said through gritted teeth, beginning to lose patience. 'We've been through this a hundred times. I've told you – Faith's not here! The Graces have sold her. You have to ride Hope.'

'But I don't like her!' Sarah retorted.

'Why not?' Josie asked. 'Hope will do exactly what you tell her, and she won't ever run away with you or go too fast. Honestly, I bet you'll really enjoy the lesson. You'll never find out unless you try.'

Sarah stared at Josie stubbornly. 'I just don't like Hope,' she repeated. 'I don't like the way she looks.'

'What difference does that make?' Josie replied, starting to feel cross herself. 'It's what she's like to ride that matters.'

Mrs Butler let out an angry sigh and drummed her fingers on the car steering wheel, while Sarah folded her arms and stared straight ahead. *Oh, this is hopeless*, Josie said to herself. *We're not getting anywhere.* She racked her brains and tried to remember what she knew about Sarah Butler. She'd been coming to the stables for ten months or so, hadn't she? She could manage sitting and rising trot but, as far as Josie could recall, that was about it.

'Never mind,' Josie said, sitting back on her heels and

looking over towards the yard. 'If you really don't want to ride, Sarah, we can't force you. It's a shame, though. I was talking to Mum just now, and she said she thought you could start cantering today. Still, maybe some other time . . .'

'Cantering?' Sarah said, her eyes lighting up in spite of herself. 'I thought your mother said I wouldn't be ready to do that for a while.'

'Not on Faith, perhaps,' Josie replied, saying the first thing that came into her head – even if it was rather unfair on Faith. 'But Hope's so steady, we thought you'd be fine. Oh well, suppose I'd better go and untack her now.' She got up, brushing some dirt from the ground off her jeans. 'See you around then,' she said, as casually as she could, beginning to walk back towards the row of loose boxes on one side of the yard. It took all the determination she had not to look back and see whether Sarah would follow her. Would the gamble pay off?

And then she heard the sound of a car door opening. 'Wait for me!' Sarah called. 'Can I ride Hope, please? If that's still all right . . .'

Josie turned round. 'Of course it is,' she said with a grin. 'Come on, or the lesson will be finished before you've got in the school.'

Hope was looking over the top half of the stable door. She gave a little whinny when she saw them coming towards her, and shook her head so that the bridle jangled. Josie saw Sarah smile, and felt a little more kindly towards her. All the same, she still couldn't understand how anyone could turn their nose up at Hope. She wasn't the prettiest pony in the world, with her broad back and bent nose, but she had to be one of the gentlest. Her sweet, steady nature made her the perfect ride for a novice like Sarah.

Josie unbolted the loose box door and led Hope across the yard to the mounting block. 'She'll always stand quietly,' she said encouragingly while Sarah pulled herself up into the saddle. 'I think you're both going to get on really well together.'

'Sorry, Hope,' Sarah said, patting the pony's grey neck as she gathered up her reins. 'I didn't mean to be rude about you.'

'Come on, then,' Josie said as she led the way towards the outdoor schooling ring. 'I'll just remind Mum about what we said.'

She was praying that her mother wouldn't think she was hijacking the lesson. Luckily, although Mrs Grace looked surprised when Josie mentioned the cantering 'they'd talked about just now', she didn't object.

'OK,' she said. 'Just fall in behind Kirsty on Charity, Sarah, and we can start practising your sitting trot. Let's not waste any more time!'

'So, what was that all about?' Mrs Grace asked Josie as

they waved the Butlers goodbye at the end of the lesson. 'Why was Sarah so late?'

'She said she didn't want to ride Hope,' Josie answered. 'She didn't like the look of her, apparently. Still, she realised by the end of the lesson how silly she'd been, didn't she?' she added, patting Hope affectionately.

'Yes,' said Mrs Grace thoughtfully. 'She did really well today and she loved cantering – though I must admit, I wasn't planning on letting her try for another couple of lessons.'

'Sorry, Mum,' Josie said, running up the stirrup leathers and beginning to unbuckle Hope's girth. 'It was the only thing I could think of to get her out of the car.' She heaved the saddle off and took it over to the tackroom while her mother held the two ponies.

'Is something wrong?' she asked on the way back, noticing her mother's anxious expression. 'You look really worried all of a sudden.'

'Oh, it's probably nothing,' Mrs Grace sighed. 'It's just that hearing what Sarah said about Hope makes me feel a little bit uneasy and rather sad, that's all. Remember the advertisement for her goes in the paper tomorrow?'

'Yes, I know,' Josie said more grimly, tackling Charity's saddle. 'I've been trying not to think about it.'

'Well, I hope that we don't get the same reaction from anyone who in *theory* is interested in buying her,'

Mrs Grace went on. 'People do judge by appearances and, let's face it – Hope isn't the best-looking pony in the world.'

'Oh, Mum!' Josie protested over her shoulder as she made her second journey to the tackroom. 'She's wonderful! Everybody knows that.'

'Everybody who knows her, knows she's wonderful,' Mrs Grace continued when Josie had come back, 'but someone who doesn't, won't simply take our word for it. Our best bet might be to go for a child who's been having lessons on Hope. But I've been asking around and I haven't had any takers so far.'

'Oh, I hate this!' Josie said suddenly, looping the reins over Hope's neck and starting to lead her back off to the loose box. 'I can't bear having to trawl around to find someone to take Hope away. I wish we could all stay here forever, exactly like we are now!'

'I know, I know,' her mother said comfortingly. 'I feel the same way, believe me, but that's life. Grace's Stables have got to close, and we'll just have to make the best of it.'

Josie experienced the same wave of shock that always came over her when she thought about the future. She found it so hard to believe that the stables were really closing. Her mother had opened them fourteen years ago, two years before Josie was born, and she'd lived all her life surrounded by ponies and the horses that were kept at livery – the 'hotel guests' as her father called them. She'd taken it for granted that things would carry on in the same way forever, but then the old lady who owned the stables and School Farm – the cottage in which the Graces lived – had died. Her nephew had inherited the land, and he'd decided to sell the property for development, so Josie and her parents now had a limited amount of time to find new homes for the ponies and for themselves. Faith, the elderly bay mare who had been at Grace's Stables from the very beginning, had left the month before, and now it was Hope's turn. Her daughter, Charity, would be the last to go.

'I can't believe we won't manage to find a good home for Hope,' Josie said as she led her into the loose box. 'Surely there's someone who will see what a great first pony she'd make.'

'Well, we'll just have to wait and see,' said her mother, tying Charity to a ring on the wall outside. 'Could you pick her feet out, love, before Tom gets here? I'll do Charity. Connie and Tubber are ready and waiting.'

The two remaining horses Mrs Grace kept at livery were standing with their heads over the half-stable doors, watching all the comings and goings in the yard. Captain, a temperamental chestnut hunter, had already been moved to another yard in the nearby town of Littlehaven.

For a while Josie and her mother worked together quietly, making sure both ponies' feet were ready for the farrier. Tom Crooke had been looking after the ponies and horses at the stables since the beginning, and he knew their feet so well that he was able to make their shoes back at his forge. He only had to bring along a portable anvil, in case any minor adjustments needed to be made before they were nailed on.

'There!' Josie said eventually, straightening up. 'She's just perfect. Aren't you, Hope?' she added, rubbing the pony's nose. 'How could anyone resist you? I think you're gorgeous!'

'At least there's no sign of sweet itch at the moment,' said Mrs Grace, looking along the crest of Hope's mane. 'That's one thing to be thankful for. She looks so much prettier when her mane's a good length.'

Hope was prone to sweet itch, an allergy to midge bites, during the summer. Greyish spots would appear around her mane and tail, and she would rub or bite bald patches as she tried to find some relief from the infuriating itching. When the rash was at its worst, she would sometimes rub away the hair on her head, too, revealing the black skin underneath.

'Waiting till it's dark before we turn her out in the field does seem to be helping,' Josie said.

'And we must keep going with the insect repellent, too,' Mrs Grace said, looking across the yard as a battered black van drew up. 'Oh, here's Tom. Come on, let's go and say hello.'

By the time they had greeted the farrier and were walking back towards the loose boxes together, Hope had stretched her head over the stable door and was nibbling along Charity's back and withers.

'Oh, there she goes, grooming again,' Mrs Grace smiled affectionately. 'She has to make sure Charity's looking her best.'

'Well, that's mothers for you,' Tom chuckled, setting the anvil up. 'They're all the same. Right – I'll get started on Charity. Won't take me too long to get them all done, will it?'

'No, only four of them waiting for you today,' Mrs Grace said. 'Now, if you don't mind, Tom, I just need to make a couple of phone calls. I'll be down in the office if you need me.'

'Oh, we'll be fine. I've got my assistant here, haven't I?' Tom said, smiling at Josie. She almost always helped Tom whenever he came to the stables and, by now, she knew exactly how he liked to work.

'So,' he said, hammering up the nails in Charity's old shoe, 'are you missing Faith? Do you know how she's getting on?'

'Oh, she's really happy,' Josie said, standing ready to pass him the pincers. 'I went to see her last weekend and she's looking great. She's sharing the field with

141

this great big black horse called Midnight, and he follows her round everywhere like a little lamb.'

'And how's Jill coping?' Tom said, taking the pincers from Josie and levering the shoe off. 'I used to look after her pony, Marmalade, you know. She was beside herself when he had to be sold.'

Jill Atterbury, Faith's new owner, had been involved in a car crash and broken her hip so badly that she wasn't able to ride any more, but she missed having a pony desperately. So when her parents had seen Mrs Grace's advertisement about an elderly mare needing a loving home, they'd thought looking after Faith might be just what Jill needed to help her get over the accident. The pony had been about to retire from the stables anyway and didn't need much exercising, so she would be perfect if Jill was able to start some gentle riding again in the future.

'Jill's getting on fine,' Josie said, watching as Tom trimmed Charity's foot with a pair of nippers and then rasped it flat with a file. 'She spends ages grooming Faith, and she's started leading her out for walks. It's lovely to see them both together. Faith slows right down to make sure Jill can keep up with her.'

'Jill's a nice girl,' Tom said, holding the new shoe against Charity's foot to see how it fitted. 'I don't think you could have done better for Faith.'

'If only we could be as lucky with Hope,' Josie said,

looking at the pony's sweet, plain face watching them from inside her loose box. 'It's her turn next. Mum's worried that we won't find anyone who'll want her.'

'She's no oil painting, that's for sure,' Tom said, following her gaze, 'but she'd be perfect for a beginner. Gentle as a lamb, she is.' He began to nail the shoe on to Charity's hoof, adding, 'You'll be sorry to see her go, but what can't be cured must be endured, as my mother used to say.'

'I know,' Josie said ruefully. 'I'm beginning to find that out.'

'Well, that's me done,' Tom said, packing his tools away an hour or so later. He'd put new shoes on Charity and Hope, but Connie and Tubber just needed their feet trimming and the old shoes put back on. 'So their owners won't need to pay so much,' he told Mrs Grace when she came over from the office. 'That should make 'em happy.'

'They won't be getting many more bills from me, anyway,' she said. 'These two are both leaving in a couple of weeks.'

Josie crossed over to the loose box and gave Tubber's skewbald coat a gentle stroke. She wasn't quite as close to the livery horses as she was to the Grace's own ponies but, even so, life would seem very strange without them. They were part of the furniture, like the hens that clucked around the barn or the ducks that waddled to and from the pond next to the schooling ring.

'Where are they off to, then?' Tom asked, undoing his leather apron.

'They'll both be joining Captain at the yard in Littlehaven,' Mrs Grace replied. 'I'm going to carry on exercising Connie, though – Jane and I have worked it all out.' Connie was a lovely black mare whom Mary Grace had been sharing with her owner, Jane Ramsay, for the past eight years.

'Well, best of luck to you,' Tom said as he prepared to carry the tools and equipment back to his van. 'I shall miss my visits here, that's for sure. Fourteen years is a long time.'

'Yes, it certainly is. We only had Faith and Tubber when you first came, didn't we?' said Mrs Grace. 'Oh well, they've been fourteen good years, and now it's time to move on. Who knows what the future holds? Come on, Tom, let's go over to the office and I'll settle up and make you a mug of tea. I've bought some doughnuts to help cheer us up. Are you coming, Josie?'

'No, thanks, Mum. I think I'll stay up here for a while,' Josie replied. 'I'll see you later.'

She felt like spending some time on her own with the ponies and, besides, she wanted to be busy when Tom left the yard for the last time. It would be too sad to watch him go and then just mope around, brooding.

Hope was standing quietly in her loose box, nibbling at the haynet. Josie picked up a brush from the kit and began to groom her with long, steady strokes, thinking back to what her mother had said. What if they couldn't find anyone able to look beyond Hope's plain appearance to see her sweet nature? What would happen then?

Two

A couple of days later, Josie was sitting on a low stone ledge that ran along the ground outside the office and the tackroom. Her back was against the office wall and she was tickling Rascal, one of the Graces' two black-and-white cats, with a piece of straw. Across the yard, Charity, Hope and Tubber were standing in their loose boxes, while Connie had already been turned out into the field. There was plenty to be done – sweeping, mucking out and the never-ending chore of cleaning tack – but Josie didn't feel like working. She'd changed into leggings and a T-shirt after a busy day at school, and she was just too warm and comfortable in the sun.

Rascal rolled on his back, grasping and kicking at the straw with all four paws before tearing it into pieces with his sharp white teeth. Then, suddenly losing interest, he curled up his tail and closed his eyes. 'Silly cat,' she said affectionately, rubbing the soft warm fur on his stomach. At least Rascal would be coming with them when they moved, along with his sister Millie, and the family's mongrel terrier, Basil. Cats and dogs were easier to take than ponies.

Josie yawned, shutting her eyes too and resting her head in her arms against her knees. She was just dozing off when she sensed a shadow looming over her. Squinting up, she saw her friend Anna Marshall standing there, with arms folded and a smile on her face.

'Come on, lazy bones,' Anna said, giving Josie's foot a little kick. 'You'll get a headache if you fall asleep out here.'

'Oh, Anna, leave me alone,' Josie grumbled. 'It was really peaceful until you came along.'

'Yes, but you're all red and grumpy already,' Anna said. 'You're too fair to sit in the sun, Josie – you ought to know that by now.'

Josie held out her bare arms. 'I suppose so,' she said, looking at the pink flush below her T-shirt's short sleeves. 'Now, if my skin was the colour of yours, I could stay out here the whole day.'

Anna laughed, shaking her glossy black hair, and stretched out a hand. 'Come on,' she said, pulling Josie to her feet. 'There must be something we could do in the shade.'

Josie gave a big stretch and looked at her watch. 'Well,' she said, 'Hope needs tacking up, I suppose. Emma Price is coming for her lesson in about ten minutes.'

'There you are, then,' Anna replied. 'Just as well I came along, wasn't it?'

They went into the tackroom. The saddles were arranged neatly on racks and bridles hung from circular pegs on the whitewashed walls, each one labelled with its owner's name. Mrs Grace had taken down Faith's name plate, but the empty peg still gave Josie a pang when she saw it.

Anna unhooked Hope's bridle while Josie heaved her saddle off the rack, together with the fleecy numnah that fitted underneath. They walked across the yard together.

'Hi, Ben,' Josie said, spotting Anna's twin brother in another of the loose boxes. Ben often took Tubber out on a Thursday after school, and he'd told Josie the day before that he'd be coming up to the stables.

'Thanks for keeping him in for me,' he said, giving the horse a quick going over with the dandy brush. 'I'll just get rid of the worst of this dirt, and then we'll be off.'

When their parents had separated three years ago, Ben and Anna had moved to the village of Northgate with their mother. On her first day at school, Anna had met Josie and discovered that she lived only a couple of kilometres away. She and Ben had turned up at the riding stables the next weekend, and begun to help out in exchange for free lessons. Although Ben had been a bit too small to ride Tubber at first, the gentle skewbald never took advantage of him and they'd soon become firm friends. Sue Collins, Tubber's owner, was only too pleased to have some help exercising her horse during the week. She taught at the same school as Robert Grace, Josie's father. They both had piles of marking and lesson plans to cope with, so it wasn't always easy to find time for a ride.

'Where are you going?' Josie asked Ben, hoisting the heavy saddle more comfortably over her arm and looking into the shady loose box. Her mother had strict rules – anyone going off for a hack on their own had to tell someone roughly how long they'd be and which route they were planning to take.

'I thought I'd go up Baker's Hill and then along the bridle path round the field and back,' Ben said, putting the brush back in Tubber's grooming kit and coming around to open the stable door. 'Shouldn't take more than an hour or so. D'you and Anna want to come too?'

'Hope's got a lesson now, so I think we'll just hang

around here,' Josie said. 'Have fun!' She liked Ben, though they weren't best friends in the way that she and Anna were. He was a lot quieter than his sister, but when he did say something, it was usually worth listening to.

'Thanks!' he said, smiling at Josie as he went off to the tackroom for Tubber's saddle and bridle.

Josie greeted Charity with a pat as she passed, then let herself into Hope's loose box. Anna was already chatting to her favourite pony, holding a chunk of apple out flat on her palm. She wasn't very confident on horseback, having had a bad fall once on a trekking holiday, but she trusted Hope completely and always chose to ride her.

'You'd spoil her if she wasn't so good-tempered,' Josie said, watching Hope stretch out and take the apple with a delicate twitch of her lips.

'Well, I haven't got much longer to make a fuss of her, have I?' Anna said, laying her face against Hope's smooth neck for a second. 'Mum showed me the ad for her in yesterday's paper. Have you had any replies?'

'A couple,' Josie said, starting to saddle the pony up. 'One probably won't come to anything, but the other lot are going to come round and see her on Saturday.'

'It's strange,' Anna said thoughtfully as she began to put the bridle on. 'You'd have thought more of the children who ride her here would have been interested.

Several of them wanted to have Faith, didn't they?'

'Yes, I suppose they did,' Josie replied, fighting a nagging sense of unease in her stomach. 'I don't know, maybe Mum hasn't asked everyone yet.' She couldn't bear to think her mother might be right – that people wouldn't want Hope because of the way she looked.

'I keep wishing there was some way she could come and live with us,' Anna went on, 'but unless my fairy godmother suddenly appears, I can't see how it's going to happen. She wouldn't be very happy in our little back garden.'

Mrs Grace came to the stable door, a peaked cap over her dark curly hair to shade her eyes from the sun when she was in the middle of the school. 'Thanks for getting Hope ready,' she said to Josie and Anna. 'Emma's just arrived, so if you bring her out, we can get started.'

'Hang on a minute, Mum,' Josie said. 'You remember how keen Emma was to buy Faith, even though we told her Faith was too old? Well, Hope would be perfect for her! She's just the right size, and she could really help Emma learn to ride. What do you think?' She looked at her mother eagerly. 'Do the Prices know we're selling her?'

'D' you know, I don't think I have said anything to them yet,' Mrs Grace said slowly, thinking it over. 'You may have hit on something there, Josie – thanks! I'll certainly have a word with Emma. Hope would suit her very well indeed!'

Josie and Anna sat together on a tree stump, watching Emma come to the end of her lesson. Mrs Grace had got her trotting without stirrups, which were crossed over the front of Hope's saddle and lying on her withers.

'But w-w-why are we d-d-doing this?' Emma asked breathlessly as she jolted alarmingly from side to side.

'So that you can feel the way Hope's moving when she trots and learn to go with it,' Mrs Grace replied briskly. 'That's the idea, anyway. It'll really help your seat. Do you remember what I told you about the trot? It's a gait with two beats. Hope's legs move in diagonal pairs – that means one front hoof and the opposite back one hit the ground at the same time, followed by the other pair of hooves.'

'Emma's going to be stiff tomorrow,' Anna said, chewing on a blade of grass.

'She looks good on Hope, though, doesn't she?' Josie commented. 'They seem to be the right sort of shape for each other.'

'OK,' Mrs Grace went on, 'pull gently on the reins now and go back into walk. Don't let Hope go to sleep, though! Squeeze with your legs to keep her walking on properly till you come to the letter B. Then you can turn in and halt. Well done, Emma – you've worked hard today.'

She opened the gate leading out of the schooling ring and Emma walked Hope through and back into the yard. Josie and Anna got to their feet and strolled around to meet them.

'Hi, Dad!' Emma said proudly as her father came over from his car. 'Did you see me?'

'Certainly did!' he replied. 'You're really coming on.'

Josie held Hope and threw her mother a meaningful look while Emma dismounted. Mrs Grace took a deep breath. 'Mr Price,' she began, 'do you remember the conversation we had about you buying Faith, the pony Emma used to ride?'

'Yes,' he replied, taking out his wallet and flicking through the notes. 'Why do you ask?'

'Well, now we're looking for a new home for Hope,' Mary Grace said, giving the pony a pat while Anna began to unsaddle her. 'I just wondered whether you'd be interested? She's so quiet and steady, she'd be ideal for Emma.'

Mr Price looked properly at Hope for the first time. 'What do *you* think?' he said to Emma. 'She's not as handsome as the other one, is she?'

Emma wrinkled her nose, smoothing out the creases in her brand-new jodhpurs. 'No offence to Hope or anything, but I think I'm outgrowing her,' she said.

'Now my riding's getting so much better, I need a pony that's a bit more lively. And I couldn't imagine taking her to a show. She's not exactly smart, is she?'

'But she's wonderful at gymkhanas!' Josie burst out. 'She does everything you tell her to and she doesn't get over-excited, or lose her head. You'd do very well with her, honestly.'

'I don't think so,' Mr Price said decisively, looking at his daughter's doubtful expression. 'As a matter of fact, we've been over to the riding school at Littlehaven and Emma's going to start having lessons there. I think they'll be able to advise us on a pony for her.' He held out his hand to Mrs Grace with a ten-pound note in it. 'Thanks for getting her this far, but we think she'll benefit from some more advanced teaching now. Keep the change.'

'Goodbye, Mrs Grace,' Emma threw over her shoulder as she was hurried off to the car. 'Thanks for everything!'

Anna, Josie and Mary Grace watched the Prices' car sweep out of the yard. 'Honestly!' Josie said angrily. 'Emma doesn't realise how lucky she is! She's had one-to-one lessons on two of the nicest ponies she could ever find! Her riding's only got better recently because Hope guesses what Emma wants her to do before she's thought of it herself.'

'I think Hope's much too good for Emma Price,'

Anna said, giving the pony a hug. 'I'm glad she's not going there.'

'But where *is* she going to go?' Mrs Grace said anxiously. 'We haven't got unlimited time on our hands to find her a new home, you know.'

'Come on, Mum!' Josie said. 'Just because Emma's turned her down it doesn't mean everyone else will. The advert only went in the paper yesterday – you can't start getting discouraged yet! There are some people coming to see her on Saturday, remember.'

'Oh, I don't know,' Mrs Grace replied. 'After what Sarah said, and now hearing the same kind of thing from Emma – well, I can't help but worry. What if everyone reacts like that?'

'Well, they won't,' Josie replied, stamping on any niggling worries before they had a chance to develop. 'After all, you wanted her when you first saw her, didn't you? Someone else is bound to feel the same way.' She stroked Hope's rippling mane. 'Besides, she's looking her best at the moment. We'll find a good home for her, just wait and see!'

Three

'Mmm, it's going to be another beautiful day,' Josie said, breathing in the sweet, fresh air. It was early on Saturday morning and she and her mother were walking through the garden towards the fields that surrounded the house, to start bringing in the ponies and horses. Beads of dew on the lawn sparkled in the sunshine and everything was quiet, except for the sound of birds singing. The Graces' brown-and-white terrier, Basil, scurried along beside them, rootling about under bushes or sniffing the air eagerly in his constant search for rabbits.

'I wonder if it's going to be like this all summer?' Mrs

Grace wondered. 'I can't believe it, the grass needs cutting again! Maybe we should look for a house with a smaller garden next time.'

Josie looked back down the path to School Farm: the low, thatched cottage in which she'd lived all her life. 'They're not going to knock the house down, are they?' she asked her mother. She couldn't bear the thought of School Farm being destroyed but, on the other hand, she didn't want to imagine anyone else living in it either.

'I don't think so,' Mrs Grace replied. 'To be honest, I'm not really sure what the developers have in mind – all I know is that we have to be out by the end of July, which only gives us another six weeks or so to find somewhere new. The trouble is, your father's so busy with this musical that we haven't had any time to go house-hunting.'

'Oh, the musical,' Josie groaned. 'Do you know how it's coming along? Dad was getting into a real state over it last week.' Mr Grace and the music teacher at his school were staging *Grease*, and rehearsals hadn't been going smoothly.

'I haven't dared to talk to him about it,' Mrs Grace said, smiling. 'Whenever I ask, he just throws his hands up in the air. It's bringing out the actor in him; that's for sure.'

By now, they'd come to the field in which the ponies

were kept. Josie took the headcollar down from her shoulder and searched for the handful of pony nuts in her pocket. Charity was grazing quietly at one edge of the field. Next to her, Hope had stuck her head under the top bar of the rail and post fencing, and was scratching her neck to and fro along it.

Josie's heart sank. 'Oh, no!' she said anxiously. 'Mum! Just look at what Hope's doing. Don't say the sweet itch has come back again!'

Her mother groaned and they both began to hurry towards the ponies. As they came closer, they could see that Hope had already rubbed away a large section of her mane, and that she'd bitten sore patches around the dock area at the top of her tail.

'Oh, why did this have to happen now?' Mrs Grace said in dismay. 'The Simmonds are coming to see her straight after lessons today. And I thought the insect repellent was working so well!'

Josie hid the head collar behind her back and approached Hope from the front, calling her name softly and holding some pony nuts on her palm. The pony drew her head out from the fence and gave a low wicker, trotting up to Josie and pushing her muzzle forward to take the titbit.

Josie's heart melted when she saw the wretched state of her. 'You poor old thing,' she said sympathetically, slipping the end of the lead rope over Hope's neck and starting to put on the head collar. 'Is that itching driving you mad?'

'She must have been bitten around dawn,' Mrs Grace said, inspecting the damage. 'From now on, we'd better keep her in the stable until later in the morning when the midges aren't so active. Come on, I'll catch Charity and then let's try and get her smartened up as much as possible. We can come back for Connie and Tubber later.'

'So who are the Simmonds?' Josie asked, as she and her mother made their way back to the yard. 'They don't come for lessons here, do they?'

'No, I've never met them before,' Mrs Grace replied. 'Mr Simmonds rang up after seeing the advertisement in the newspaper. From what I could tell over the phone, he seemed nice enough. He used to ride when he was a child, and they've got a boy of nine who's desperate for a pony of his own. There's a field with stables near their house, and a couple of other horses in it. One's only a yearling, so Hope would have a baby to keep in order.'

'She'd like that,' Josie smiled, rubbing the pony's nose affectionately. 'Well, let's keep our fingers crossed. Who knows, maybe Hope will find her perfect home, too!'

Josie tried hard to get Hope looking her best. She groomed her for ages, arranging the bedraggled mane as nicely as she could over the pony's neck, and polishing her coat with a damp stable cloth until it gleamed. Apart from one patch of spots on her hindquarters and the area round her tail, it was mostly Hope's mane that had been affected; her face, luckily, was clear. Josie could tell Hope was really enjoying all the fuss by the way she put her head in the air and blew gently down her nose when her neck and withers were being brushed.

'Does that make you feel better, poor old itchy thing?' she said, painting some oil on her hooves as a finishing touch.

'What's happened to her mane?' Anna gasped, putting her head over the stable door and gazing at Hope in horror. 'It looks awful!'

'Oh, thanks, Anna. Tactful as usual,' Josie said, throwing a handful of straw at her. 'Some people are coming to look at her after the lessons are finished and I've just spent hours trying to make her beautiful.'

'Oops! Sorry,' Anna said. 'I've put my foot in it again. Well, they probably won't mind a little bit of sweet itch. She's still dear old Hope underneath, after all.'

Josie shook her head, smiling. She was used to Anna's habit of saying just what you didn't want to hear. 'Could you start getting Charity ready?' she asked. 'I haven't touched her yet and lessons start in half an hour.'

'OK,' Anna said. Then, as Ben appeared behind her,

she added, 'Come on, little brother, let's work as a team.' Anna had been born first by twenty minutes, which she always tried to use to her advantage, telling Ben he should respect his elders.

'Hi, Josie,' Ben said. 'Hope looks great!'

'Thanks, Ben,' she replied, giving him a broad smile. 'This is a big day for her. There's a family coming to look her over later on.'

'Oh, I'm sure they'll like her,' he said. 'What does it matter if she's going bald, after all?'

'Ben!' Anna called from the loose box next door. 'I'm not meant to be doing this all on my own. Come and help!'

Soon, the stables were much livelier. Jane Ramsay arrived to ride out on Connie, and had a quick cup of tea and a gossip in the office with Mary Grace before saddling up and clattering out of the yard. Then, as it was time for lessons to begin, cars started pulling into the driveway.

'Could I have someone to take Jessica round on Charity, please?' Mrs Grace said, hurrying over to the loose boxes. 'She's just arrived, and Emily's here for Hope, too. Oh, and Ben, could you be a love and get Tubber ready? Mary's coming up at eleven for a hack.'

Josie and Anna took it in turns to lead beginners round for the next few lessons, and soon Josie began looking anxiously round towards the yard to see if the

Simmonds' car had arrived. Just as the last lesson was ending, an unfamiliar car drove in.

'Mum! I think they're here,' Josie hissed from her lookout post by the tree stump, and Mrs Grace nodded to show she'd heard. Anna, whose turn it was on the lead rein, turned to look and gave Josie a thumbs-up sign.

'Just before we finish, John,' Mrs Grace said to the boy who was riding Hope, 'could you take her for one last trot round the school?'

Hope had a smart, springy trot, and Josie realised her mother wanted to show it off to the Simmonds. She felt very proud of Hope as she watched her trot along at a snappy pace, her head high and her tail held out behind her. It did look rather untidy, but Ben was right – what did that matter? She looked over at the yard to see if Ben was there, but he was nowhere to be seen. Shading her eyes, she gazed around and eventually spotted him out in the field, picking up droppings with a wheelbarrow and spade.

A middle-aged man with thin brown hair and glasses got out of the car, followed by a boy who immediately walked over to the school to watch the ponies. Seconds later, a short, harassed-looking woman, whom Josie assumed was the boy's mother, got out of the front passenger seat. A shrill ringing sounded from her shoulder bag and she muttered something and took out a mobile phone, hanging back to answer it.

'Very nice,' said Mrs Grace back in the ring as John finished. 'Now, if you can both turn in and halt, I'll tell you each a couple of things to remember for next week.'

If there is a next week, Josie thought to herself. *Hope might not be here then.* She had another look at the Simmonds family, to see if she could find out what they were like. The man was chatting to his son, and the boy listened with a determined expression on his round, freckled face.

She went over towards them, ready to open the gate and let the ponies through when the lesson was over, and gave a smile that she hoped was cheerful and welcoming.

'My mother won't be a minute,' she said. 'The lesson's nearly finished. I'm Josie Grace, by the way.'

'Oh, don't worry, we're happy to wait,' the man replied. 'I'm Bill Simmonds, and this is Luke. My wife's in the middle of a crisis at work, I'm afraid, but I'm sure she'll be over in a minute.' He smiled too, but the boy just stared at Josie and didn't speak. 'And which is the pony you're selling?' Mr Simmonds went on.

'The slightly smaller one that the boy's riding,' Josie said, pointing Hope out. 'Did you see her trotting just now? She's got a lovely action.'

'But I don't want *that* one,' Luke said. 'I told you, Dad, I like the other one better. Why can't I have her?'

164

'Oh, no, Hope is the pony we're looking to re-home at the moment,' Josie said, horrified. It had taken her long enough to get used to the idea of parting with Hope – she wasn't ready to consider letting Charity go yet. 'Besides, Hope is the perfect first pony,' she went on. 'She's wonderful with beginners.'

'I'm not a beginner,' said Luke rudely. 'I've had five lessons.'

'Now then, Luke,' said his father mildly. 'Five lessons aren't really enough to teach you all you need to know. It takes a long time to learn how to ride. I think you should listen to what Josie says. Why don't you have a turn on Hope? That would give you a better idea of what she's like.'

By now Mrs Grace had stopped talking to her pupils and they were making their way over to the gate. Anna was still holding Charity on the lead rein.

'Anna, could you help Sophie dismount in the yard, please, and then take Charity back to her box?' Mrs Grace called. 'John, you can hop off Hope here, if you wouldn't mind.' She smiled and waved at Mr Simmonds, hurrying over to say hello. 'I won't be a second,' she said, shaking hands with Luke and his father. 'I just need a word with John and Sophie's mother about next week. My daughter, Josie, can introduce you to Hope.'

'But I told you, I don't want her,' Luke grumbled to his father. John, who had jumped down and was giving

Hope a pat, stared at him in surprise. '*That's* the one I want,' Luke went on, pointing after Charity as she went through the gate and over to the yard. Anna carried on walking, raising her eyebrows at Josie as she passed. It was pretty clear what she thought of Luke Simmonds.

'But Hope's lovely,' John said earnestly. 'She tries really hard, and she does just what you tell her to.'

Good for you! Josie said to herself, smiling at him. She'd always liked John Butcher, but now she decided he was even nicer than she'd thought. 'Bye, Josie,' he said, handing her the reins and going off to join his mother and sister in the yard. 'See you next week.'

'Why don't you have a ride?' Josie suggested to Luke. 'Then you'd see what John means.' She took the reins and looped them over Hope's head, then she patted the pony's neck, which was damp with sweat from all her hard work in the lesson. 'Come down with me and I'll take her over to the mounting block.'

'All right,' Luke said gracelessly, sticking his hands in his pockets.

'How long have you had Hope?' Mr Simmonds asked as they walked down to the yard. 'And why are you selling her?'

'We've had her for nine years,' Josie replied. 'My mum bought her when she was five. The stables and land are about to be sold, so that's why we've got to find a new home for her. She's very gentle and affectionate – she'll nuzzle and groom anyone who'll let her.'

Mrs Grace waved goodbye to the Butchers and came over to join them at the mounting block. 'Sorry about that,' she said, a little breathlessly. 'There seems to be quite a lot to sort out at the moment. Now, are you going to have a ride on Hope?'

'I suppose so,' said Luke, grabbing Hope's saddle without any warning and sticking his foot into the stirrup so roughly that he prodded her in the side.

'Wait just a minute!' Mrs Grace said quickly. 'You're the wrong way round and you've got the wrong foot in the stirrup, too. You'll end up back to front in the saddle if you get on like that! Here, take the reins in your left hand and stand facing her tail. Then put your *left* foot in the stirrup. That's it!'

'Ugh!' said Luke suddenly, dropping the reins which Josie had looped back over Hope's neck. 'What's the matter with her mane? Half of it's fallen out and she's got spots everywhere!'

'Oh, yes,' said Mrs Grace. 'I was going to mention that Hope can get sweet itch in the summer. It's a reaction to midge bites, you know – she doesn't suffer from it too badly and you can ride her without any problem, but sometimes she rubs patches away in her mane and tail when she scratches. There's a liquid we put on her to help, and we're going to start keeping her in overnight.'

Luke was rubbing his hand against his jeans. 'I'm not touching her! I might catch something,' he said.

'Now, just a minute,' Mr Simmonds began, but he was interrupted by his wife, who'd finally finished her phone call and was walking over from the car. She took a brief look at Hope and then said brusquely to Mrs Grace, 'We're going to have to leave you, I'm afraid. I need to get back to the office straight away.'

'Oh, Mum!' Luke protested. 'There's this other pony here—'

His mother cut him off quickly. 'We're just wasting time,' she said to her husband. 'It's perfectly obvious there's something wrong with this pony and I don't know why you're even bothering to discuss this, Bill. Besides, she's very plain.'

Josie drew her breath in sharply and felt herself going red with anger. How dare this horrible woman insult her lovely Hope! Instinctively, she stood closer to her and put an arm round the pony's neck.

'But you can tell she's got a sweet nature, darling,' protested Mr Simmonds, flushing and looking embarrassed. 'She might be just the thing for Luke – at least he could try her out.'

'Look, I have to get back to the station in time to catch the next train into London,' his wife told him sharply. 'I don't know why you insist on wasting all our time. This pony's obviously not right for Luke. I don't care how good-natured she is, she looks like a fright and we're not having her. That's all there is to it.'

Mrs Grace had had enough. 'You're absolutely right,' she said, drawing herself up and standing very straight. 'There's no point in discussing this further. Your son would be very lucky to have a pony with such a perfect temperament as this, but I wouldn't dream of letting you buy her. There are plenty of people around who know about ponies and would never judge Hope at face value, like you just have.'

'Oh, are there?' said Mrs Simmonds, with a brittle smile on her face. 'Well, I hope you find one of them to take her off your hands. Good luck – you'll need it!' And she turned and marched smartly back to the car, followed by her sheepish-looking husband and sulky son.

'Well said, Mum!' Josie told her mother as they watched them go. 'Why did she have to be so rude?' She laid her head against the pony's neck, glad her good, kind Hope couldn't understand the insults that had been thrown at her.

Four

'I thought the boy was bad enough,' Anna said as she walked up the path to the cottage with Josie and Ben, 'but it sounds as though his mother was even worse.'

'Oh, she was awful!' Josie told them. 'She was so rude about Hope – you should have heard her! All she wanted to do was get back to her stupid office.'

'Well, Hope's had a lucky escape, then,' Ben said. 'I wonder what your dad's made for lunch, Josie? I'm starving!' Robert Grace was a wonderful cook, and Josie's mum was more than happy to leave the family meals up to him.

'I wouldn't expect too much,' Josie replied. 'He's so

busy with this musical they're putting on at his school he hardly goes near the kitchen these days. They're doing a version of *Grease* – you know, that rock and roll musical. John Travolta was in the film.'

Her father taught at a different school from the one they all went to – much to Josie's relief. Otherwise there would have been no escaping the musical, at home or at school.

By now, they were nearly at the front door to School Farm. 'What on earth's he doing?' Anna exclaimed, peering through the leaded windows into the sitting-room. 'Get out the straitjacket, Josie – I think your father's gone mad!'

Ben and Josie crowded round behind her, and they all looked through to see Robert Grace leaping around the room like a maniac, blond hair falling over his face as he twirled and twisted. 'Oh, he's dancing,' Josie groaned. 'Don't look – it's too embarrassing!'

'He's actually not that bad,' Anna said, cupping her hand on the glass to cut down the reflection. 'Not exactly John Travolta, but quite good for an old crumbly. Oh, he's gone down on his knees – could be tricky! Can he get himself back up again? Yes! He's done it. Oh dear, straight into the bookcase. What a shame. Just when it was all going so well . . .'

'All right, Anna!' Josie said, laughing and dragging her away from the window. 'We don't need a running commentary, thanks very much.'

They opened the front door, and the strains of 'Summer Lovin' came drifting out on the air. 'If I hear that song one more time, I'm going to scream,' Josie said, looking through the sitting-room door to see her father sitting on a chair, cradling his knee in both hands.

'Great!' he said enthusiastically as he caught sight of them. 'Just in time! I need two volunteers to try out these new dance steps. Ben and Anna, you'll do.'

'Oh, no! He's my brother,' Anna said, drawing away. 'I don't want to touch him!'

'All right then, Josie and Ben,' Mr Grace said, arranging them both in position with Ben standing back to back with Josie and holding her right arm up with his left.

'I'll watch and criticise,' Anna offered, perching on the sofa. 'That's what I'm best at, after all.'

Soon, though, Anna was laughing too hard to speak. Josie managed to follow her father's instructions, but Ben seemed to have two left feet and kept forgetting which way he was meant to turn.

'All right,' Mr Grace sighed, after Ben had gone lumbering off in the wrong direction yet again, leaving Josie holding on to thin air, 'perhaps we should call it a day.'

'I don't think I could take much more,' Anna gasped,

holding her stomach. 'I haven't laughed so much in ages!'

'Well, let's see how good *you* are,' Ben said, pulling his sister to her feet and spinning her off round the room. 'Now we can all enjoy ourselves at your expense!'

'Enough! Enough!' shouted Mr Grace, as Anna's flailing arms toppled a lamp and threatened to knock over a vase. 'Time for lunch, I think.'

'Thank goodness that's over,' Josie said, heading for the door. 'Mum's coming in a minute – she's just making a couple of phone calls in the office.'

'No, I've finished and I'm here,' Mary Grace said, looking into the room from the hallway. 'What's going on? Sounds like you've been having a party!'

'You don't want to know,' her husband said, putting an arm round her shoulder and taking her off to the kitchen. 'Come and have some lunch and tell me about these people who came to see Hope.'

'They were horrible,' Josie said, following her parents down the hall with Ben and Anna close behind. 'The boy was really spoilt and the mother was unbelievable!'

'It *is* the very worst time for Hope to have sweet itch,' Mrs Grace said anxiously. 'I've just been on the phone to the vet about it. That new lotion we've got just doesn't seem to be working.' She sat down at the kitchen table, which was covered with plates of salad, ham and salami, different kinds of cheese and crusty bread. 'Oh, Rob, this looks great – thanks for getting it all ready.'

'You'd think people would realise sweet itch is just a temporary thing, though,' Josie said, pinching a tomato and popping it into her mouth. 'I mean, it's only in the summer because of the midges. And it's not as if it affects the way Hope behaves.'

'Yes, but unfortunately first impressions matter,' her mother replied. She picked up a slice of cucumber and crunched on it absent-mindedly. 'I am getting more worried about where Hope's going to go,' she admitted, looking up at Josie. 'There's no one else lined up to see her, and we haven't had any phone calls about the advert for a couple of days.'

'Oh, well, something'll turn up,' Josie said, rattling around in the cutlery drawer for knives and forks to lay the table. 'Remember, it took the Atterburys a while to get in touch with us about Faith.'

'I know, but just in case it doesn't,' Mrs Grace said carefully, 'I've also been on the phone to Mrs Peabody. At the animal sanctuary.'

'The animal sanctuary?' Josie said, pausing with a serving spoon in mid-air. Ben and Anna glanced up from their seats at the table, too. They looked as shocked as Josie felt.

'Only as a last resort,' her mother said. 'I think it would be a good idea for us to have something up our sleeve if we can't find Hope a home anywhere else.

She'd have lots of company, and Mrs Peabody looks after those animals really well.'

'But isn't the sanctuary for animals who've been mistreated?' Anna asked.

'Not necessarily,' Mrs Grace replied. 'They also take in pets whose owners can't keep them any more, for one reason or another. I've arranged to go and see her on Monday afternoon, Josie. Why don't you come along and have a look, too? We can go after school. Might be interesting.'

'OK,' Josie said mechanically. She sat down at the table, but her appetite seemed to have vanished. Hope at the animal sanctuary? Something about the thought made her feel terribly sad. They'd loved and looked after Hope for years – if they took her to the sanctuary, it would feel like they were abandoning her. Like they didn't care any more.

A tall, plump woman with an exploding bun of wispy grey hair came out from behind a counter in the small shop at the entrance to the Peabody Animal Welfare Sanctuary.

'Lovely to see you!' she beamed at Josie and her mother, shaking their hands. 'Welcome to PAWS! Of course, I suppose we should be known as Paws and Hooves! Or, strictly speaking, Paws, Hooves and Claws,' she added, beginning to look rather flustered, 'as we have birds, too. And there is actually a snake at the moment, though I don't know where he'd fit in. Anyway,' she finished with some relief, 'I'm Elizabeth Peabody, as you've probably realised, and I'm delighted to meet you.'

'Mary Grace,' smiled Josie's mother, 'and this is my daughter, Josie. Thanks so much for letting us have a look round.'

'Not at all,' said Mrs Peabody, turning the sign on the door to the 'Closed' side and locking it. 'Only too glad to help. Your pony sounds lovely, and I do hope you'll manage to find a family to take her – but if you don't, I think we might be able to squeeze her in here.'

'Thank you very much for the offer,' said Josie dutifully. She'd been coached by her mother in the car about looking grateful and appreciating what Mrs Peabody was prepared to do for them. 'It's very kind of you to—' Then she couldn't help letting out a scream, and clapping her hand over her mouth. There was something moving in Mrs Peabody's bosom! She could just see the top of a small, black, scrawny *thing*, wriggling around.

'Josie! What *is* the matter with you?' said her mother, horrified, as Josie pointed wordlessly towards whatever it was.

'Oh, this!' said Mrs Peabody, fishing down inside her shirt. She came out with her hand closed gently around something, and opened her fingers slowly for Josie to see. A tiny baby bat, only about eight centimetres long, flopped around on her palm. 'I'm keeping him warm,' she went on softly. 'Someone found him in a garage and brought him in yesterday. We're feeding him milk with an eye dropper.'

'He's so small!' Josie breathed, quite captivated now that she'd got over the initial shock.

'He is indeed,' said Mrs Peabody, popping him back down her front. 'When he's a bit stronger we're going to see how he gets on when he tries to fly, but this is the best place for him at the moment. Now, come and meet the others.'

Josie decided she rather liked Mrs Peabody. They followed her through the back of the shop and into a small courtyard, with wire cages all around. 'Birds on this side,' she announced with a wave of her arm that Josie was frightened would send the bat into orbit sooner than planned. 'Rabbits and guinea pigs over here, and we even have a badger at the moment, though we're hoping to release him back in the wild very soon.'

'Where's all the noise coming from?' Josie asked, as a cacophony of yaps and howls rose on the air.

'Come this way and I'll show you,' said Mrs Peabody, leading them towards a doorway in the far wall of the courtyard. They went through it to find a long, low building, with caged runs all along one side. About twenty dogs of various shapes and sizes were pressed up against the wire, wagging their tails and barking eagerly at the visitors.

'Do you try and find homes for them?' Josie asked, her hands over her ears. She couldn't bear the thought of all these creatures, desperate for company and attention, living out their lives here.

'Well, some of them can be re-homed,' said Mrs Peabody, 'but others just aren't suitable as family pets, unfortunately. If they're nervous already, the way they've been treated can make them aggressive towards people. You wouldn't believe the injuries I've seen. Cigarette burns, rope marks, scalds from boiling water – we've had them all.'

'Oh, how awful!' Josie said, looking at her in distress. 'How could people do things like that to animals? What have they ever done to hurt anyone?'

'It is very upsetting,' Mrs Peabody agreed. 'Still, we do our best for them once they've arrived here. Now, I expect you'd like to see our horses and donkeys, wouldn't you?' She led them on past another covered building – 'Cats!' – then a large shed – 'The reptile house!' – and out into a pleasant-looking field which sloped downhill. There were about ten donkeys in it, and a horse and a pony grazing near the fence.

'I won't try and name all the donkeys,' Mrs Peabody

said, 'but the chestnut horse is called Hercules and the dun pony we've named Sally. We found her in the water, trapped in a river.'

'What happened to her legs?' asked Mrs Grace, looking at the nasty scars all over them.

'We think she must have torn them on some barbed wire,' Mrs Peabody said. 'That's why she'd fallen in the river. She was lucky not to get tetanus. The wounds are healing up now, but I don't think the hair will ever grow back.'

'And what about Hercules? Where's he come from?' Josie asked, watching the big chestnut. He lifted his head and returned her gaze with big, sad eyes, then went back to eating the grass.

'Someone found him in the basement of a derelict house in the city,' Mrs Peabody answered. 'From what we can make out, he was going to be part of some plan to offer carriage rides that went wrong, and he was just abandoned to starve to death. He nearly did, too. Here, boy! Come on, Hercules!' She whistled, and the horse came walking slowly and hesitantly over to them, his head held low.

Josie held out her hand and Hercules sniffed it suspiciously. 'Can I give him a mint?' she asked.

'He'd like that,' said Mrs Peabody, patting Hercules' neck. 'After all, he deserves a bit of spoiling. Just be careful when you hold it out to him – he's head shy.

Someone's obviously beaten him around the face at some time in his life.'

Mrs Grace shook her head sadly, while Josie cautiously held the mint out on her palm. 'You poor old thing,' she whispered, as Hercules snatched it up and crunched it between his teeth. 'How could anyone do that to you? I'm so sorry.'

But the horse just flicked back his ears and wandered away.

'We had to have our other resident pony put down a couple of weeks ago,' Mrs Peabody said, 'so we do have room for one more at the moment. If you're interested, you should let me know quickly – I could get a phone call at any time and that place would be gone.'

'Thanks very much,' said Mrs Grace, with a look at Josie's downcast face. 'We'll give you a ring just as soon as we can.'

'Mrs Peabody's quite a character, isn't she?' Mrs Grace said as they drove away from the sanctuary. 'You can tell she loves the animals, though. It's good to think of some creature that's been badly treated getting a second chance with her.'

'Oh, sure,' Josie agreed. 'For a horse like Hercules, it must be great to end up there. But our Hope? Come on, Mum – she's not that old, and she hasn't been abused or anything. She's been a part of our family for most of her life. The sanctuary's just not the right place for her, it really isn't!'

Mrs Grace gazed at the road ahead and didn't speak for a while. 'Look,' she said eventually, 'I do think we ought to have some plan in mind for Hope in case nothing else turns up. Let's face it – time's running out and we've got to be realistic. I think we should consider Mrs Peabody's offer very seriously, Josie. I don't want to lose what might turn out to be Hope's only chance by dragging our feet over it.'

Josie wasn't sure at first quite how to reply, but she knew better than to risk a head-on clash with her mother. Once Mrs Grace had made up her mind, she wouldn't budge, and Josie didn't want to push her into a decision. It would be better to play for time. 'Today's Monday,' she said. 'Why don't we wait until this weekend? If nothing else has turned up during the week, we can talk to Mrs Peabody again. What do you think about that?'

'OK, then,' said her mother. 'But I'd say Friday at the latest. If there are no other offers by then, we go for the sanctuary.'

Five

'Come on, Josie,' Anna said as they walked down the road towards the village. 'We're meant to be doing this project together. You could at least help me decide which explorer to choose!'

'Did any of them go on horseback?' Josie asked absent-mindedly.

'Well, I suppose the ones who went overland would have done,' Anna replied, with a touch of impatience. 'They couldn't exactly hop on a train, could they? But you don't have to bring horses into *everything*, Josie. Couldn't you think about something else for a while?'

'Oh, I suppose so,' Josie said, as they turned off

Northgate's high street and started down a narrow lane on the edge of the village. 'I'm just so worried about Hope, it's hard to concentrate on anything else.' She'd told Anna all about their visit to the animal sanctuary the day before, and her mother's deadline. 'Don't you feel the same?' she added.

'I know what you mean,' Anna replied, serious for once. 'But I don't see what we can do about it – worrying isn't going to get us anywhere. Why don't you think about this Geography topic instead? It might take your mind off things. And Ben's playing football at school, so the computer's free for a while.' She stopped at the end cottage in a row of three, and pushed the front door open.

'Hello there, love – and hi, Josie!' said Lynne Marshall, the twins' mother, who was sitting in a chair by the window with a huge book of paint swatches on her lap. 'I haven't seen you for a while. How are you?'

'Oh, fine, thanks, Lynne,' said Josie. She knew how much Anna's mum disliked being called Mrs Marshall, especially since she and her husband had separated. It was true – she hadn't been to Ben and Anna's house for ages, and now she realised how much she'd missed her visits. She'd been so involved in everything that was happening at the stables lately, there hadn't been time for much else.

The cottage was lovely – it might have been small,

but Lynne arranged everything so beautifully that it always felt cosy and welcoming. She was a trained artist, though these days she worked mainly as a painter and decorator, and she had filled the house with light and colour. In winter there was almost always a fire burning in the open grate when Anna and Ben got back from school. On sunny days, the French windows looking out on to the paved courtyard at the back of the house were thrown open. Today, the scent of honeysuckle floated in and a bumble bee buzzed around a tub of white lilies.

Josie looked round the peppermint green walls of the sitting room. 'Something's different in here,' she said. 'What is it?'

'Aha!' Lynne replied with a grin. 'See if you can work it out.' With her short fair hair and blue eyes, she looked totally unlike Ben and Anna. They got their dark colouring from their father's side of the family.

'Got it!' said Josie after a couple of minutes. 'That's a different painting over the fireplace, isn't it?' She gazed at the bright, swirling landscape. 'Is it one you've just done?'

'I wish,' said Lynne, getting up and casting a critical eye over the picture. 'It's been gathering dust in the studio for the past five years. I felt like a change, that's all.'

'I like it, Mum. Those poppies are wonderful,' Anna

said. 'I always love your flowers. You should do a few more like that and see if your agent could fix up another exhibition.'

'And when am I going to get the chance to do any more painting?' Lynne said as she went back to her chair. 'I'm worn out with all this decorating work and there's no time for anything else.'

'Give it up, then,' Anna suggested. 'Just paint for a while.'

'And what would we live on? Fresh air?' came the reply. 'At least the business brings some regular money in. Painting's going to have to wait for a while, I'm afraid. Now, can I fix you both a sandwich?'

'Not just at the minute, thanks, Mum,' Anna said. 'We're going to do some work on the computer.' She took Josie's arm and steered her towards the dining room-cum-study on the other side of the staircase. 'Come on,' she said. 'I've decided for us. We're going to write about Mary Kingsley – she's the only female explorer I could find. She paddled up the Congo in a dug-out canoe. How about that for girl power?'

An hour later, Anna pushed the computer keyboard back across the desk and rolled her stiff shoulders around in a circle. 'Well, I think that's covered everything,' she said. 'I'll just print out what we've typed and we can copy the maps at school tomorrow.'

'You were right, Anna,' Josie admitted, cutting out the picture of Mary Kingsley that they'd downloaded and were planning to put on the cover of their project. 'It's been good for me to think about something different for a change. And I never realised how useful the Internet is.' Anna and Ben had been really excited when they got the computer as a birthday present from their father, but it was the first time that Josie had expressed any real interest in it.

'It's great, isn't it?' Anna agreed. 'And it's done wonders for our project.'

'Wait a minute!' Josie said suddenly, putting down the scissors and looking excitedly at Anna. 'Why don't we see if there's anything about sweet itch on the Internet? Mum says she's tried everything for Hope, but maybe there's some new treatment she hasn't heard of!'

'That's not a bad idea,' Anna said, catching her enthusiasm. 'Hang on, I'll just get connected again and give it a go.'

In a few seconds, she was hooked back on to the Internet. Josie pulled up her chair, looking eagerly at the screen as Anna typed in the words 'sweet itch' and clicked on the 'Find It' button.

'Got it!' she said a minute or so later. 'Josie, you're brilliant! There's a whole web site just for sweet itch.' Together they waited for the site to be opened and then, as if by magic, the latest information began to appear.

'This is amazing!' Josie said, reaching for a pad of paper. 'We'd better make some notes – there's so much to take in!'

They scrolled down the screen, copying out any remedies that seemed effective. There were extracts from scientific journals and photos of horses suffering from the complaint which made them both wince. 'At least Hope doesn't look quite as bad as some of these poor things,' Josie said. What she found most exciting, though, were the firsthand reports from people who'd tried out the various cures on their own animals.

'This person says castor oil's good for helping the hair grow back,' Anna said. 'Have you seen that? Halfway down the page?'

'Hang on,' Josie said, scribbling furiously, 'I'm still copying this bit about the cream and zinc oxide powder.' She looked back at the screen – and then let out a yelp as her eye caught sight of an entry near the bottom. 'Anna!' she said, grabbing her arm as she read on. 'There's a woman who's developed a spray that's meant to be 98 per cent effective. She's used it with her own horses, and now she's looking for people to test it out – for free! Here, read it for yourself.'

Anna ran her eyes over the words flickering in front of them and turned to smile at Josie. 'Bingo!' she said.

'Let's send her a message now! After all, what have we got to lose?' She clicked on the e-mail address and began to type.

'This spray couldn't be dangerous, could it?' Josie asked, getting cold feet all of a sudden. 'What if it makes Hope worse?'

'I don't think that's likely,' Anna replied confidently. 'It seems to have been thought out very scientifically. Anyway, if it shows any signs of harming her, we can just stop using it. Oh, Josie, maybe this will really help Hope. We've got to give it a try!'

At that moment, Lynne Marshall's voice came through the open door. 'You haven't been on the Internet all this time, have you?' she said crossly, poking her head in. 'For goodness' sake, Anna – remember the phone bill! I'm not made of money, you know.'

'No, we've only just gone back on, Mum,' Anna replied, turning round from the desk. 'Josie just had this brainwave about finding out if there's anything—'

'Well, whatever it is, do it as quickly as possible, please,' her mother said sharply, and went back out of the room.

Anna sighed as she carried on typing the message, finally showing it to Josie for approval.

'That looks fine,' Josie said. 'Thanks! It might not work but, like you say, what have we got to lose?' Then she took another look at Anna's glum face and added,

190

'Is anything wrong? You were really excited a second ago.'

'Oh, I'm just a bit worried about Mum at the moment,' Anna replied. 'She gets grumpy out of the blue and she's tired most of the time – I think she's working too hard. It's tough, all that stripping wallpaper and sanding and painting. You should see the muscles in her arms.'

'Maybe she needs another evening out with my mum,' Josie suggested, after thinking for a while. 'You and Ben could always stay overnight at our house.'

'Yes, she'd like that,' Anna replied. 'They get on really well, don't they?'

'Just like we do,' Josie said, giving her friend a quick hug. She felt guilty: Anna had problems of her own, and she hadn't even noticed. 'Look,' she said, 'why don't we have that sandwich now and then take the ponies out for a ride? There's still plenty of time before it gets dark, and I feel like some fresh air after all this work. What do you say?'

'Good idea!' Anna replied, jumping up. 'I'll just get changed and then we can grab something to eat.'

So, after a peanut butter-and-banana sandwich and a lecture from Lynne about rules for going on the Internet – 'after six o'clock and for half an hour at the most' – Josie put the notes they'd taken in her school bag and the two of them began to walk back to the stables. Mrs

191

Grace was busy polishing a saddle in the tackroom when they arrived.

'Mum!' Josie said, bursting in. 'We've found out all sorts of information on the Internet about sweet itch. Look, I've made loads of notes! And we've contacted someone who's developed a new spray and wants people to test it out. Anna's asked for it to be sent here!'

'I'm a bit doubtful about miracle cures,' Mrs Grace said, scanning the pages Josie had given her. 'In my experience, they don't often do much good. Still, thanks for taking all this trouble. I hadn't heard of using castor oil on the scars, I must say, but let's give it a try!'

'Can we take the ponies out for a quick ride, Mum?' Josie asked, reaching for a couple of headcollars.

'Just so long as you're back before dusk,' Mrs Grace said. 'We've got to have Hope safely in the stable before those midges start biting.'

'Yes, we won't go for long,' Anna replied. 'I'll catch the ponies while you get out of your school gear,' she said, taking the headcollars from Josie.

'Bring them in one at a time, remember,' Mrs Grace called after them. 'You can't handle them both at once, Anna!'

'So, where shall we go?' Josie said as they turned out of the stables. It felt great to be on horseback after spending so long in front of the computer. Charity

192

began to pull, eager to be off, so she shortened her reins, patted the pony's neck and spoke quietly to calm her down.

'Why don't we go through the village and then up Baker's Hill and back through the fields?' Anna replied, falling in behind her on Hope. 'Ben said he had a great ride with Tubber there the other day, and it won't take too long.'

'Fine,' Josie said, turning on to the road and back towards the village. 'Oh, Charity, stop mucking about!' The pony was beginning to take little steps backwards, making a fuss about a piece of plastic flapping in the hedgerow. Josie squeezed her outside leg behind the girth to stop Charity's hindquarters swinging out into the road and soon got her walking on. 'I think she's been having too much of that young grass,' she said, turning back to smile at Anna. 'We'll have to keep her in overnight with Hope.'

The ponies' shoes struck smartly on the tarmac as they trotted along the road, quiet now the rush hour traffic had gone. Josie felt her spirits rise as they went. It was good to be out in the open with Anna. She took another quick glance behind and Anna gave her a thumbs-up sign. Hope's poor bedraggled mane and sparse tail weren't looking any better, but Josie told herself that she and Anna were going to help her get over the sweet itch, if it was the last thing they did. One

193

of the cures they'd read about was bound to work, even if the spray didn't turn out to be a miracle. And someone would offer Hope a home, she was sure of it – she'd have another word with a few of the pupils who came to the stables.

And then she looked forward again, and groaned. Hanging around by the bus shelter were Mark Lee, a big bully in the year above them at school, and a fair-haired boy in a leather jacket she hadn't come across before. They were sitting on mountain bikes, watching as Josie and Anna approached, obviously bored and looking for trouble.

'Try and ignore them,' Anna called softly behind her, and Josie tried to relax. She didn't want Charity to sense her tension – she was high-spirited enough this afternoon as it was.

'Well, what have we got here?' Mark sneered as they came closer, narrowing his eyes and staring at them. 'Two little girlies out for a ride. How sweet!'

'Look at the ugly one!' crowed his friend, as Anna rode past on Hope. 'What's the matter with her? Looks like all her hair's dropping out. Couldn't you find a better pony to ride than that old nag?'

Josie bit her lip, furious but determined not to lose her temper. Anna, though, had forgotten her own advice about staying calm. 'She's got a horse version of acne,' Josie heard her say sweetly. 'Something you'd know all about. Perhaps there's a good cream you could recommend?'

Josie looked back and saw the boy's spotty face flush a deep red. *Oh no!* she thought to herself. *Anna, that's not going to do any good!*

'Very funny,' he said, riding his bike out into the road behind them. 'Think that's clever, do you? You're out of your league here, Miss Stuck-up Princess. Come on Mark, let's have some fun!'

They rode along some distance behind the two ponies, circling their bikes from one side of the road to the other, whistling and shouting. Charity put her ears back and her tail began to swish angrily. She snorted a couple of times, but Josie didn't dare turn around and tell the boys to get lost.

And then, disaster struck. Either Mark or his friend – she couldn't tell which of them it was – suddenly let out a piercing blast on a hooter. With a squeal of fear, Charity reared up in panic, throwing her fore legs frantically out in mid-air.

'Josie!' she heard Anna scream, as she desperately fought to keep control of the terrified pony.

Six

Josie tried to sit as deep in the saddle as she could, to tell Charity that she was still there and still in charge. She was relieved that, after her first terrified lunge, the pony was no longer rearing. But her ears were right back and she was obviously very nervous. What frightened Josie most of all was the thought that if Charity bolted straight through the village, they'd come out on to a busy main road, where the traffic thundered along at all times of the day and night. She kept a tight contact with the reins, but Charity was throwing her head around and dancing all over the road with jumpy little steps.

Thinking quickly, Josie tried to turn her around in a circle, so that even if she did take off, she'd be galloping away from the main road. Unfortunately, that meant she was facing the boys, who were still shouting and laughing behind them, but she felt it was the safest option. She patted Charity's neck and spoke soft reassuring words to her, but the pony was spooked and wasn't going to be calmed down easily.

'Charity! It's OK,' called Anna, trotting towards her on Hope. She brought the calm, steady mare up to stand beside her daughter. 'Look!' she said soothingly. 'Hope's not frightened. She knows they can't do you any harm.'

'Oh, can't we?' shouted the lad in the leather jacket. 'Do you want some more of this?' And he put his hand threateningly on the big black hooter fixed to his handlebars. 'Doesn't like that, does she?' he jeered.

Don't blow that again, you idiot! Josie thought to herself. She knew that if there was another blast, she'd have no hope of keeping Charity under control. How could that stupid boy be so thoughtless? Didn't he realise the danger he was putting her in?

'Don't be such a fool!' Anna shouted at him. 'Somebody could get hurt!'

'Well, it won't be me,' he sneered, 'so what do I care?'

'Oh, won't it?' Anna muttered under her breath. She

shortened her reins, as though about to move off. 'I've a good mind to—'

'Anna, don't go!' Josie said urgently. 'Hope's the only thing that's stopping Charity from bolting. Please, stay with me!' As soon as Hope had walked up to them, she'd felt some of the tension go out of her pony. Hope seemed to sense how frightened Charity was and stood squarely between her and the boys, shielding her from their shouts and blocking her way as if to stop her bolting. Without Hope's reassuring presence, Josie didn't know what might happen.

'Come on, Steve,' said Mark Lee uneasily. 'Give it a break now. Let's go back to my place and watch the telly – I've had enough of hanging about with stupid horses.'

He turned his bike around and began to pedal back down the road. With one last defiant gesture to Josie and Anna, the other lad followed him. 'We'll be waiting for you another time!' he called over his shoulder.

'Oh, will you?' Anna said grimly. 'Big coward! I'm a match for you any day of the week.'

Josie let out a long shaky breath. She knew now that Charity wasn't going to gallop off – her breathing was steadier and her ears were flicking back and forth as she watched the danger going further and further away. She obviously felt safer standing next to her mother.

'Hope's amazing!' she said to Anna, her voice

quivering. 'I think she must be the bravest, calmest pony in the world. Charity was about to bolt, I know she was.'

Anna patted Hope and then slipped her feet out of the stirrups and jumped off, looping the reins over her neck. She stood by Charity's head, rubbing her nose and speaking softly to her. 'You can tell by her eyes she's still quite frightened,' she said. 'I think we should go back, don't you? What if I lead Hope and walk next to Charity? Then I can take hold of her if anything goes wrong or we run into those morons again.'

'Thanks, Anna,' Josie said gratefully. 'I'm just so glad Hope was here. I don't know what I'd have done without her.'

'She's one in a million, isn't she?' Anna replied, kissing the pony's neck.

'It makes me so angry when people are horrible about the way she looks,' Josie went on. 'Why can't they see how special she is underneath? I can't bear to think of Hope going to the sanctuary, Anna, I just can't!'

However, enquiries from people interested in buying Hope seemed to have entirely dried up. Josie asked her mother anxiously on Wednesday whether anyone else had phoned, but Mrs Grace just shook her head. Try as she might, Josie was finding it hard to keep feeling positive – she had to admit that Hope's chances of finding a new home in the next few days seemed slim.

Then, just as she was bringing her in from the field to spend the night in her stable, she heard the phone ring in the office, where her mother happened to be working.

'Who do you think that is, Hope?' she said as she cleaned out the pony's feet with a hoof pick, checking to see she hadn't picked up any stones. 'Could it be someone asking about you?'

She called in at the office when she'd finished topping up the water bucket and putting some more straw in the loose box. 'That wasn't a call about Hope, was it?' she asked her mother. 'I heard the phone ring about ten minutes ago.'

'Well, as a matter of fact it was,' Mrs Grace said, pushing back her chair.

'And–?' Josie asked eagerly. 'Come on, Mum, don't keep me in suspense!'

'I'm afraid it wasn't a serious offer,' her mother replied. 'Some children who are friends of John and Sophie – you know, the Butchers – rang up to see if we'd sold Hope yet. They want a pony more than anything else, and John had told them all about her.'

'So what's the catch?' Josie said.

'They live in a block of flats,' her mother replied with a smile, 'and they wanted to keep Hope in the lift. She's so laid back she'd probably think that was just fine, but I don't really think it's an option, do you?'

'No, I suppose not,' Josie sighed, slumping in a chair on the other side of the desk.

'Cheer up, love,' her mother said gently. 'If Hope does have to go to the sanctuary, she'll probably be perfectly happy there, and we could go and visit her whenever we wanted. There are worse places she could end up.'

'Maybe you're right,' Josie said dispiritedly. 'I've worried about this so much I can't seem to think straight any more.'

'Hello, you two,' said Robert Grace, appearing at the office door with a bulging case and an armful of exercise books. 'Everything OK?'

Josie looked at him for a moment without speaking. Her face must have shown how dejected she was feeling, for he dumped the books he was carrying on the desk and drew up a chair next to her. 'What's all this doom and gloom, then?' he asked gently. 'Come on, if anyone's depressed, it should be me. I've just had a truly terrible rehearsal – Sandy doesn't know her lines, Danny's lost his voice and there's only just over a week to go. Beat that for worries!'

'It's Hope,' Josie said. 'We can't seem to find anyone who wants her.'

'OK, you win,' said Mr Grace immediately, and Josie couldn't help smiling. Her father had a knack of cheering her up.

'I have told Josie, though, that I think the animal

sanctuary isn't such a bad prospect,' said Mrs Grace, closing her accounts' book. 'I'm sure Hope would be well looked after there.'

'And it might only be for a little while,' Mr Grace suggested. 'After all, we could still carry on looking for a family to take Hope whilst she stayed at the sanctuary, couldn't we?'

'I guess so,' Josie said, leaning back in her chair and pushing her feet against the desk. 'It's just so unsettling, not knowing what's going to happen to her and whether she'll be gone in a few days or not.'

'I agree with you there,' said her mother with feeling. 'I'm not sure whether to take any bookings for next week, or how much more feed to order. Everything seems to be up in the air. We don't even know where we're going to be living in a couple of months!'

'Look,' said Mr Grace, 'this is a difficult time for all of us to get through, nobody could deny that. We'll just have to take it step by step and tackle the problems one at a time. At least Hope has somewhere to go, even if the sanctuary isn't perfect, and who knows – something else might turn up.' He looked earnestly at Josie and her mother. 'The most important thing is, we've still got each other. If we stick together, we can come through this!'

Josie knew in her heart of hearts her father was right. Besides, moping around wasn't going to do Hope any good. 'You're right!' she said, stretching out a hand to hold each of her parents'. 'Things could be better, but they could be a lot worse, too.'

'Well done, sweet pea,' her father smiled. 'That's the right way to look at it.' Then suddenly he jumped up and announced, 'I know what we need – a party! There are a hundred good reasons for throwing one. Well, three at least. We could thank everyone who's come to the stables over the years, and everyone who's helped me with the musical, and cheer ourselves up at the same time! Let's have it the weekend after next, straight after *Grease* has finished.'

'But will that give us enough time to organise everything?' Mrs Grace objected. 'When there's so much else to be done, do we really need a party too?'

'Yes, we do!' Josie exclaimed. 'I think it's a brilliant idea. Come on, Mum – let's have some fun and try to forget our problems for a while!'

The next day, though, Josie came back from school to a sight that sent all those good resolutions flying out of her mind. There, parked in the yard, was a van belonging to the Peabody Animal Welfare Society. Her heart lurched. What was going on? Hope still had another day's grace, didn't she, before her mother rang the sanctuary? Surely she wouldn't have gone back on their agreement without some warning . . .

She rushed up the path to School Farm and burst through the front door and down the hall into the kitchen. Her mother and Mrs Peabody were sitting over mugs of tea at the big pine table.

'It's all right, love,' said Mrs Grace, holding up a hand as soon as she saw Josie's face. 'You don't have to worry – we're not deciding anything. Mrs Peabody's just called round with quite an interesting proposal.'

'For Hope?' Josie said breathlessly, letting her school bag drop to the ground.

'That's right,' Mrs Peabody said, smiling. 'I was just telling your mother that I had a visit yesterday from a group of handicapped children. There's a respite centre called Friendship House not far from us – have you heard of it?'

Josie shook her head, joining them at the kitchen table.

'Well, they take mentally handicapped children for holidays, to give their carers a break,' Mrs Peabody went on. 'The place is run by a wonderful young woman called Liz Tallant. She's quite an extraordinary person – full of energy and ideas.'

Mrs Peabody took a sip of her tea and seemed to be lost in thought for a moment.

'And . . .?' Josie prompted her, almost bursting with impatience. What *was* this interesting proposal? She was dying to find out.

'Oh yes,' Mrs Peabody said, gathering herself together again. 'Well, they've got a couple of donkeys at the centre – I've heard it's a very pleasant place, lots of lovely grounds – and Liz's keen to adopt a pony. She was asking about Sally, but I'm afraid the poor thing's much too nervous to cope with lots of boisterous children.'

'Apparently they need a very steady, gentle pony who doesn't mind noise,' Mrs Grace put in. 'Does that ring any bells, Josie?'

'Yes, it does,' Josie said slowly. There were a hundred questions buzzing round in her head, but a small, excited feeling was also growing in the pit of her stomach.

'I'm sure there's a lot you need to find out,' said Mrs Peabody, as though she could read her mind. 'If you agree, I'll talk to Liz and she can give you a ring and arrange to meet. If she's interested in Hope, that is.'

'I think that sounds like a good plan,' Mrs Grace said. 'What do you think, Josie?'

'I agree,' Josie said, her eyes shining. 'Thanks, Mrs Peabody!'

What Hope enjoyed most of all was being useful, and Josie was sure she'd love to carry on working. The donkeys at the centre would be company for her, but she'd still get plenty of care and attention. It sounded wonderful. Liz Tallant had to be interested in Hope – she just had to!

Seven

'What do you think, Josie?' said her mother as they sat in the car outside Friendship House. 'It seems a nice place, doesn't it?'

'Lovely,' Josie agreed, looking at the sprawling, honey-coloured stone building in front of them. The original house must have been quite old, but it had obviously been added to over the years. On one side, a single-storey extension in the shape of a rectangle with three sides lay around a small lawn. Tubs of bright red geraniums were dotted along the drive and on either side of the front door, and the sound of piano music floated out through an open window.

'It's very peaceful,' Josie added, looking around for signs of life. 'I wonder where everyone is?'

'Well, Liz said this was their changeover time,' Mrs Grace said. 'She's expecting a new group of children tomorrow, and the last lot have just left. That's why she asked us to come today, so we'd have a chance to talk without too many interruptions. Come on, let's get going. We don't want to keep her waiting!'

They rang the bell, and a minute or so later the door was flung open by a slim, brown-haired young woman in a striped T-shirt and jeans. 'Hi, there, I'm Liz Tallant,' she said, ushering them in with a broad smile that lit up her face. After Josie and her mother had introduced themselves, she went on, 'I'm so glad you could come! Let's go straight to my office and we can talk.'

She led the way into a pleasant-looking room near the front entrance. There was a large desk by the window, and several armchairs and a sofa along one wall. 'Have a seat,' Liz said, settling in one of the armchairs herself.

'We'll try not to take up too much of your time,' Mrs Grace said politely as she and Josie sat down. 'I'm sure you must have plenty to do.'

'Oh, don't worry about that!' Liz replied warmly. 'It's great to meet you and I can't wait to hear all about your pony. But let me tell you a bit about Friendship House first, so you can see if you think it might be the right place for her.'

Josie took the other chair and gazed round the office while her mother and Liz talked. There was so much to look at! Paintings, drawings and cards were stuck over every inch of the walls, and a huge cork pinboard was covered in photographs. She could see children at the beach, in a swimming pool, covered in mud, cooking, painting – all of them looking busy and really happy.

'We take mentally handicapped children, to stay for a week or two at a time,' Liz was saying. 'This should be a holiday, so we try to make it as much fun as we can, and it's also a break for the children's carers. Looking after them can be a twenty-four hour job, and everyone needs some time off, don't they?'

She jumped up, saying, 'Look, why don't I show you round, so you can get more of an idea of the place? That'll give you a much better idea than me just droning on.'

Josie got the feeling Liz was much happier doing something than sitting still and talking. She seemed to radiate energy and enthusiasm as she showed them into a big, airy room with lots of comfortable armchairs and a few low tables arranged in groups around it. The music Josie had heard when they'd first arrived was coming from a CD player in the corner, and it gave the place a lovely tranquil feeling. She looked around, imagining the room full of life and activity.

'This is our sitting-room, where we have a few singsongs and generally chill out,' Liz said. 'We try to make music and art a part of everyday life here. The children seem to love it, and some of the work they produce is incredible.'

'Yes, so I see,' Mrs Grace said, looking at the framed pictures hanging along the walls. 'These are beautiful. Look at the colour and movement!'

'I love this one!' Josie exclaimed, pointing at a wonderfully detailed and intricate pen-and-ink sketch of the front of Friendship House. 'It must have been done by a proper artist, though.'

'You'd think so, wouldn't you?' said Liz, looking over her shoulder. 'In fact, that picture was drawn by a fourteen-year-old boy. He can't read or write, but he's fascinated by buildings, and he can draw them like you wouldn't believe.'

'It's incredible!' Josie breathed, examining the picture even more closely and then turning to look at Liz in surprise.

'Great, isn't it?' Liz said proudly. 'I tell you, I'm always finding myself amazed here. Billy's an exception, of course, but all of the children seem to enjoy their sessions so much. I'd really like to get an art teacher to help us, though that's just one of my dreams at the moment. Now,' she went one, 'let me show you the studio where it all happens. Then we can see the children's rooms and I'll take you outside for a look at the field and the stables.'

They followed Liz around the building, while she told them about the children who came to stay there and the kinds of things they enjoyed doing. The more she talked, the more enthusiastic she became, and Josie realised that working at Friendship House was more than just a job for Liz – it was her whole life.

'You've got fantastic facilities here,' Mrs Grace said, as they walked through one of the bedrooms in the modern extension. Most of the rooms had two or three beds, but some were just for one person, and there was a warden's room at the end of each corridor.

'I know – we're lucky, aren't we?' Liz replied. 'The centre was set up by a wealthy couple with a handicapped daughter who discovered what a huge need there was for a place like it, and we've kept going by private donations ever since. Most of the families whose children come here give us something, but we don't insist if they can't afford it. Now, follow me and I'll show you one of my favourite places.'

She opened a door at the back of the building and led Josie and her mother through to a wide terrace. There were more tubs spilling over with flowers all the way along it and beyond lay a small field, in which two donkeys were grazing.

'Jack and Jill,' Liz said, waving an arm towards them. 'Not very original, I'm afraid! Over there—' and she pointed across the paddock to a large wire enclosure with several hutches in it, 'we've got the rabbits and guinea pigs. The stables are on the other side, at the back of the main house. It used to be a coaching inn,

and three of the old loose boxes are left. Shall we go and say hello to the donkeys first?'

'Yes, please,' Josie said eagerly.

'I always like bringing the children out here,' Liz said, following on behind her with Mrs Grace. 'Meeting the animals really seems to help if they feel homesick or lonely – and many of them do, at first.'

'Oh, I love donkeys,' Josie said, as she reached the fence and the two of them trotted towards her. 'It's just something about their furry ears . . .'

'I know exactly what you mean,' Mrs Grace said, feeling in her jacket pocket for a sugar lump. 'Who looks after them?' she asked, turning to Liz. 'I shouldn't think you have time!'

'No, I don't,' Liz answered. 'We've got a couple of men in charge of the grounds and the building and Sid, the older one, takes care of the two of them. They're his pride and joy! I'm sorry he's not here at the moment, or he'd talk to you about them for hours. He's been nagging me for months about getting a pony for the children to ride.'

Josie and her mother both looked at Liz, aware that they were getting to the heart of the matter. 'So, tell us more about what you're looking for,' Mrs Grace asked her.

'Well, *anyone* who works here needs to be very even-tempered,' Liz replied, scratching a donkey's nose.

'Some of the children can be quite noisy, particularly when they're excited, and we couldn't risk having an animal who might hurt them out of fear. And to be honest, plodding up and down giving rides isn't the most exciting thing in the world, so a high-spirited pony would probably go mad with boredom. But some horses seem to thrive on it. Somehow they realise they have to be patient, and they'll put up with almost anything.'

She smiled sympathetically, looking at Josie's thoughtful face. 'There's a lot for you to think over – I do understand,' she said. 'I realise you might have been imagining your pony would go to a family, rather than somewhere like this. Why don't I leave you both to have a chat? You can wander around and explore. Come and find me inside when you're ready.' And without further ado, she strode back off towards the modern building.

'Well, where shall we go first?' Mrs Grace asked Josie as they watched Liz's determined back disappear into the distance. 'Rabbits or stables?'

'Stables,' Josie said promptly. 'That's really what we're here for, after all.'

They walked back along the terrace, looking out at the peaceful scene. Behind the rabbits' enclosure were a couple of swings and a climbing frame that faced towards the field. Jack and Jill were now standing under a large oak tree in one corner, their grey coats perfectly camouflaged against its trunk.

'I wonder how many horses have been put up here over the years?' Mrs Grace said as they approached the row of loose boxes that were covered by a mossy tiled roof. She peered into the dark stables. 'Just imagine what it must have been like – passengers sleeping in the inn while the horses stayed out here, then harnessed up and off again in the morning. More exciting than catching the train! A lot slower, too, mind you.'

'Come on, Mum,' Josie said, tapping her back. 'Stop trying to avoid the issue. What do you think of Friendship House?'

'I think it's a wonderful place,' Mrs Grace replied, turning around to lean against the stable door and look along the terrace. 'Liz is lovely, and the grounds are perfect.'

'But . . .' Josie prompted. 'There is a "but" in your voice – I can hear it.'

'OK,' her mother smiled. 'I've got two "buts", I suppose. Firstly, we really can't tell how Hope is going to react to the children. We're assuming she'll be fine, because she's so placid, but we don't know for certain. She hasn't really had any experience with handicapped people – Grace's Stables have always been too small for that.'

'Oh, Mum, I'm sure she'll be perfectly happy,' Josie protested. 'Remember me telling you how calm she was when those boys were mucking about? I bet none of the children can yell any louder than that bike hooter!'

'Yes, but you know ponies. They're just like people, with their own funny little likes and dislikes,' Mrs Grace replied. 'It may be that Hope doesn't respond as well as we expect, that's all I'm saying.' She put her arm round Josie's shoulder and they began to walk back towards the house.

'And I still think you're worrying about nothing,' Josie replied. 'Anyway, what's the second problem?'

'Well, what if Liz decides she doesn't want Hope once she sees her, like the Simmonds family did?' Mrs Grace said, frowning into the distance. 'I can't bear it when people reject her – I think I'd sooner let her go to the sanctuary now than risk that again. At least Mrs Peabody loves animals for what they are.'

'Oh, but so would Liz!' Josie exclaimed. 'I'm certain of it. She's not one to judge by appearances, is she? You can tell that just by talking to her for five minutes.'

'Yes, you're probably right,' her mother said, thinking it over. 'But what with the sweet itch, too—' Then she suddenly clapped one hand to her forehead and said, 'Of course – I keep forgetting to tell you, Josie! The spray you found on the Internet arrived yesterday! What with Mrs Peabody being there when you got back from school, it went right out of my head, and then you rushed off before I could talk to you this morning.'

'So what's it like?' Josie asked eagerly. 'Have you been using it?'

'Well, it's too early to tell for sure, but I've been spraying Hope every few hours and I think it might – just might – be making a difference,' Mrs Grace said. 'Her skin certainly isn't getting any worse.'

'Yes!' Josie said, feeling a tingle of excitement. 'Everything's going to work out, I know it will!'

'Now look, love,' Mrs Grace said seriously, 'I don't want you to get too carried away, in case we're disappointed again. Maybe Friendship House *is* the right place for Hope, but there's still an awful lot to be decided.'

'Then let's go and find Liz and start talking!' Josie said, propelling her mother with a firm hand on her shoulder towards the back door of the main building.

'Don't you want to see the rabbits and guinea pigs?' Mrs Grace asked, laughing, as she was pushed along.

'No, I don't!' Josie replied definitely. 'How can we possibly think about rabbits and guinea pigs at a time like this? Hope's future is lying in the balance!'

They found Liz in the kitchen, sitting on a stool and talking to a capable-looking older woman in an overall. 'This is Joan,' she said. 'She handles all our catering – and a fantastic job she does, too.' Everyone smiled and said hello, and then Joan made a pot of tea before disappearing off to the dining-room.

'So,' Liz said, 'what do you two think? Would Hope be happy here? Tell me more about her.'

'We *think* that she would,' Mrs Grace said cautiously, taking a sip from her mug. 'She's a very gentle, calm creature and nothing usually bothers her. But as I was saying to Josie, she hasn't come across disabled children before, so we can't be absolutely sure how she'll react.'

'We're ninety-nine per cent sure, though!' Josie put in, worried that her mother sounded too pessimistic. 'At least, I am. Hope's the most wonderful pony, Liz – she's so kind and patient, and she's marvellous with beginners.'

'Well, she sounds perfect!' Liz smiled.

'Josie!' said her mother, shooting her a warning look. 'What did I say about getting your hopes up?' She turned to Liz. '*We* think she's lovely because we know her so well, but I ought to tell you that you could probably find a prettier pony. Hope's a sweetheart, but she's no great beauty. And at the moment, she's having a few problems with a skin complaint—'

'Though that's improving,' Josie interrupted.

'Plus, she's a bit of a barrel, with quite a broad back,' Mrs Grace went on, determined that everything should be out in the open.

'Then she really *is* perfect!' Liz said, laughing. 'That's just what most of our children need. A lot of them have problems with their vision, and what they want is a solid base to sit on. Helps with their balance. And for goodness' sake – as if I cared about her looks! I can tell you that none of the kids will, for a single second.'

'Well then,' Mrs Grace said thankfully, 'perhaps you could bring some of them round to meet her.'

'I'd love to,' Liz said, jumping off her stool. 'I'll go and fetch my diary from the office and we can fix it up. Oh, I've got a good feeling in my bones about this!'

'Yes,' said Josie, beaming at her. 'So have I!'

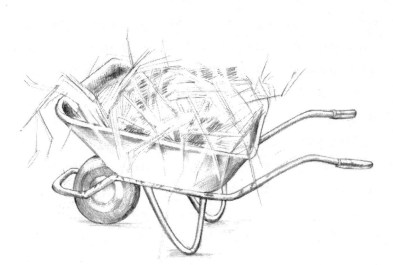

Eight

'Right! Let's get this lot down to the muckheap,' said Ben, wheeling the barrow and its towering load of dirty straw away from the loose boxes.

'Thanks, Ben,' Josie said, coming out of Charity's loose box and rubbing her aching shoulders. She leaned against the wall and took a few minutes out to watch everyone else working.

It was Sunday afternoon, and lessons had finished half an hour earlier. Grace's Stables were a hive of activity: Ben and Anna were busy mucking out the stables and grooming the ponies. Lynne Marshall had come over to help Robert Grace paint the scenery for the musical – after he'd spent fifteen minutes charming her into it over the phone. She and Josie's mum were now unloading overalls, brushes, tins and cans of spray paint from her van and taking them to the barn, where the painting would take place.

'That's it, I think,' Lynne called on her way up there with a final load of buckets, rags and sponges. 'We should have everything we need.'

'Then I'd say it was time for a tea break,' Mary Grace replied, appearing from the barn. 'Come on, you need to keep your strength up, and I feel like a chat. It seems like months since I've seen you.'

'Tea break?' Robert Grace said indignantly as they added to the pile of equipment on the barn floor. 'But we're just ready to start! You're not due a break for at least another couple of hours.'

'Slave driver!' Lynne called back, as she and Mary began to walk over to School Farm. 'We won't be long, I promise!'

Josie smiled and went to see if she could help Anna groom Hope.

'Don't you think the two of us are incredibly, fantastically brilliant?' Anna asked as she came over.

'Well, we are, of course,' Josie replied, 'but for any reason in particular?'

'Check out Hope's mane,' Anna replied, pointing towards it with a body brush. 'Is that spray making a difference, or what?' The spots had nearly disappeared and the dark, shabby patches on Hope's light coat were fading as new hair grew over them.

'I know, it's great,' Josie said with satisfaction, as she stroked Hope's neck. 'I thought her coat was improving yesterday and today it's even better. Mum's taking photos every day to send back to the person who's developed the formula and she's keeping a diary, too.'

'It'd be good to get the sweet itch sorted out before Hope's sold,' Anna said. 'Do you think she's really got a chance of going to Friendship House?' Josie had told her all about the respite centre.

'We'll have to see how she gets on with the children,' Josie said, looking anxiously over at the yard. 'They should be coming any minute.'

'Oh, I'm going to miss her so much,' Anna said, throwing her arms round Hope's neck and giving her a big hug.

'We all will,' Josie said sadly. 'Still, she's got to go somewhere, and Friendship House is near enough for visits.'

'Sorry, Josie,' Anna said, looking round at her. 'Here I go again – making you feel worse. Mum keeps telling me to think about other people's feelings, but I just can't seem to help blurting things out.' She put her arm around Josie's shoulders. 'So, tell me, how are *you* finding all this?' she asked solemnly. 'Is there anything you'd like to share with me?'

'Oh, get off!' Josie said, laughing and shrugging her arm away. 'I think I like the old tactless Anna better!'

She took another body brush from the kit in Charity's stall and began to untangle Hope's tail a section at a time. 'But, since you ask,' she went on, 'I'm not really sure how I feel. Half the time I worry that Friendship House might be the perfect place for Hope but that for some reason she won't be able to go there. And then, the rest of the time I think that they'll want to have her but she won't be happy, surrounded by lots of noisy children.'

'Well, it's nearly make-your-mind-up time,' Anna said. 'Look, here they come.'

They watched as a white minibus with 'Friendship House' painted on the side pulled up and parked in the yard.

'Why don't you go and meet them?' Anna said to Josie. 'I'll fetch your mum from the house.' And she set off towards the path to School Farm.

Liz Tallant was climbing out of the driver's seat of the minibus, and she smiled and waved when she saw Josie coming over. A couple of other adults were already starting to open the doors and help the children out, and soon a small group was standing in the yard.

'I won't introduce you to everyone straight away – you're bound to forget all the names,' Liz said to Josie.

'But these are the lucky few who most wanted to meet Hope, and Marion and Pete who've come to help.'

'Hello, there,' Josie said brightly, to a little girl of seven or eight who was holding Liz's hand tightly. At once she shrank back and hid her face.

'Charlotte's feeling a bit shy at the moment,' Liz explained. 'She's going to stick very close to me.'

Just then Mrs Grace and Anna appeared and Ben came over from the muckheap, and soon the ice was broken and everyone was chatting. The children were beginning to wander off in different directions, so Josie's mum made a suggestion. 'Why don't we go and say hello to Hope now? She's over here, ready and waiting.'

Josie smiled at the tall girl standing next to her, not quite sure whether she should offer to help. 'It's this way,' she said. 'Shall we go together?'

'Yes!' said the girl firmly, taking hold of Josie's hand in her own much larger one. 'My name's Cathy. What's yours? I've brought my bag with all my special things in. Do you want to know what they are?'

'Yes, please,' Josie said, delighted that Cathy was so easy to get on with. They obviously weren't going to have a problem making conversation.

'Tommy! What are you up to?' Liz suddenly called to a dark-haired boy who had started to run jerkily after a couple of hens. They squawked in alarm and scattered

225

across the yard, much to his obvious delight.

'Don't frighten those poor chickens!' Liz said to him, but Anna was already on her way over. 'I think you'd better come with me, Tommy,' she said, taking his arm. 'I've got a brother, and I know just what to do with cheeky boys.'

'Cheeky boys!' Tommy crowed, grinning all over his face and clapping. Anna laughed and towed him off, while Ben followed on behind, promising to get his own back.

'Why don't you tell us about Hope, Josie?' Liz suggested, walking along beside her with Charlotte.

'Well, my mum bought her at an auction nine years ago, when I was three,' Josie began, aware of Cathy and Charlotte listening intently. 'We already had a pony called Faith, who isn't here any more—'

'Is she dead?' Cathy asked seriously.

'No, she's just gone to a new home,' Josie reassured her. 'Anyway, Mum thought Faith was bound to get on with a pony called Hope, because they had the same sort of name. And she liked her anyway, because she looked so calm and gentle.'

Cathy smiled approvingly. 'That's nice,' she said, shifting her bag to the other shoulder.

'Then Hope began to get fatter and fatter,' Josie went on. 'Nobody could work out why, until the vet told us she was going to have a foal. And a few months later she gave birth to Charity.' By now they'd reached the loose boxes, and she added, 'Charity's in the stable and this is Hope, tied up outside. Would you like to stroke her?'

'No, I'll just look for now,' Cathy said, quite contentedly. 'I've got some special things in my bag and

I don't want them to get broken.'

So Josie stood back with Cathy and watched as the children surrounded Hope – all patting, stroking, talking and laughing, at once. Josie held her breath. How would the pony react? There was such a lot of noise and movement! But Hope patiently stood still, only sometimes lifting her head away from the more eager arms that were stretching up to her.

And then, overcome with excitement, Tommy let out a high squeal – so loudly that it made Josie jump. The other children were startled into silence. Charity, who had been watching everything that was going on over her stable door, snorted in alarm and retreated to the depths of her loose box. Hope, though, just took one step backwards and shook her head a couple of times as she avoided Tommy's waving hand.

'Do you like dogs, too?' Anna asked, taking him quietly away. 'There's a lovely dog called Basil, somewhere around. Shall we go and find him?'

'Well!' Liz said wonderingly to Josie. 'Hope really is a superstar! You weren't exaggerating when you said how special she was.'

Josie just smiled. There was something about seeing Hope standing there with the children that filled her with a pride she couldn't quite express.

'Would you like to pat the pony now, Charlotte?' Liz said, bending down. 'Come on – she's lovely!' Gently, she led her forward into a space among the other children. Then, taking her hand, she guided it towards Hope's neck, and Josie realised with a shock that Charlotte was blind.

She watched as the little girl began to stroke Hope – timidly at first, then gradually becoming more confident. Her tight, anxious face began to relax as she concentrated on the feeling of the pony's silky, warm skin under her fingers. Fascinated, she began to explore Hope's mane, and Josie could imagine just what a surprise the thicker, wiry hair there must be to Charlotte.

Hope turned her head around and gently blew down her nose, sniffing at Charlotte's hand. Josie felt Liz take an anxious breath and Charlotte froze for a second that seemed to last for minutes. Then her intent face broke into a beaming smile. 'Tickles!' she said.

'Does it?' Liz said delightedly. 'Do you like it?'

'Yes!' Charlotte said, and laughed.

Liz turned to Josie and whispered, 'That's the first thing she's said since she arrived yesterday morning.'

Josie had to bite her lip to stop that choking feeling in her throat that was threatening to overflow. She was glad to hurry away to fetch a couple of hard hats from the tackroom when her mother suggested the children might like to take turns having pony rides.

* * *

From that moment on, the visit turned into a huge success. All the children who wanted to had a ride on Hope, and she carried them as steadily and patiently as Josie had thought she would. Those who weren't riding explored the stables. They were fascinated by the tackroom, and loved watching the ducks on the pond. The Graces' cats, Millie and Rascal, kept well out of the way, but Basil was another big hit – particularly with Tommy. He and Anna spent ages throwing a tennis ball for the terrier to fetch, though it was difficult for Tommy to control his arm movements and it was anybody's guess where the ball would end up. Both he and Anna thought this was a great joke, and they were soon laughing fit to burst.

Later, while they were all standing around having a drink in the sunshine, Liz suddenly looked around the group and said, 'Hang on, we're missing a couple of people. Where are Cathy and Lee?' Then her anxious expression relaxed a little as she added, 'Oh, Marion's not here, either – she's probably with them. Still, I think I'd better go and see where they've got to.'

'I'll come with you,' Josie offered, 'just in case you get lost.'

They looked in the outdoor schooling ring, the tackroom and the office, and down at the duck pond, without any success.

'I know!' Josie said, as a thought occurred to her.

'Let's try the barn. My dad and our friend Lynne are painting in there. Perhaps the others are with them.'

They hurried past the loose boxes towards the big covered building and, sure enough, the sound of several voices came from inside. Propped against a couple of hay bales at the barn entrance was the plywood cut-out of a long, flashy car. It was shiny with silver foil metalwork and metallic red paint, and the words 'Greased Lightning' ran along the side. Robert Grace and one of the boys from Friendship House were crouched at one end, carefully spray-painting the front wheel.

'Lee! That's fantastic!' Liz exclaimed, but he was too absorbed even to turn around.

'Lee's been a great help,' Mr Grace beamed, putting down the can and coming over. 'We needed someone who knew a bit about cars and, as if by magic, there he was!'

'This is my dad, Robert Grace,' Josie said, introducing Liz. 'He's putting on a musical next week – no prizes for guessing which one.'

'We've roped in Cathy, too,' he said cheerfully, shaking hands and then waving an arm behind him into the barn. 'She and Lynne are in charge of the backcloth for our American diner.'

'Lynne is Anna and Ben's mother,' Josie explained, as Liz looked across to see her and Cathy busy painting a huge sheet of canvas that was draped over some more hay bales. Lynne stopped to explain something to Cathy, waving big circles on the air with her brush. 'She's an artist,' Josie added, in case Liz thought she was just rather eccentric.

'She's been marvellous,' put in Marion, the helper, coming over for a quick word. 'Both the children are in seventh heaven. You know what Lee's like about cars, and Cathy's even given me her bag so she has both hands free. Sorry – I should have come over and told you where we were.'

'Oh, don't worry about that,' Liz said, still watching Lynne intently. 'It's great to see them so happy.' Then she turned back to Josie and said, 'I'm glad you brought me here. I've got a feeling Lynne and I should have a chat before we leave. It could turn out to be quite interesting for both of us!'

Nine

'I feel worn out!' Josie groaned, resting her head in her arms on the kitchen table.

'That makes two of us,' said her mother, yawning. 'But we have been on the go since early this morning, after all.'

'Is anyone else just a little bit hungry?' Ben asked hopefully, looking round the empty kitchen for any sign of food. He'd already polished off a packet of biscuits.

'Ben!' Anna and her mother exclaimed together, while Mr Grace smiled and went to get the Chinese takeaway menu down from the pinboard. 'Right, let's have your orders!' he said, looking at the exhausted group around the kitchen table.

'Crispy chili beef, please,' Ben replied promptly, 'and spring rolls to start off with.'

'The usual, please, Dad – sweet and sour pork,' Josie asked, while Anna requested prawn toasts, chicken with cashew nuts and a spinach and noodle dish for Lynne, who was vegetarian.

'And for you, Madam?' he asked his wife, with a pencil poised over a piece of scrap paper.

'Oh, I'll have anything, thanks,' Mrs Grace replied, wrinkling her nose. 'I'm a bit bored with takeaways, to be honest. The sooner this musical of yours is finished, Rob, the better, as far as I'm concerned.'

'Well, you only have to wait till Friday,' Mr Grace said, studying the menu. 'I'll get going on Saturday with the party food and it'll be good home cooking from then on, I promise. Oh, before I forget – I invited Liz to the party.'

'Great,' Josie said. 'I think she's really nice.'

'Yes, and she's going to bring the children, too,' her father added as an afterthought, scribbling down his order.

'Rob!' Mrs Grace said, staring at him in alarm. 'How many children is she bringing? Will we have enough food? Not to mention enough room?'

'Oh, relax,' he said airily. 'It'll be fine – you worry too much. The best parties are always crowded, and you can leave the food to me.' Then suddenly he stopped writing down numbers from the menu and looked up, a gleam in his eye. 'Of course!' he said. 'I'll get the cast to come in costume and they can perform a couple of songs. The kids will love it!'

Mrs Grace just shook her head, lost for words. Lynne laughed and laid a hand over her friend's. 'Give in gracefully and let him get on with it,' she advised.

'People are going to talk about this party for years to come,' Mr Grace said happily. 'A live performance will be the finishing touch!'

'So, how are you getting on with the musical?' Lynne asked, dabbing half-heartedly at the spot of paint she'd just noticed on her denim shirt.

'Well, I *think* it's all coming together – at last,' he replied. 'There are a couple more songs we need to work on, but the dancing is fantastic now. They're really catchy tunes, and Jane and I have worked out some great moves. She's the music teacher, by the way. You should see the roller-skating waitresses in the diner!'

'We will see them,' Josie reminded him. 'We're coming to the opening night, remember? On Wednesday?'

'Sounds cool,' Anna said. 'Can we come too?'

'Of course,' said Mr Grace, going out to the hall to phone the order through for the takeaway. 'Your mother's the official set designer. Tickets are on the house.'

'Come on, Mum,' Josie said, while they waited for her father to return with the food. 'You still haven't told us how you left things with Liz. What did she say? Does she want Hope?'

'Yes, she does,' Mrs Grace replied. 'She thought Hope was lovely, and she'd really like to buy her. But she wants us to be absolutely sure in our own minds that it's the right thing to do. So – what does everyone think?'

'Well, *I'd* say–' Anna began, before catching sight of her mother's face and biting back the words. 'How do you feel about it, Josie?' she asked instead, and Lynne smiled her approval.

'I'm *almost* sure that Hope ought to go to Friendship House,' Josie said carefully. 'It was really moving seeing her with the children, wasn't it? Nothing they did seemed to bother her.'

'I know what you mean,' Ben said. 'I was watching her, and she was even more gentle with them than she is with beginners at the stables here. It's like she has some sixth sense that tells her they need some help.'

'Even that little blind girl plucked up the courage to go for a ride,' Mrs Grace added. 'She just loved Hope, didn't she? The look on her face when she was sitting up in the saddle so proudly nearly broke my heart!'

'Don't, Mum,' Josie said. 'You'll set me off again.' She jumped up to start laying the table and crashed the knives and forks about for a while to relieve her feelings. Then she went on, 'I would like to know more about how they'd look after her, though. Who's going to groom and feed her? Her sweet itch does seem to be almost better, thank goodness, but it still needs a careful eye kept on it. And would there be anybody to take her out for a good long ride every now and then? I'm sure she'll need it.'

'I talked to Liz about all of that while we were having tea,' Mrs Grace replied. 'She does know something about horses herself, through work she's done with Riding for the Disabled, but Sid would be mainly looking after them. He's the groundsman in charge of the donkeys,' she explained for Ben and Anna's benefit, 'and a real animal lover, apparently. He's been suggesting they get a pony for ages.'

'Do you think Liz would let us come and take Hope out sometimes?' Anna asked, reaching into the cupboard for glasses while Ben looked for cans of cold drinks in the fridge. By now, they were as familiar with the Graces' kitchen as their own.

'I'm sure she wouldn't mind if you came to ride her,' Mrs Grace said, 'though it might be difficult for you to get up there regularly. Friendship House is about half an hour away by car.'

'What sort of place is it?' Lynne asked casually. 'Liz seems so nice, I'd imagine the children love being there.'

'When we saw it, none of them were around,' Mary Grace replied. 'Even so, you can tell the place has a really good atmosphere. There's a happy feel to it – the rooms are all bright and cheerful.'

'The children have done some of the most amazing paintings,' Josie put in, laying down the last fork. 'And the studio is brilliant! There's even a kiln for firing pots. You ought to go and have a look sometime, Lynne.'

'Yes, maybe I will,' she murmured.

Anna looked at her curiously as she searched in the cupboard for some soy sauce. 'Are you planning something, Mum?' she asked.

'Oh, not really,' Lynne answered vaguely. 'Anyway, let's get back to the point. It certainly sounds as though Hope would be well looked after. But do you think she'd be happy?'

'I bet she would,' Anna said. 'She'd have the donkeys to keep her company, and lots of attention. I say we should let her go to Friendship House – I think they deserve her. A lot more than Emma Price, anyway.'

'I'll second that,' said Ben, while his mother added, 'And I'll vote in favour.'

Mrs Grace looked at Josie. 'Do you agree?' she asked her. 'We need you on side, too.'

'Oh, I suppose it's the best option,' Josie replied, thinking everything over for the hundredth time. 'After all, aside from the sanctuary, this is her last hope, isn't it?'

'That's settled, then,' her mother said. 'Don't worry, Josie, I'm sure Hope will love it at Friendship House. As soon as I saw her with Liz and all the others this afternoon, I felt it was the perfect place for her.'

'Yes, you're probably right,' Josie said, trying her best to feel cheerful and almost succeeding.

The next few days seemed to pass in a blur, which was almost a relief for Josie. Now that they'd decided on Hope's new home, she was anxious to get her settled in at Friendship House. If there were going to be any problems, it would be better to know about them sooner rather than later.

Mrs Grace had rung Liz Tallant on Monday to say they'd be delighted to accept her offer, and it was arranged that she and Josie would bring Hope round on Sunday, the day after the party. 'That's if we all survive it,' she said darkly to Josie. 'As far as I can make out, your father's invited anyone who's ever set foot in the stables, plus most of his school. I don't know where we're going to put them all. If it's raining, we're finished!'

Then, before Josie knew it, Wednesday had arrived and they were setting off with Lynne and the twins for the opening night of *Grease*.

'I don't know about Rob, but I'm certainly feeling nervous,' Mrs Grace said as they sat on rows of chairs in the packed school hall. 'I do hope the musical's a success – he's put so much effort into it.'

'I'm sure it's going to be great, Mum,' Josie reassured her. 'Dad's productions always are.'

'And even if it's not, in a couple of days it'll all be over,' said Anna, from the next seat. 'Just think – you won't have to listen to "Summer Lovin" ever again.'

'Shh!' Josie whispered, giggling, as the lights dimmed and a band began to play. 'It's about to begin!'

Slowly, the black curtains in front of the stage drew back, and there was a gasp from the audience as the opening scene was revealed. Around twenty students were arranged in two groups on the steps leading up to the high school entrance. The girls were all wearing tight-fitting tops and brightly-coloured flouncy skirts that swirled out from wide belts at the waist. They sat to one side, while the boys in leather jackets, sunglasses and greased-back hair swaggered around on the other.

'Wow!' Lynne breathed admiringly. 'Great costumes!'

'Great set design,' Josie said, smiling at her.

'Great music!' Anna added, as the strains of 'Summer Lovin' filled the hall, and Josie snorted with laughter so loudly that her mother had to dig her in the ribs.

'I think you could say the musical's more than just a

success,' Lynne said to Mary Grace as they all queued up for drinks in the interval. 'It's a complete and utter triumph!'

'I know,' she agreed happily. 'Thank goodness for that! The dancing is amazing, and we've still got the roller-skating waitresses to come.'

'Oh yes, in the diner,' Josie said. 'I want to see the backcloth you were painting with Cathy, Lynne.'

'As a matter of fact, I've got something to tell you all which is connected with that,' Lynne said mysteriously. 'I didn't want to say anything until it was settled.'

'I knew it!' Anna pounced on her mother. 'I could tell you were hatching some little scheme. Come on, Mum

241

– out with it! What have you been up to?'

'Well, I've got a new job,' said Lynne, looking very pleased with herself. 'At Friendship House. I'm going to run the art sessions there.'

'Congratulations!' Mary Grace said. 'What wonderful news! When did you fix all that up?'

'I had a chat with Liz on Sunday when we were in the barn,' Lynne told her, 'and she invited me round on Monday to see the studio and have an interview. This morning she rang to say the trustees have agreed to appoint me. I can't wait to start – it's just up my street. I did an art therapy course at college, you see.'

'Well done!' Josie said, delighted. 'I can just see you at Friendship House, it's exactly your kind of place.'

'Brilliant, Mum!' said Ben, and Anna gave her a hug. 'It sounds perfect,' she said. 'You won't be so tired and maybe you'll have a bit more time to paint, too.' Then suddenly she grabbed Josie's arm in excitement.

'That's it!' she exclaimed, so loudly that several people turned round to look. 'Of course! This means we'll be able to keep in touch with Hope! We'll know if she's happy or not, and in the holidays, we can go with Mum and exercise her. I'm sure Liz won't mind. Oh, what could be better?'

'I couldn't possibly imagine!' said Josie, with a broad grin.

Ten

Josie sat on the desk in her bedroom, her back against the corner wall and her feet on a chair, and looked out of the window. Hope and Charity were standing in the field below. Lessons for the weekend had finished that Saturday morning, and now the stables were shut to give everyone time to prepare for the party. Josie smiled as she saw Hope move closer to Charity and begin to groom her, scratching and nibbling her withers. Charity stood still at first, then eventually walked away, tired of being fussed over. *Never mind, Hope,* Josie said to herself, *just wait till you see those two donkeys in your new field. They're going to need a lot of looking after.* The motherly pony swished her tail a couple of times, gazing after Charity, them dropped her head and began grazing again.

Josie sighed, looking round her room for something to do. She couldn't settle to anything. Ben and Anna and their mother were coming over later to help decorate the stables, and she didn't feel like starting the job without them. Her father had gone out shopping early that morning and come back with the car piled high with bulging carrier bags. They'd had a quick sandwich for lunch and then he'd shooed Josie and her mother out of the way. Enticing smells had already begun to waft up the stairs.

Josie decided to go down and see if he needed a hand. 'How's it going, Dad?' she asked, wandering into the kitchen. 'Do you want some help?'

Her father turned round from the stove, his face red and a stripe of flour on his cheek. 'Oh, hi, love,' he said distractedly. 'Let me think – what needs doing? Chicken's in the oven, the flans are next, sausages and pizza we won't cook till later. How about puddings? You can make meringues. Yes, that's a good idea. Eggs in the fridge – we'll need about two dozen to start off with, if they'll fit in the bowl.' He rushed over to the cupboard and reached down a couple of bowls and mugs. 'They'll need separating,' he instructed Josie. 'Whites in the big bowl, yolks in the smaller one. Better break the whites into this mug first, in case some of the yolk gets in by mistake.'

'OK,' Josie said, taking two large egg cartons out of the fridge. She began to crack the first smooth shell on the side of one of the mugs, and dug in her thumbs to break the two halves apart. 'I thought *Grease* was great, Dad,' she said, slopping the yolk from one eggshell cup to the other. 'I haven't really seen you since, to tell you. Are all the cast coming to the party?'

'Most of them,' said her father distractedly, flicking over pages in a recipe book.

'The girl who was playing Sandy has a fantastic voice,' Josie went on. 'She's not so good at dancing, though, is she?'

'Mmm,' her father replied, reaching past her to the cupboard above the work surface.

'Oh dear,' Josie said, looking into the big bowl. 'I've got a little bit of yolk in this egg white. Now how did that happen? D'you think it'll matter? It's only a tiny trace . . .'

'Josie,' her father said firmly, taking the bowl out of her hands, 'thanks for the offer, love, but I think I'm better off on my own. I've got to concentrate, or I'll never get anything done. Why don't you see where Mum is?'

'Oh, OK,' Josie said. 'If you're sure.' But he was already busy fishing yolk out of the bowl and didn't reply.

She ambled out to the yard and caught sight of her mother's bent head through the tackroom window.

'What are you doing cleaning tack, Mum?' she asked, putting her head round the door. 'Why don't you leave that till tomorrow?'

'Well, we're taking Hope to Friendship House in the morning,' her mother replied. 'Might as well give this bridle a good polish now. Don't want her to start off on the wrong foot!' And she smiled rather sadly.

Josie sighed again and slumped on to a stool. 'This is so weird,' she complained. 'Everyone's busy but I can't think of anything to do except sit here and wait. Wait for everyone to arrive and the party to start. Wait for Hope to go off to her new home. In some ways, I wish it was all over.'

Her mother looked at her sympathetically. 'You're bound to be feeling a bit strange,' she said. 'I do, too. After all, everything's beginning to wind up, what with Connie and Tubber having gone to Littlehaven yesterday and Hope going away tomorrow. That leaves us with just Charity. This party is a kind of goodbye to the stables, isn't it?'

'Are you going to carry on giving lessons with Charity?' Josie asked. She hadn't really considered what would happen after Hope left the riding school.

'Well, maybe for a few more weeks,' her mother replied, rubbing the bit vigorously with some metal

246

polish. 'Kirsty's keen to carry on for as long as possible and some of the other pupils may be, too. The thing is, Dad and I really ought to start house-hunting now the show's done with. It's not that long till we have to be out of here.'

'Oh,' said Josie, thinking it over. It still seemed amazing that they were going to be moving out of School Farm. She'd lived there all her life.

'Don't forget what Dad said in the office,' Mrs Grace reminded Josie, giving her hand a squeeze. 'We've got each other, and that's the main thing. Everything else is going to work out OK.'

'And you've got us, too!' came a cheerful voice through the door. It was Anna, her arms full of bunting and packets of balloons and streamers. She blew on a hooter that unrolled to reveal a bright red feather at the end. 'Come on, Josie – there's work to do!'

'Well, I think you've made a fantastic job of the yard,' said Mr Grace, looking round a couple of hours later. 'It looks great!'

Brightly coloured bunting zig-zagged across from the loose boxes over to the office and tackroom on the other side, and balloons were pinned up everywhere. Mrs Grace was always worried about fire risks, so outdoor candles and lanterns were stuck safely in buckets of sand, ready to be lit later on. The 'Greased

Lightning' car was back at the barn, propped up by the entrance next to a huge stereo sound system that Mr Grace had borrowed from the music department. Lynne Marshall had also brought along several trestle tables in her van. Now they stood in a line along one side of the yard, covered by tablecloths and groaning with bottles, paper plates and cups, alongside huge bowls and platters of food shrouded under tea towels and plastic wrap.

'You've outdone yourself, Rob,' said Mrs Grace admiringly. 'I've never seen so much delicious-looking food!'

'There's plenty more in the kitchen,' he said. 'We'll just have to nip back for more supplies when they're needed.' He turned to Josie, Ben and Anna. 'Could you three keep an eye on people's glasses and go round with bottles if they need a refill?'

'Sure, Dad,' Josie replied, when an idea struck her. 'I know! Why don't your roller-skating waitresses help as well?'

'I'm not so sure about that,' her father replied with a grimace. 'Judging from the number of near-misses we had on stage, I think it might be better if they just stood in a corner somewhere until it's time for their number. I'd sooner rely on you lot, if you don't mind.'

'Perhaps we should sample a few dishes first,' Ben suggested, lifting up the corner of a tea towel and pinching a sausage. 'So we'll know what to recommend.'

'Ben! Don't eat everything before people start arriving,' Lynne scolded.

'Oh, help yourself,' Mr Grace replied in his usual laid back way. 'We may be too busy soon.' He reached under the table and brought out a couple of bottles. 'And now we're all together and it's just family, so to speak, I think it's time for a toast. Champagne for us, Coke for you.'

He lined up some glasses, unscrewed a bottle lid and popped a cork. The six of them held up their brimming glasses and clinked them together as he announced, 'To the future, whatever it holds!'

'And let's drink to Hope,' Josie added. 'This is her last night here, remember.'

They looked over to the loose boxes, where Charity and Hope had been installed for the night, and burst out laughing. 'Oh, Anna!' Mrs Grace said. 'What have you been up to?'

Apples, carrots and turnips had been hung across the lower part of the stable doors, and the two ponies were busy nibbling them off their strings.

'Well, *we're* having fun – why shouldn't they?' Anna protested. 'It's their party too!'

'And here come the first arrivals,' said Mr Grace, going forward to meet a group of people who were walking up the drive. 'Now let's just enjoy ourselves and forget everything for a few hours.'

'Sounds good to me,' Josie said, feeling her spirits beginning to lift. 'I think we deserve some fun!'

'Josie, can you give me a hand, please?' Mr Grace said, rushing over to where she was standing, chatting to Jill Atterbury. 'Sorry to interrupt, but we need more white wine and soft drinks from the kitchen.'

'Sure,' Josie said. 'Don't go away, Jill – I'll see you in a minute.' She hurried up the path to the cottage with her father.

'Seems to be going well, doesn't it?' he flung over his shoulder. 'The joint's jumping.'

'Oh, Dad, it's great,' Josie said. 'There are so many people here! I never knew Jill was going to come. And guess what? She was telling me she might be able to start riding Faith side-saddle before too much longer. It won't put so much strain on her hip, apparently. Isn't that fantastic?'

'It's a great idea,' Mr Grace said as they came into the kitchen. He started piling bottles into Josie's outstretched arms. 'Nearly all the cast have turned up, too,' he added. 'And the Friendship House children should be here soon. I've told Liz she can bring the minibus right into the yard. Then we can get the singing and dancing going.'

'I bet they'll love that,' Josie said.

'Seeing Hope again's going to be a treat for them,

too. After all, they've got to know her a little bit now,' her father added, as he fetched a case of wine from under the table and led the way out of the kitchen.

'I suppose so,' Josie said, a little more doubtfully than she'd intended.

'What's the matter, love?' her father asked, pausing to turn and look back at her. 'You *are* feeling OK about Hope going there, aren't you? You were so struck with Friendship House at first, but you don't seem so certain now.'

'Oh, I don't know – it's hard to explain,' Josie said with a sigh as they walked on down the path to the yard. 'I can see Hope giving the children rides and everything, and I'm sure she'll be very good with them. She likes working and being useful. It's just that she's been our pet, too, hasn't she? One of the family. I'm sure she'll be a part of the team at Friendship House, but do you think they'll really love her?'

'Something tells me you don't need to worry about that,' said Mr Grace slowly. He nodded his head towards the yard. 'Take a look over there, and I think you'll find the answer to your question.'

The Friendship House minibus was parked in the far corner, and Josie saw her mother standing next to it, talking to Liz Tallant. Over at the loose boxes, Hope was surrounded by several excited children. Tommy was standing stock still, his face buried in her mane and his arms round her neck. A girl was stroking her soft nuzzle and Cathy was patting her plain carthorse nose and kissing it over and over again. Hope's eyes were closed and she looked blissfully happy.

Anna came up from the crowded yard and stood next to Josie, watching the scene with her. 'Dear, sweet Hope,' she said fondly. 'I'd say there was a pony in seventh heaven! She's the centre of attention, and loving every minute of it. You're not still having doubts, are you, Josie?'

Josie laughed and shook her head, a feeling of huge relief washing over her. 'Not a single one!' she said joyfully. 'Do you know, I think Hope's last hope is going to be the best home she could possibly have!'

Sweet Charity

One

Josie Grace and her pony, Charity, were riding through the wood in the early evening sunshine. There was no one else around, and everything was quiet except for the pounding of the grey mare's hooves as she cantered along the bridle path. They had just turned the corner when suddenly a riderless horse came bolting towards them, causing Josie to scream out in alarm. The horse skidded to a halt and stood, snorting, in the middle of the path, his coat glistening with sweat.

Josie calmed the frightened animal and led him back up the bridle path alongside Charity. She had to try and find his rider – whom she realised might be injured or even lying unconscious somewhere in the wood.

A few minutes later, after they had covered only a short distance, Josie heard a faint cry from up ahead and, as they came nearer, she saw a young man, lying by the side of the track and clutching his leg. His face was white with pain, but he managed to tell her what had happened. His horse, startled by a rabbit, had reared and thrown him off, and he thought his leg might have been broken. If Josie could find his aunt at the nearby riding stables, she would send help.

Josie and Charity galloped off down the path and quickly found the stables. There they saw a frail old lady, struggling to muck out one of the loose boxes. No, Josie thought to herself, *that doesn't sound right. An old lady wouldn't muck out loose boxes. What else could she be doing? Ah yes, this was better, . . . saw a frail old lady, watering flowers in a beautifully kept front garden.*

Josie must have had this daydream at least twenty times. The old lady turned out to be the owner of the stables and was tremendously grateful for Josie's help. She would ring an ambulance immediately, and then, while they were waiting for it to arrive, she would tell Josie about a troubling problem she had. The stables urgently needed a well-schooled pony and a qualified instructor to give riding lessons and occupy the vacant house next door. Josie would then tell her what an incredible coincidence this was, because her mother was a riding instructor and sadly, *they* had to leave the stables in which they currently lived.

She had just reached this triumphant moment when her father's voice interrupted her thoughts from the end of the table. 'Josie!' he said. 'I've asked you to pass the milk three times. Wake up!'

'Oh – sorry,' Josie said, coming back down to earth with a bump. 'What's that?'

'The milk, please,' Robert Grace said slowly and clearly, and then smiled at her. 'For my cornflakes. It's in the jug in front of you.'

'Oh, right,' Josie said, passing the china jug.

'Thanks, love,' he said. 'You were miles away! What were you thinking about?'

'Oh, just daydreaming,' Josie sighed, taking a bite of her toast and jam. It was Saturday morning and she was sitting in the kitchen with her mum and dad. She sighed. There were no magical solutions to the problems they were facing. They had to leave School Farm, the cottage where Josie had lived for all of her twelve years, and she was going to have to part with her very special pony, Charity.

Josie had been over this a hundred times in her head, but there seemed no alternative. For fourteen years, her parents had been renting their house and the riding stables her mother ran from an old lady, Mrs Wetherall. She had died suddenly a few months before, leaving the place to her nephew. His solicitors had sent the Graces a letter saying that he would be selling the cottage and land to a developer; they had three months to close the stables and move out.

Those three months were flying by. Josie had already said goodbye to the two other ponies at Grace's Stables: Faith, the elderly bay mare who'd been there from the very beginning, and Hope, the sweet-natured grey who was Charity's mother. Now they had less than three weeks to find a new home for Charity, as well as themselves. Josie's mum and dad had explained to her that they just couldn't afford to keep a pony once the riding school had closed.

Josie gave another deep sigh and stared out of the kitchen window. The advertisement for Charity would be in the local paper that Wednesday.

'I've got a couple of lessons this morning and then we're going house-hunting in the afternoon,' Mary Grace told her daughter. 'You'll come with us, won't you?'

Josie shook her head. 'No thanks,' she said, looking down at her plate. 'I don't really feel like it. You just find somewhere and tell me when it's all decided.' She didn't want to think about living anywhere else until she absolutely had to.

'I wish you would come along,' her father said. 'I don't like the thought of you here on your own, feeling miserable.'

'It's all right, Dad – I won't be on my own,' Josie said,

seeing his anxious expression. 'Anna's coming over after lunch.'

Anna Marshall had been Josie's best friend for three years now. She lived a couple of miles away in the village of Northgate with her mother and twin brother, Ben.

'Good! If anyone can cheer you up, it'll be Anna,' said Mrs Grace, starting to clear away the breakfast things. 'Something tells me we won't be away too long, anyway. We've only got a couple of houses to see, and I don't think either of them are very likely.'

'Right. I'm going to fetch Charity in from the field and get her ready for the first lesson,' Josie said. She put her plate in the sink and headed out of the kitchen with Basil, the family's terrier, scurrying along at her heels. She wanted to spend as much time as possible with her pony while she still had the chance.

'We're not starting until ten today, so there's no need to hurry,' Mrs Grace called after her.

Josie walked down the path from School Farm to the stable yard. Basil gave a playful bark at Millie, one of the Graces' two black-and-white cats, who was sitting outside the tackroom, her tail curled neatly around her paws. She glanced away disdainfully and stalked off to join her brother, Rascal, who was playing in the straw in one of the loose boxes on the other side of the yard.

'Never mind, Basil,' Josie said, giving his smooth head a pat. 'Maybe there'll be a rabbit for you to chase in the field.' She felt under the flowerpot outside the tack room door for the key to unlock it.

'Hi, Josie,' came a soft voice, making Josie nearly jump out of her skin.

She whirled around and saw a young blonde-haired girl standing just behind her, smiling rather uncertainly. 'Oh, Kirsty!' she said. 'You nearly gave me a heart attack. Where did you spring from?'

Kirsty Fisher had been coming to the stables for nearly two years. She lived in Northgate too, so it was easy for her to walk up to the stables. Recently, she'd been spending more and more time there. Charity had always been her favourite pony, and she'd asked if she could carry on riding her right up until the Graces sold her. Mrs Grace was happy to agree – she wanted to give lessons for as long as possible, and she knew how fond Kirsty was of Charity.

'Sorry, Josie. I didn't mean to frighten you,' Kirsty said, twisting her hands together awkwardly. 'I thought I could help you bring Charity in from the field. I've got a lesson later on but your mum said it would probably be all right if I came up early.'

Kirsty had one sister who was much older than she was, and Josie guessed she was sometimes quite lonely at home. 'Of course you can help me,' Josie said, trying not to feel irritated. She'd really been looking forward to some quiet time alone with Charity. Still, there would be other days. She unlocked the tackroom door and they went in.

'It looks so bare in here now there's only Charity's things left,' Kirsty said, looking round the whitewashed walls. Besides Hope and Charity, Mrs Grace had kept three horses at livery that she looked after and helped to exercise. Their owners had recently moved them and all their tack to another yard, and now Grace's Stables seemed very empty.

'I know,' Josie replied, unhooking a head collar and scooping up a handful of pony nuts from the bag by the door. 'Come on, let's go and see what she's up to.'

Together they walked back across the yard and past the outdoor schooling ring towards the field. Charity was grazing in a far corner, swishing her tail to keep away the flies that were settling on her every now and then. Josie noticed Kirsty's pale face light up when she caught sight of the pony. Making a huge effort to be generous, she passed her the head collar. 'Here,' she said. 'Do you want to try catching Charity?'

'Oh, yes, please!' Kirsty answered, obviously delighted.

'Just hide the head collar behind your back and hold out some of these pony nuts,' Josie advised. 'I'll give her a call.'

Charity had lifted her head when she'd first seen them and now decided to trot over, her mane flowing

and the muscles beneath her grey coat rippling as she moved. 'She is so beautiful, isn't she?' Kirsty said, as Charity pushed her soft pink muzzle forward to take the tit-bit.

Charity's silver-grey coat was speckled with darker hairs, and Josie had always thought 'flea bitten' – which was the proper term – hardly did it justice. She had a paler blaze running down her face, and a pure white mane and tail. Her legs were long and straight, her body was perfectly proportioned, and she carried her head proudly on a gracefully arched neck.

'I love her eyes best of all,' Josie said, helping Kirsty buckle up the head collar. 'They've got such a sparkle in them. You can tell just by looking at her how much fun she is to ride, even if she does get up to mischief.'

Josie and her mother had grown used to Charity's little tricks over the years. When Charity was still only young, she had worked out how to open the bolt on her loose box door with her teeth, and was discovered cantering round the yard. Mrs Grace had had to fit another bolt at the bottom of the door after that, to keep the frisky mare out of trouble.

Kirsty took the lead rope and began to lead Charity carefully back across the field. When they were nearly there, she said to Josie, who was walking alongside, 'Charity's not really going to be sold, is she?'

'I'm afraid so,' Josie replied, opening the gate. 'We're going to be pretty hard up with the stables closing.'

'I always thought you had loads of money, living here with all your ponies and horses,' Kirsty said, looking at the fields and paddocks that surrounded School Farm as she led Charity out of the field.

'Well, the livery horses didn't belong to us, and the ponies all had to work for their living,' Josie replied. 'Besides, Mrs Wetherall didn't charge much rent because she was just glad to see the stables put to good use. So, we're going to have to pay a whole lot more to live somewhere else.'

'But your parents know how much Charity means to you,' Kirsty said. 'They won't really make you give her up, will they?'

'I don't think they've got much choice,' Josie sighed. 'Come on now, let's start getting her ready for your lesson.'

'Thanks for letting me bring her in,' Kirsty said, as they walked Charity over to the loose boxes. 'It was great!'

'That's OK,' Josie said, slightly ashamed of how annoyed she'd felt when she'd first seen Kirsty. On an impulse, she added, 'Look, Mum's told me to clear out some of my old things and I thought I'd do it this afternoon. Do you want to come over? I think there's a pair of jodhpurs that might fit you.'

'Yes, please!' Kirsty said eagerly. 'I'd really like that, Josie. Thanks!'

'Great,' Josie replied. Then she remembered, too late, that Anna was coming over too, and Kirsty really got on her nerves. Never mind. Anna would just have to put up with her for one afternoon.

Two

Josie was sitting up in her room later that day when she heard someone calling her name. Throwing open the window, she saw Anna standing on the path below, her glossy dark hair falling back from her face as she squinted up into the sun.

'Locked in the tower, Rapunzel?' she called, laughing, as Josie held back her wavy auburn hair with one hand while she looked down.

'Ha ha, very funny,' Josie replied, feeling her spirits lift at once. She *had* been feeling rather lonely, all on her own in the empty house. 'Hold on a minute – I'll come and let you in.'

'It's so quiet in the yard now!' Anna exclaimed, following Josie down the hall. 'D'you know it's exactly a week since the party? Think how many people were here then.'

Josie's dad had just staged the rock and roll musical, *Grease*, at his school. After the last performance the Graces had thrown a big party at the stables. It was partly to thank everyone who'd been involved and partly to say goodbye to the pupils and friends who'd supported the stables over the years. Since that night, it seemed as though the place was really winding down. Charity's mother, Hope, had gone off the next day to begin her new life at Friendship House, a respite centre for mentally handicapped children. The livery horses left the same weekend, too.

'It was a fantastic evening, wasn't it?' Josie said, remembering all the fun. 'I couldn't believe how many people turned up!'

'I know – it was great,' Anna replied, as they climbed the stairs. 'So, what's going on today?'

'Mum and Dad are off looking at houses and I'm under strict instructions to sort out my old stuff,' Josie replied. 'I can't go out for a ride until it's all done. Do you want to help?'

'Yes, definitely,' Anna said, looking quite pleased at the prospect. 'You know what a magpie I am. Do you think there's anything that would fit me?'

'I'm not sure,' Josie said as they thudded up the stairs. 'You're not that much smaller than me. Kirsty's probably the right size for most of the clothes – she's coming over later.'

'Oh, Josie!' Anna said, making a face. 'Why did you ask *her*? I thought it was just going to be the two of us. Kirsty always seems to be here these days and she really gives me the creeps, hanging around the place so much.'

'I felt sorry for her,' Josie confessed as they went into her bedroom. 'I don't think she's got many friends. It's all right for you, Anna – you're popular at school and you've got Ben to keep you company at home. I used to get lonely sometimes before you moved into the village, so I know how it feels.'

'Feeling sorry for someone isn't a good way to start off being friends with them,' Anna said, kneeling on the floor and sifting through a pile of Josie's old clothes. 'Besides, the nicer you are to her, the more time she'll spend up here. Soon you'll never be able to get rid of her.'

'Well, think of all the time *you*'ve spent here, Anna!' Josie exclaimed, sitting on the floor with her back against the bed. 'You and Ben ended up helping out at the stables every weekend. Why shouldn't Kirsty?'

'But you like me, and you can put up with Ben,' Anna said, holding a T-shirt up to the light and eyeing it critically. 'I didn't think you felt the same about Kirsty.

267

Anyway, she's younger than us, isn't she?'

'Yes – I think she's ten,' Josie replied. 'Oh come on, Anna, let's change the subject. It won't kill you to be nice to Kirsty for an hour or so.'

'You don't know that,' Anna said darkly. 'It might.'

By the time Kirsty turned up, Josie had sorted out a pile of things she thought might fit her and Anna was lying on the bed, deep in a magazine. She managed to give Kirsty a cheerful enough smile though, and said hello nicely.

'Thanks, Josie,' Kirsty said shyly, picking up the jodhpurs and holding them against her skinny legs to see if they were long enough. 'These look perfect!'

'I've got some jeans that might fit you, too,' Josie said, dropping to her knees on the floor and picking them out of the heap. She could tell Kirsty felt rather awkward about taking too much, but they'd soon filled a carrier bag with clothes and a pair of riding boots Josie had grown out of.

'Are you sure you don't mind me taking all this?' Kirsty asked. 'It'll be great to have some proper clothes for riding.' She got up and went over to the window. 'I've never been in your room before,' she went on. 'It's lovely! You can watch Charity outside and everything.'

'Creep!' Anna mouthed in mock-horror, looking at the carrier bags and piles of clothes all over the floor.

Josie threw her a death stare before replying, 'It's a bit of a mess at the moment, but I love it up here.'

Kirsty started to rummage through a bag full of books under the window. 'Oh, you're not throwing out your old pony stories, are you?' she said. 'Don't you want to keep them?'

'Not really,' Josie said, sprawling out on a bean bag. 'I've read them so many times, I know them off by heart. Besides, I don't think I'm going to feel like reading about other people riding if I can't do it myself.'

'But you *can* still do it yourself!' Anna said, putting down the magazine and swinging over her legs to sit up on the bed. 'Even if you don't have Charity, we can go and ride Faith – Jill invited us round at the party, remember. And we can visit Hope at Friendship House, too. Mum's going to start working there next month, and she'll take us over there with her.' Anna and Ben's mother Lynne was an artist and, since meeting Liz Tallant, who ran the respite centre, she'd got the job as art teacher.

'I suppose so,' Josie said doubtfully. 'It's just that—'

She was interrupted by Kirsty, holding up a large hardback book and asking curiously, 'What's this?'

'Oh, it's a scrapbook I made a couple of years ago about Charity,' Josie replied. 'I found it last night when I was clearing out the bookcase. You can have a look, if you like.'

269

The book was filled with dozens of photos of Charity, charting the first five years of her life. There were captions under each picture and lots of information about the pony's health and the food she ate, the prizes she'd won at Pony Club shows, and all her likes and dislikes.

'Wasn't she a cute foal?' Kirsty said, admiring the photos on the first few pages. 'And there she is, sucking from Hope. That is so sweet!'

Josie smiled and then frowned sternly at Anna, who was silently putting her fingers down her throat, pretending to be sick. She looked over Kirsty's shoulder at the album. 'I remember that day,' she said, pointing to a picture of Charity wearing a saddle and a very suspicious expression. 'She hated the saddle to begin with! And look – there I am, sitting up on her. I was the first person to ride her, you know, when she was four.'

'You look so young there!' Anna said, becoming interested in spite of herself and craning over to see the photo, too. 'It must be that fringe and those chubby little cheeks.'

'Well, it was four years ago,' Josie said, giving her a playful shove. 'I was only eight – what do you expect?'

Soon they had leafed through the entire book and Kirsty closed it gently. 'I just can't believe Charity's going to be sold,' she said, looking seriously at Josie.

'Surely your parents will find the money for you to keep her somehow!'

'They might not be able to,' Josie said, inwardly wishing Kirsty would stop going on about it. She was just making her feel worse. 'Look, we can't possibly afford to keep Charity at a livery stables and we don't have the money to move to a house with a field. So the simple fact is that Charity has to go.'

'No!' Kirsty said. 'I won't let them take her away from you!'

Something about her pale, determined face made Josie feel slightly uneasy. 'Listen, Charity's going to be advertised in the paper on Wednesday,' she told Kirsty firmly. 'We don't have any choice but to wait and see what happens after that.'

'Bye, then,' Josie said to Anna and Ben as they all got off the bus after school on Wednesday afternoon. She waved and started to turn away from the village and up towards Grace's Stables.

'Hang on!' said Anna, hurrying after her. 'We're coming with you.'

'We thought you might need some moral support,' Ben added, getting a football out of his bag and kicking it ahead as he walked along. 'Charity's being advertised today, isn't she?'

'That's right,' Josie said, touched that they'd

remembered. 'You might get a bit bored, though,' she went on. 'There's not much to do at home these days. Now there's only Charity left, Mum and I are arguing over who's going to muck her out.'

'Well, we can just hang out and watch some TV or something,' Anna said. 'At least you won't be moping around on your own.'

'Thanks,' Josie said, giving her a grateful smile.

'Everything does feel strange at the moment, like we're in a sort of limbo. I'm just trying not to think about what's going to happen. I've already decided I'm not going to look at the paper.'

They walked into the yard. Charity, who was standing in her loose box, neighed, just as she always did when Josie came back from school. 'She looks so lonely, all on her own,' Anna said as they made a big fuss of her. 'She must be missing Hope and Faith.'

'I'm sure she is,' Josie agreed. 'I was watching her in the field last night and she doesn't seem to know what to do with herself.' She sighed. 'I ought to be hoping we get a new home sorted out quickly, for her sake, but in reality, I want to keep her for as long as possible. From the moment she was born, she's always been my special pony. It was hard enough saying goodbye to Faith and Hope – I don't know how I'm going to manage it with Charity. It's not fair – this is her home, here with us!'

'But you're not going to be here for much longer, are you?' Ben asked as they went into the cottage. 'Don't you have to move out of School Farm soon?'

'Yes, and we still don't know where we're going,' Josie told him grimly. 'Dad's got some estate agent friend who told him there was loads of property to rent on the market, which is why they left it this late, but he and Mum have been looking for nearly two weeks and 'nothing's turned up. I think Mum's getting quite worried.'

'Mum's getting quite worried about what, exactly?' Mrs Grace asked, looking up from the paper as the three of them came into the kitchen. She gave Ben and Anna a smile. 'Hi there, you two!'

'Worried about where we're going to live,' Josie told her after the twins had said hello. 'You must be – we've got to be out of here in two weeks' time.'

'Yes, I am,' Mrs Grace admitted. 'After what Jim told Dad, I thought we'd have no trouble finding a house, but there's hardly anything around that we can afford! I don't think he realised what a tight budget we're on. Still, he's promised to let us know the second anything suitable turns up.'

Josie fetched some apple juice from the fridge and put it on the table with three glasses and the biscuit tin, trying to avoid looking at the newspaper. Her mother must have realised how she felt, for she hastily gathered the paper together and folded it up. 'No houses in there today, anyway, and no jobs for me either,' she said, and then went on casually, 'Charity's ad has gone in, but we haven't had any phone calls yet.'

Josie nodded, as she sat down at the table with Ben and Anna and began to pour drinks for them all. She idly picked up some papers from the estate agent that had been hidden underneath the newspaper. 'What are these, Mum?' she asked, looking at the photos of identical-looking houses on each one and reading the information typed below.

'Some places I had a look round today,' Mrs Grace replied. 'None of them is ideal, but I think this one is the best of the bunch so far.' She extracted a sheet from the pile Josie was holding and put it on the top.

'This one's the best?' Josie said, reading through the details and feeling her spirits sink even lower. 'What makes you say that?'

'Because it's in between Dad's school and yours, it's quite cheap and it's got three good-sized bedrooms,' her mother replied. 'All these modern houses are packed together very tightly, but there's actually quite a lot of room inside.'

Josie turned over the sheet and then looked up at her mother, horrified. 'Mum!' she exclaimed. 'It says there's a "small patio garden at the rear". What about all our animals? How can we fit Basil and the cats, plus all the ducks and chickens, in a small patio garden at the rear?'

'We can't,' her mother replied in a final tone. 'Listen, love. We're just going to have to accept that we can't carry on with things being exactly the same as they are now. Of course Basil and the cats can come with us – luckily he's not a big dog and I'll walk him every day – but there's no way we can keep the ducks and chickens. It's simply not an option.'

'Oh, great!' Josie said angrily. 'That's wonderful news.' She knew she wasn't behaving very well, but she couldn't help herself. It all seemed so unfair.

'*We*'ve only got a small patio garden at the rear,' Ben said mildly, eating a biscuit. 'It's better than nothing.'

'The thing is, love,' her mother went on, 'we've got rather out of touch with reality, living here for years on such a low rent. We've been lucky to have had a house like this for so long. Now it's time to join the real world, I'm afraid.'

'I should have seen this coming, I suppose,' Josie said gloomily, reading the house details through again.

'Come on!' Anna said. 'It might not be as bad as all that. Our mum will help decorate the place, and you know how good she is at making houses look wonderful.'

'She can't do much with a small patio garden at the rear, though, can she?' Josie grumbled.

'Look, Kirsty's coming for her lesson in half an hour,' Mrs Grace said in a determinedly bright voice. 'Why don't you saddle Charity and get her warmed up in the schooling ring? That might take your mind off things.'

'I thought she only usually had lessons at the weekend, Mum?' Josie asked.

'I said I'd throw in a couple of extra ones for nothing before we really do have to close,' Mrs Grace replied. 'Kirsty's so fond of Charity. It's a pity the Fishers can't buy her – I'm sure they could afford to keep her at livery somewhere.'

'So why won't they?' Josie asked, draining the last of her apple juice.

'I don't think anyone in that family is really interested in Kirsty's riding,' said her mother. 'She's so keen and she's been coming here every weekend for ages, but she still hasn't even got her own hard hat. And seeing as the Fishers live in a big house with two expensive cars, it can't be the money.'

At that moment, the phone began to ring outside in the hall.

'Let's go!' Josie said to Ben and Anna, jumping to her feet. She didn't feel like hearing her mother talk to all those lucky people who were looking for a pony to buy. One of them would probably end up taking her beloved Charity away, and that was something she just didn't want to think about right now.

Three

'Bye, Mum!' Josie called as she swung lightly up into Charity's saddle. 'See you later.'

'Hang on a minute,' Mrs Grace said, putting aside the broom she'd been using to sweep the yard and hurrying over. 'You haven't said where you're going yet.'

'Oh, no – I forgot. Sorry!' Josie replied, sorting out the reins.

'You know how important it is for me to know where you'll be,' her mother said. 'How many times do I have to remind you?' It was one of Mary Grace's strict rules – she insisted on knowing the route anyone going out riding planned to take, in case of an accident.

'Sorry!' Josie said again, shifting her leg forward and reaching under the saddle flap to check Charity's girth. 'I thought we'd cut through the fields and then along the river as far as the boathouse and back. Shouldn't take more than a couple of hours.'

'I hope it doesn't,' her mother said, giving the pony a pat and a quick inspection. 'There are some more people coming to see Charity this afternoon, remember? The Taylors. I want her looking nice and fresh when they arrive.'

'OK,' Josie called over her shoulder as she rode off down the drive. It was a sunny Saturday morning and, despite all her worries, she couldn't help feeling a surge of happiness. 'I'm going to forget everything for a couple of hours and just enjoy myself,' she told Charity, and the pony's ears flicked back and forth alertly as if she agreed that was exactly the right thing to do.

The mare trotted smartly along the road, her tail swishing jauntily behind her. Josie soon found her rhythm, enjoying the fresh air and sunshine while she kept a steadying hand on the reins. When they turned off the road into a field that sloped gently uphill, she let Charity take off in a gallop. There was nothing to beat that wonderful feeling of flying over the ground, with the wind in your face and the sun on your back.

Before long they had reached the wood at the top of the hill. Now that Charity had worked off some of her energy, she was happy to trot steadily through it, and then down a lane and along a bridle path that led to the river. Apart from one solitary fisherman sitting on the bank and staring out at the water, there was no one in sight. Not many people came to this stretch of the river because it was quite far from the lane and took a while to reach on foot. It was quiet and peaceful, and one of Josie's favourite places. She used to come here often with the twins. Anna always rode Hope and Ben would follow behind on steady old Faith – when he wasn't riding Tubber, his favourite amongst the livery horses.

Josie smiled to herself as she remembered some of the fun they'd had. About a mile farther on was the derelict boathouse that they'd discovered on one of their first hacks out together. They'd enjoyed exploring its interior until Ben had put his foot through one of the floorboards and Mrs Grace had declared the place out of bounds.

On one side of the boathouse stood two rooms which had remained in fairly good condition, with a couple of benches and even a decaying life jacket under one of them. An unsteady-looking verandah led off the back room, raised on stilts over the river racing along beneath. The other half of the building, consisting of one large room where the boats would have been kept, hadn't lasted so well. A corner of the outside wall had rotted away altogether and most of the roof had gone, making a kind of open, grassy courtyard.

Josie rode on until she reached the boathouse, which lay in between the path and the river. She brought Charity to a halt and they stood for a while, watching the water as it swirled in the grip of a powerful current. 'I wish we could stay here forever, just you and me,' Josie whispered, stroking the pony's silky smooth neck. Aware that this might be one of the last times they'd ride out here together, she gave a deep sigh, and then turned Charity around to take her back to the stables.

Mrs Grace was working in the office and came out to greet them when Josie trotted into the yard. 'Good ride?' she said, giving Charity a pat.

'Great, thanks, Mum,' Josie replied, dismounting. 'Do you mind just holding Charity for a second while I take off her tack?'

'No problem,' her mother replied, looping the reins over Charity's neck. 'Could you turn her out when you've finished, though, instead of putting her in the loose box? The Taylors want to see how easy she is to catch, so they've asked to watch us bringing her in.'

'Oh, OK,' Josie said, running up the stirrup leathers before she took Charity's saddle off. 'That's fair enough, I suppose.' If she was buying a pony, that was exactly what she'd want to do. 'What are the Taylors like?' she asked when she'd come back from the tackroom with a head collar. 'Do they know anything about horses?'

'They certainly seem to,' her mother said. 'They've got an older boy who's had a horse for a while and now they want a pony for his younger sister. She's been having riding lessons for ages, apparently.'

Josie unbuckled Charity's bridle and quickly slipped on the head collar. 'Thanks, Mum,' she said, tying the rope to a ring on the wall. 'I'll just sponge her down and give her a rub over before she goes back out in the field. She might not be looking so smart by the time they arrive, though.'

'Oh well, I don't think that should bother them too much,' said Mrs Grace, taking the bridle from her and going to hang it up in the tackroom. 'Lunch in an hour or so – Dad's making lasagne.'

'OK,' Josie replied automatically. Her father was a brilliant cook and lasagne was one of his specialities, but she was beginning to feel nervous and the appetite that she had worked up on her hack suddenly disappeared. The Taylors were the first people to come and see Charity. It sounded as though they were serious about buying her, and the moment when she'd finally have to leave was drawing ever closer.

After a quiet lunch, during which nobody spoke very much, the Graces were tidying up when they heard a car pull up in the yard. 'I think that must be the Taylors,' said Mrs Grace, putting down a tea towel and taking Josie's arm to shepherd her out of the kitchen. 'Come on, let's go and say hello. We might as well get this over and done with.'

Josie took a long, careful look at Emily Taylor as she got out of the car. She was a girl of about Josie's age with short brown hair. They might be selling Charity, but Josie wasn't prepared to let her pony go to anybody she didn't trust. Emily smiled hello rather shyly, but Josie decided that was OK. There would have been nothing worse than a bossyboots who thought she knew it all. Matthew, Emily's older brother, was quite aloof and offhand but, as he wouldn't be the one looking after Charity, Josie felt it didn't matter so much what he was like.

'Well, shall we go out to the field?' Mrs Grace said, after they'd all said hello. 'I'm sure you're keen to see Charity.'

Josie found herself walking next to Emily on the way over to the field while her mother chatted to Mr and Mrs Taylor and Matthew wandered along on his own. 'You're so lucky to live at a riding stables,' Emily said, breaking the slightly awkward silence. 'That would be my dream come true!'

'I *have* been lucky, I suppose,' Josie said. 'But we've got to move soon because the stables are being sold. That's why we have to find a new home for Charity.'

283

'Oh, I'm sorry,' Emily said, blushing pink. 'I didn't realise. How stupid of me!'

'It's all right,' Josie said. 'You weren't to know. Don't worry about it.' And she gave Emily a smile to show there were no hard feelings. 'There she is,' she added, waving a hand towards Charity, who was grazing in a corner of the field.

Emily caught her breath as she stared eagerly over. 'Oh, she's lovely!' she exclaimed. 'I've been trying to imagine what she'd look like ever since we saw your ad in the paper. She's even better than I imagined she'd be! Don't you think so, Matthew?'

'I suppose so,' her brother replied cautiously. 'But you can't tell much from appearances. Wait till you've ridden her.'

Josie started to speak and then stopped and bit her lip. She was so proud of Charity that she couldn't help wanting to tell them both what an utterly wonderful and marvellous pony she was. On the other hand, she still had a last wild hope that if her parents couldn't sell Charity she'd somehow be able to stay with them. Josie decided not to say anything that would encourage the Taylors to buy her.

'What do you think, Emily?' said Mrs Taylor. 'She looks all right, doesn't she?'

'She's lovely!' Emily repeated. Josie took one look at her face and realised nothing she said or didn't say would make the slightest difference – Emily had already fallen for Charity.

'Come on,' Josie said, starting to open the gate into the field. 'Let's catch her and then you can see what she's like to ride.'

As if she knew her every move was being watched, Charity behaved perfectly. She neighed and trotted up to the two girls as they walked over, allowing Emily to pat her while Josie slipped on her head collar. 'Here you are,' Josie said, handing Emily the lead rope. 'Do you want to take her back to the yard and we can get her saddled up?'

'Yes, please,' Emily said enthusiastically, giving Charity one last stroke and then leading her confidently back across the field, a broad smile on her face.

'Now don't make your mind up straight away, Emily,' Mrs Taylor warned her when they reached the gate. 'Matthew's right – you need to see how you feel about riding Charity. Take your time. This is a big decision.'

Mary Grace gave Josie's hand a quick squeeze as they all leaned on the fence around the outdoor schooling ring, watching while Emily put Charity through her paces. Josie was used to seeing other people on Charity, but this was desperately hard to take. 'She's my pony really!' she wanted to shout. 'I should be riding her, not you!' Somehow, she managed to stifle the urge.

'She obviously knows how to ride,' Mrs Grace murmured in her ear, and Josie had to agree. Emily had got Charity moving in a good balanced trot and, without any fuss, was making sure the pony did exactly as she was told. Charity was wonderful to ride but she was quite 'forward-going', as Mrs Grace put it – she didn't

need much encouragement to go faster. It was obvious she wanted to canter now, but Emily firmly reined her back. Then, at the next corner, when she was ready, she gave Charity the gentlest of touches with her heels and they struck off into a graceful canter.

'Looks like they're made for each other,' Josie heard Mrs Taylor say to her husband.

Even Matthew commented, 'That's not a bad little pony. Em could do a lot worse.'

Enough was enough. Muttering something vague to her mother, Josie turned on her heel and walked back to the cottage. She didn't want to make a fool of herself in front of the Taylors but she just couldn't bear to watch Emily and Charity together any longer. It was like torture.

'Oh, Josie!' her father said as she stomped down the hall after flinging open the front door with a crash. 'I'm so sorry. Getting on well, are they?'

Josie nodded, pushing his arm away while she struggled to hold back the tears and control herself. 'This is *so* hard!' she eventually managed to say as she paced up and down the kitchen.

'I know,' her father said sympathetically. 'And I wish I could do something to help! Listen, why don't we ask the Taylors whether you could ride Charity every now and then?'

'No,' Josie said, sitting down at the table and burying

her head in her arms. 'I think that would only make things worse,' she went on in a muffled voice. 'I'll get over this, Dad, but not just yet. Right now, this is the worst thing that's ever happened in my life!'

Four

Josie heard a gentle tap on her bedroom door an hour or so later and then her mother's voice asking, 'Are you OK?'

'Yes,' she called, giving her mum a wan smile as she came into the room. 'I'm sorry,' she said, sitting up. 'I know it must have looked bad, me rushing off like that, but seeing Emily on Charity suddenly really got to me.'

'It's OK,' said Mrs Grace, perching on the bed next to Josie and stroking her thick, coppery hair. 'Everyone understands how you feel. Emily said she'd be exactly the same if she had to part with her pony.'

'She was all right, wasn't she?' Josie said. 'I didn't

particularly want to like her, but I couldn't help it.'

'Yes, she was,' Mrs Grace sighed. 'And her parents were fine, too. I was half-hoping there'd be some reason why we couldn't let them buy Charity, but I couldn't find a single one. There are stables and a field not far from their house, with a couple of other horses there to keep her company. Emily's a good rider too, and you can tell she adores Charity already. It's just hard to accept that we finally have to let her go.'

'Do the Taylors definitely want to buy her?' Josie asked.

'They seem very keen,' Mrs Grace replied. 'I told them a couple of other people were interested but hadn't come to a decision, and they asked us not to sell her without ringing them first. Before they say yes for certain, though, they've asked if they can have her seen by a vet, just to make absolutely sure she's OK.'

'And we know she will be,' Josie said gloomily, 'so that's that.'

'Looks like it,' her mother replied. 'I think the Taylors are really keen. They offered to leave part of the money for Charity in advance, but I've given my word we won't sell her to anyone else before she's passed her health check. They've got a friend who's a vet, apparently, and they'd like her to call by as soon as she can next week.'

'Well, I suppose if we've got to sell Charity to anyone, it might as well be them,' Josie said, getting up from the bed and walking over to the window.

'I think so,' agreed Mrs Grace. 'We probably won't get a better offer. And they don't live very far away, so I'm sure you could go and visit her after we've moved to wherever we end up living. Emily did say you'd be welcome to ride her sometimes, if you wanted to.'

'I don't know about that,' Josie said, looking at Charity all by herself out in the field again. 'It might make things worse, seeing her settled into a new home and having to leave her there. I'd sooner remember her like she is now, here with us.'

Her mother came over to the window and they watched Charity together for a while. She was standing with her head up in the air, as though she were listening to some sound being carried on the wind.

'You can tell she's missing the other ponies,' said Mrs Grace with a sad smile. She put her arm round Josie. 'I know how much we're asking of you, having to give her up,' she said. 'And I can't stand the thought of saying goodbye to her myself.'

'Oh, why did everything have to change?' Josie said, leaning her head on her mother's shoulder. 'We were so happy before, with Faith, Hope and Charity all together. Why couldn't things just stay the way they were?'

'Because life's not like that, I'm afraid,' Mrs Grace replied. 'Come on, though, we've still got each other!

And there are a lot of people much worse off than we are.'

'I suppose so,' Josie said, taking a tissue out of her pocket and blowing her nose.

'Look, why don't you give Anna a ring and see if she can come and sleep over?' her mother suggested. 'We could get a video to watch, if you like.'

'That's a good idea,' Josie said, brightening a little. 'Let's go for a comedy, though. I don't think I could face anything too serious tonight.'

'Well, here's something to cheer us all up!' said Robert Grace, coming into the kitchen. 'That was Jim on the phone.'

Anna's mother Lynne had just dropped her round to stay the night, and they were all sitting in the kitchen drinking tea and eating crumpets. Lynne Marshall was one of Mary Grace's best friends, and they had as much to talk about as Josie and Anna.

'Oh yes?' Mrs Grace said, pulling out a chair and pouring a mug for her husband. 'We could do with some good news.'

'Who's Jim, when he's at home?' asked Lynne Marshall.

'He's an estate agent friend of mine,' Mr Grace explained, taking a sip of tea. 'He promised he'd let us know if he heard of any good properties to rent, and it sounds like one might just have appeared.'

Josie listened intently. She'd been denying the fact that in a couple of weeks they'd have to move, but it looked like now it was time to face up to it.

'Tell us more,' Lynne was saying. 'What's the place like?'

'Jim hasn't even seen it yet,' Mr Grace said, 'so he couldn't go into much detail. The owner only came in this morning.'

'Well, he must know something!' Mrs Grace exclaimed. 'Come on, Rob – don't keep us in suspense!'

'Is it like those other houses you've been looking at?' Anna asked, exchanging a meaningful look with Josie.

'No, it isn't,' said Mr Grace. 'That's the interesting part. It's quite different, in every way.' He sat back smugly, obviously having decided to enjoy teasing them for a while – much to Josie's irritation.

'Dad, I can't stand this any more!' she burst out, jumping up and attacking him from behind. 'If you don't tell me everything you know right now, I'm going to tickle you to death!'

'OK, OK! I give in,' her father gasped, laughing as he tried to defend himself. When Josie had gone back to her seat he went on, 'Well, the house is quite old, for a start. It used to be the gate lodge for some stately home that was knocked down years ago.'

'And are you prepared to tell us where it is, exactly?' Mrs Grace asked.

'On the other side of Littlehaven, just off the main road. It would be easy for Josie to get the bus into school,' Mr Grace replied. 'The bad news is, it's not as big as some of the houses we've seen. There are three bedrooms, but one of them is tiny, and the kitchen's not enormous either.'

'That doesn't bother *me* much,' Mrs Grace smiled. 'You know how I feel about cooking.'

'Our kitchen's miniscule,' Lynne added. 'You just have to train yourself to be tidy.'

'What's the good news, then?' Josie asked. 'If the house is so small, why are you getting worked up about it?'

'Quick thinking, clever daughter of mine,' said her father, taking the last crumpet. 'Well, apparently the lodge has a big garden and it's in a lovely setting. I think that makes up for a small kitchen, don't you?'

'Mmm,' Josie said thoughtfully. 'That does sound nice.'

'It sounds brilliant!' said Anna, beaming at her. 'When are you going to see it? Can we come too?'

'It's empty at the moment because they've been having some work done, and Jim's got the keys so he can show people round,' Mr Grace said. 'He's completely booked up with appointments at the moment, but he did say that we could take a quick look on our own if we wanted to – seeing as he knows us.

The estate agent's office is shut tomorrow, but maybe we could go round on Monday after school.'

'Why don't we go now?' Anna suggested. 'Someone else may have snapped it up by Monday next week!' She looked at her watch. 'Come on, there's at least an hour till the office closes for the weekend, isn't there? We can pick up the keys and go straight there.'

'Yes, why don't we, Dad?' Josie said. Now that she had started thinking about moving and was getting involved, she was curious to see the house. 'Besides, if we go now, Lynne can come too and tell us how to make it look nice. You will, won't you?' she asked, looking appealingly at Anna's mother.

'I'd love to,' Lynne replied, draining her mug of tea. 'Ben's playing cricket, so I've got a few hours to spare, and you know how much I like poking round other people's houses.'

'What do you think, Mary?' Mr Grace asked his wife. 'Do you want to go now?'

'Absolutely!' she replied, unhooking her shoulder bag from the door knob. 'Time's running out – we can't afford to hang about and miss a chance like this. Anyway, on Monday I've arranged for us all to look around that other house I found. It would be useful to have seen this one first, because we need to make a decision in the next few days.'

'Then let's not waste any more time!' Josie said,

jumping up. 'Anything to save us from a small patio garden at the rear!'

'This must be it,' said Mr Grace, pulling off the main road through a pair of tall iron gates and parking outside a cottage covered in terracotta tiles. He squinted at the sign next to the front door. 'Yes – Lime Tree Lodge. Can anybody see a lime tree?'

Josie got out of the car and stared at the house. There was no garden at the front, and the main door opened straight on to the pavement. To the left, a black-painted wooden bench had been built into the wall, and on the other side of the door was a big bay window with diamond-leaded panes of glass.

'I suppose that's where the gate-keeper would have waited for the carriages to come down the drive,' said her father, nodding at the bench.

'I like it,' said Josie, sitting down and making herself comfortable. She could imagine herself bringing a book out there in the summer, or chatting with Anna while they watched the world go by. 'What's up there, Dad?' she went on, pointing up the narrow road that stretched off into the distance with fields on either side of it.

'I think it's a modern estate,' he replied. 'Look, you can just see a couple of houses on the edge. It's not too built up round here, though – most of the land is still farmed.'

'What are we waiting for? Let's go inside,' said Mrs Grace from the doorstep. 'You can't tell much from out here.'

It was strange, walking into an empty house that until recently had been somebody else's home. Even Anna spoke in a whisper as they walked around the ground floor. 'It feels as if someone's going to spring out and ask us what we're doing here,' she hissed, and Josie nodded in agreement.

Lynne and Mary Grace had made a beeline for the kitchen. 'Well, it's bigger than ours,' Lynne said, looking round. 'You couldn't get a table in here, but there's a dining room to eat in. I wonder if the owner would let you put a hatch into the wall? Or an arched window would look good, with glass shelves.'

'Now, hold on a minute,' laughed Mrs Grace. 'Don't get carried away! A coat of paint's the most I was thinking of.'

'Let's go and explore upstairs,' Anna said, taking Josie's arm. 'You want to get the best bedroom, don't you?'

They made their way up to the first floor. 'Well, this is big enough,' Anna said, going into a bedroom overlooking the front of the house. Seconds later, she called out, 'Oh, Josie, this is perfect! You've even got a walk-in wardrobe for all your clothes!'

'All what clothes?' Josie asked, looking over Anna's

shoulder. 'My things wouldn't even fill up one corner, especially now I've cleared all the jumble out. No, something tells me this is the room Mum and Dad would choose.'

She went back out on to the landing and examined two other doors leading off it. One led to the bathroom and the other to a tiny room not much bigger than the walk-in cupboard she'd just seen.

'You could just about fit a bed and a desk in here, I suppose,' Anna said, putting her head round the door. 'You'd have to keep your clothes somewhere else, though, even if you don't have that many.'

'But I'm sure there were meant to be three bedrooms,' Josie said, squeezing past Anna out on to the landing again. 'Yes! There's another door here, in the corner. How could I have missed it?'

She opened the door and together they looked up the steep, winding staircase behind it. 'This must lead to the third bedroom,' Anna said in a hushed voice. 'Come on, let's go and see.'

'Feels like we're intruding again,' Josie whispered as they cautiously climbed the stairs and emerged in a large attic room with sloping ceilings. The faint sounds of their parents moving around and chatting floated up from downstairs, but otherwise the room seemed quite cut off from the rest of the house. It was painted white, and sunlight streamed in through the two large loft windows overlooking the back garden.

'This is wonderful!' Josie said, looking around with shining eyes. 'Don't you think so, Anna? I can just imagine myself here.'

'You haven't seen the best bit yet,' Anna replied, looking out of the windows. 'Come and look!'

Josie hurried over and gazed through the dusty glass at the cottage's long back garden below. There were a couple of sheds on the left, and flowerbeds waist-high in weeds curved around from the other side, with a tangle of shrubs and bushes beyond. The grass was very overgrown, but she could make out the borders of a lawn with a huge tree in the middle. Her father was sprawled underneath it, lying in the long grass with his

hands behind his head and his eyes shut.

'Looks like Dad's found the lime tree!' she said to Anna, with a laugh. 'Honestly, he's hopeless! He hasn't even been upstairs to look at the bedrooms.'

'But have you seen what's on the other side of the garden?' Anna said eagerly. 'There! Past those bushes at the end.'

At the bottom of the garden was a fence and on the other side of that, a field. A field that seemed to stretch on for miles, with two horses grazing in it.

Josie felt her heart leap when she saw them. 'Oh, Anna!' she said. 'Are you thinking what I'm thinking? Do you think there might be room for a pony in that field?'

'Well, it would be worth talking to your mum and dad about it, at least!' Anna said. 'I mean, it just seems so perfect, having a field right there. If Charity could share it with those horses, you wouldn't have to pay for her to be kept at a livery stables after all!'

Josie's eyes lit up. Her parents couldn't deny her this chance, could they? 'Come on!' she said to Anna. 'Let's go and ask them right now!'

Five

'But it would be ideal, Mum!' Josie said despairingly. 'There's a huge field right at the bottom of the garden. Surely there'd be room for Charity there? We could easily find out who owns it and ask them if we could rent a space.'

'I'm so sorry, love,' her mother replied, looking anguished. 'If there was any way of us hanging on to Charity, of course I'd say yes. But it isn't just a matter of living next to a field. It's what we'd have to pay for her feed, and shoeing, and vet's bills, and worming, and tack – quite apart from the cost of renting the field. You know how expensive it is to keep a pony!'

'But what if we both got a job?' Anna asked, looking from Josie to her mother. 'There must be something we could do!'

'I don't think there is,' Mary Grace replied. 'It's not easy to find work round here, and I should know – I've been searching hard enough and I haven't come up with anything. You're not old enough to babysit yet and something like a paper round wouldn't earn you enough.'

'It can't just be a question of money!' Josie cried desperately.

'I'm afraid it is,' said her father, his footsteps echoing on the bare floorboards as he walked into the room. 'Things are going to be very difficult for us for a while, Josie. There'll be no income from the stables, and it may take some time before Mum can start earning again. This house is at the top of our price range, and it's going to take every penny we've got. But even if we rented the cheapest one we've seen, we wouldn't have enough money left over to keep Charity.'

'I'm so sorry,' Mrs Grace said again, putting a comforting arm round Josie's shoulder. 'It must seem hard, but I think we'll have to put having a pony of your own on hold for a while. You never know, circumstances may change later on and things could be different.'

But Charity will be sold by then, and she's the only pony I'll ever want! Josie felt like saying, desperately trying to make the lump in her throat disappear.

'We *could* find out who owns the field, though, and who the horses belong to,' Mrs Grace suggested. 'Perhaps they need someone to help look after them? And who knows, you might be able to do some riding, too.'

'Don't bother,' Josie muttered. 'I don't really want to.' Not looking at anyone, she added, 'I'm just going to sit on the bench for a while.' She didn't want to be anywhere in sight of a field that would make a perfect home for Charity – not with her parents telling her there was no way she could ever live there!

Everybody else had plenty to say in the car on the way home, so it was easy for Josie just to sit and stare out of the window. She didn't feel like joining in the conversation.

'I thought the cottage had a really comfortable, friendly feeling about it,' her mother was saying, turning round in the front passenger seat to talk to Lynne. 'Especially with that bench at the front! It seems so welcoming, somehow.'

'I know what you mean,' Lynne answered. 'The paintwork needs touching up in places, but the house doesn't look at all uncared for and depressing, like some empty places do. The downstairs rooms might not be very big, but the two main bedrooms are a good size.'

'That loft room is brilliant!' Anna said, flashing Josie a smile and squeezing her arm to try and cheer her up.

'It's the garden I like best,' Mr Grace put in. 'I'm sure we could get it into shape over the summer holidays. Think of the picnics we could have under that tree! I'll get Jim to ask the landlord if we can keep the chickens in one of those sheds, and maybe he'll let us make a pond for the ducks.'

'What do you think, Josie?' Mrs Grace asked tentatively. 'It's much better than those other houses, isn't it?'

Josie looked at her anxious face and suddenly felt a pang of guilt. Her mother was losing her job as well as her home and having a depressed, grumpy daughter must only be adding to her worries.

'It's a lot better,' she said, trying to summon up a smile.

'And you don't have to worry about a small patio garden any more,' her mother added encouragingly. 'We'll probably be able to keep all the birds, and Basil could root about in the shrubbery to his heart's content.'

'Well, sounds like we're all agreed,' Robert Grace said. 'I'll ring Jim at home when we get back and tell him we want to take it.'

'And you'll have the whole of August to get settled in,' Lynne said. 'Term finishes on Wednesday, doesn't it?'

'Yes, it does,' Josie said, half-heartedly. This must be the first summer holiday ever that she wasn't particularly looking forward to.

'I'm going to be working at Friendship House for a couple of days a week soon,' Lynne said. 'Why don't you and Anna come with me? You can help with the children and visit Hope. Oh, I forgot to tell you – I went in to talk to Liz Tallant yesterday, and I went to say hello to Hope.'

'Mum! You should have said,' Anna exclaimed. 'How was she? Is she happy?'

'She looked wonderful,' Lynne said cheerfully. 'She's bossing about those two donkeys in her field like an old mother hen, and Liz says the children all love her to pieces.'

'I bet they do,' Josie said with a real smile this time, beginning to feel a little happier in spite of herself. 'Dear old Hope – it would be brilliant to see her again.'

'Then let's do it!' Anna said. 'That's a great idea, Mum. We could ring Jill and arrange to go round and visit Faith over the holidays, too.'

'Yes, I think we should,' Josie said, making a huge effort to be more positive. 'And we can spend some time fixing up my room, and exploring—'

'And gardening,' Mr Grace added.

'And I won't be so busy, so we can all do things

together,' said Mrs Grace. 'I bet you'll find the holiday flies past, Josie.'

'Yes, perhaps you're right,' Josie said, deciding then and there not to think too deeply about anything, but just get through the next few weeks as best she could.

The next day, Mary Grace brought out all the cardboard boxes and tea chests she'd been collecting in the barn, ready to begin the task of packing up. 'If we do some every day next week, we won't be completely exhausted by the time we have to leave,' she said. 'I'll make a start with your books on Monday, Rob.'

Mr Grace had spoken to the estate agent as soon as they'd got back from looking at the house. Now it was just a question of paying a deposit and signing the contract, and Lime Tree Lodge would be theirs to live in from the beginning of August, in ten days' time.

'Are you feeling better about things?' Anna asked Josie that morning while they were grooming Charity.

'I've decided to try and take each day as it comes,' Josie replied, getting to work with the dandy brush on a patch of mud over Charity's withers. 'I don't really want to think about the future too much.'

'That's probably the best thing to do,' Anna agreed. 'Anyway, you've got nearly another week with Charity still, haven't you? That's good news.' The Taylors had rung earlier to say the vet they knew was away at a

conference all week and wouldn't be able to check
Charity over until Saturday morning.

'Besides,' Anna went on, carefully brushing out
Charity's mane, 'you never can tell what the vet might
find. I know!' she said suddenly, her face lighting up.
'Why don't we bribe her to say Charity's got some awful
disease?'

'That's a terrible idea,' Josie said in dismay. 'For a

start, we've got nothing to bribe her with, and I bet she wouldn't agree even if we had. And say she did make something up – who'd believe her? The Taylors aren't stupid, they can see Charity's healthy and fit.' It was true: Josie was spending so much time riding the pony and grooming her that she was in top condition.

'You're right. But it was worth a try,' Anna admitted, not at all put out. 'I'm surprised Kirsty's not here by now,' she added, looking at the yard. 'What time's her lesson?'

Josie checked her watch. 'In about half an hour,' she said. 'When she does turn up, try not to say anything about us having found a buyer for Charity, OK? Mum thinks she'll be really upset and that we shouldn't tell her until it's definitely settled.'

'You know me,' Anna grinned. 'I'm not one to blurt things out.'

'Ha ha,' Josie replied sarcastically. 'That is a joke, isn't it? You've got the biggest mouth in the history of the world, Anna Marshall.'

For the whole of the next week, Josie tried really hard to keep as calm as she'd told Anna she would. She floated through the last day of school on Wednesday and said goodbye to her friends, promising them she'd ring with her new address and phone number. She carried on riding Charity every day, feeding, grooming and mucking her out. All the time she was telling herself not to think about what she'd be doing next week, when there wouldn't be a pony to look after any more.

And then, before she knew it, Saturday had arrived and the Taylors' vet was parking her car in the yard. Mrs Grace took her over to where Charity was waiting, tied up outside the loose boxes, while Josie hovered around in the background. She didn't want to miss anything but, at the same time, she wasn't in a hurry to hear Charity declared fit and well and able to be sold.

'Hello there, gorgeous,' the young woman said, giving the pony a stroke. 'I can see why Emily was so taken with you. You're beautiful!'

She began to check Charity over, taking her pulse and listening to her heart. Then she felt each of her legs for abnormal swelling or scars, lifted up each hoof in turn to check her feet, and carefully opened her mouth to examine her teeth. Josie had to try and soothe Charity down at this point, because she'd begun to fidget and toss her head.

'That's all right,' smiled the vet. 'I don't like strangers poking around in my mouth, either. Could you take her for a trot on the lead rein now?' she asked Josie. 'Just so I can watch how she moves.'

At the end of the examination, she began to pack all her equipment away and gave Josie and her mother a smile. 'That's one lovely pony,' she said, 'as I'm sure you already know. She's got tons of personality, hasn't she? There are no problems there that I can see, and I'm happy to let the Taylors know. I'd just like to see her vaccination record, and then I'll pass her with flying colours.'

'Of course,' said Mrs Grace. 'It's down in the office with the rest of the paperwork. I'll show you the way. You could put Charity back in her loose box, Josie,' she added. 'Kirsty's coming for a lesson this afternoon. It looks like we'll have to tell her it'll be the last one.'

Josie led Charity back into the stable, feeling numb. So this was it. The final hurdle had been crossed and, unless a miracle happened, Charity would be going to the Taylors. It was like some horrible dream.

Mrs Grace rang the Taylors after lunch. 'We've agreed that they'll come and pick Charity up on Tuesday,' she said, coming into the loose box where Josie was saddling the pony up for her lesson. 'As I thought you might like to keep her until just before we move.'

'OK,' Josie said mechanically, buckling up the girth.

Mrs Grace gave her a quick hug, saying, 'Keep going, love.' Then she added, 'I'll have a word with Kirsty after the lesson – I don't want to spoil it for her. And I think I might give her mother a ring and ask her to take Kirsty home this time, rather than letting her walk back on her own. She might be pretty upset.'

* * *

'That was wonderful!' Kirsty said to Josie, jumping down from Charity at the end of the lesson. 'I didn't think your mum was going to let me start jumping yet!'

'Well, I did promise you could take Charity over a couple of jumps at some stage,' said Mrs Grace, walking up with Mrs Fisher. 'And it had to be this afternoon, Kirsty, I'm afraid. You know we have to leave the stables soon?'

Kirsty nodded, her eyes wide.

'Well, next week we're moving to our new house, and now we've found someone who wants to buy Charity. She'll be going to *her* new home next week, too.'

'But, I didn't realise—' Kirsty stammered, looking desperately from Mrs Grace to her mother to Josie. 'I mean, I never thought you'd really—' Her eyes brimmed over with tears and she couldn't say any more.

'Why don't you give the pony a hug goodbye?' Mrs Fisher said. 'You are making rather a fuss, dear – this isn't the end of the world. You can carry on having lessons at Littlehaven, after all.'

'It is the end of the world to me!' Kirsty blurted out angrily to her mother. 'What do you know about it? You don't understand anything!' And she turned and ran out of the yard.

'Kirsty!' her mother shouted after her. 'Come back here!' Then she turned to Mrs Grace. 'I'm so sorry,' she said, looking embarrassed. 'I've been trying to tell her for weeks that this would happen, but she refused to believe me. I suppose she thought you couldn't ever bring yourselves to sell Charity.'

Well, that makes two of us, Josie said grimly to herself. *I know exactly how you feel, Kirsty, if that's any consolation.*

'Poor Kirsty,' Mrs Grace said, when the Fishers had both gone. 'Still, they've got some nice ponies at Littlehaven. I'm sure she'll soon find one to take Charity's place.'

'Maybe,' Josie said shortly, starting to heave off the saddle. An unspoken thought hovered on the air between them: Charity couldn't ever be replaced, as far as the Graces were concerned.

'Look, why don't the two of us go out for a hack together tomorrow?' Mrs Grace offered. 'I could do with a break from packing, and I can ride Connie over from Littlehaven. Mary's asked me to take her out.' Connie was the black mare who used to be kept at livery at Grace's Stables. Mrs Grace had carried on exercising her, even though she'd moved to another yard near by.

'OK,' Josie said, buckling up Charity's head collar. 'Whatever you like.' She couldn't bring herself to feel that anything mattered, not even how they spent these last few days. Charity was going, and nothing could alter that final, awful fact.

* * *

Josie spent a restless night. It was heavy, thundery weather and her bedroom felt airless and stuffy. She tossed and turned, her mind racing with all kinds of strange dreams. At one point, she was with Charity at the airport, trying to load her on to the revolving luggage belt. Her hooves kept slipping on its smooth black surface. 'This pony should be packed in a suitcase,' the air hostess was saying. 'Why haven't you prepared her for the journey? The plane leaves in ten minutes.'

She woke up early, feeling anxious and panicky. Finding her way between the half-filled boxes that covered her bedroom floor, she looked out of the window, hoping the sight of Charity grazing quietly in the field would calm her down. The storm clouds had broken, and a misty grey drizzle hung in the air. But Charity was nowhere to be seen.

Josie rubbed her eyes, thinking she must be still half asleep, then looked again. There was no sign of the pony anywhere. *She must be right over by that curve in the hedge*, Josie thought to herself, craning to see the outermost edge of the field. Quickly, she pulled on some jeans and a T-shirt and ran downstairs, grabbing a pair of wellies from the porch on her way out of the house. Basil leapt out of his basket in the kitchen when he heard the door opening and scurried along beside her.

She climbed over the gate and ran towards the middle

of the field. When she was certain she could see every inch of it, she stopped and looked around for some flash of white that would tell her Charity was there. Basil stopped to search, too, one paw lifted and his black nose sniffing eagerly. Josie's heart was thumping so loudly it threatened to burst out of her chest, and the palms of her hands prickled with sweat. Whirling around, she stared at every hollow, every corner, every bend in the hedge, before coming to the final conclusion she was almost afraid to make.

'Mum, Dad!' she screamed, running at top speed back towards the house. 'Charity's gone! She's not in the field!'

Six

'Maybe there's a gap in the fence somewhere that we haven't noticed,' Mrs Grace said, her dark curly hair already beaded with raindrops as she and Josie hurried towards the field. 'Don't panic yet – she's probably not far away.'

'But we checked the fencing the other day!' Josie said frantically, searching for some sign of Charity. 'I suppose she could have found a weak spot in the hedge and got into the field where we used to keep the livery horses. She's never done that before, though.'

'I'll look in the jumping paddock and the yard,' Mr Grace called. The striped pyjama top he hadn't stopped to change billowed out over his jeans as he rushed towards the loose boxes.

Josie climbed over the damp, slippery fencing around the field, too impatient to wait for her mother to open the gate. Her mind was racing with all sorts of horrible scenes – Charity lying in some ditch with a broken leg or a gash from a barbed wire fence, or galloping on to a busy road, or maybe even being loaded into a trailer and taken off by some gang of thieves. Where on earth was she?

'Now don't just rush off,' Mrs Grace said. 'Let's get organised. I'll walk along the back hedge and see whether she might have got through at the side into the other field. Basil can come with me – he might pick up her scent. You look at the fence round the front and by the schooling ring. Don't worry, love, I'm sure we'll find her soon!'

'You don't think she might have been stolen, do you, Mum?' Josie asked, hardly daring to put her fear into words.

'Oh, I don't think so,' her mother replied. 'It's more likely she's wandered off somewhere.'

Josie forced herself to slow down and look carefully along the front boundary of the field for any broken posts or white hairs caught in the wood that would show where Charity might have broken through.

Perhaps she realised we were going to sell her, she thought as she walked along, anxiously scanning the fence. Charity was so intelligent, she had probably picked up on the unusual atmosphere at the stables. First Faith and then Hope leaving must have worried her, too. Charity was lonely – they'd noticed how she seemed to be looking around for the other ponies. Maybe now she'd gone to find them! *Oh, why did we leave her on her own?* Josie asked herself. *Why didn't we guess something like this would happen?*

She was jolted from her worries by a shout from her father, who was running over from the yard. 'Come here!' he called urgently, waving to summon Mary Grace from the far end of the field as well.

'What is it, Dad?' Josie asked, scrambling back over the fence to join him. 'Have you found something?'

'Yes and no,' he replied breathlessly, his face pale. 'I *haven't* found something would be more accurate.' He took Josie's arm and hurried her over to the tackroom. 'There!' he said, pointing towards it.

'Oh no!' Josie said, as she looked at the door swinging open. 'I'm sure I locked up last night!'

'It's not that. Go inside,' her father said, following closely behind her as she headed into the dark little room. Apart from a couple of spare head collars and a show saddle they didn't often use, it was empty. Charity's tack had gone.

Josie gasped and fell back against the wall. She felt as

though someone had punched her in the stomach.

'You know what this means, don't you?' Robert Grace said, putting a steadying arm round her shoulders.

'Yes,' Josie replied, in a voice that sounded to her own ears as though it was coming from very far away. 'It means someone *has* stolen Charity.'

At that moment, Mrs Grace came through the door. She glanced round the bare tackroom walls and then said grimly, 'I think we'd better go back to the house, don't you? We'll need to ring the police.'

Josie and her father sat at the kitchen table while Mary Grace used the phone in the hall.

'I can't believe it!' Josie said, sipping the hot sweet tea her father had made. 'Why didn't we hear something? My bedroom overlooks the field, after all, and I didn't sleep very well last night.'

'I just can't understand it,' Mr Grace said, holding his head in his hands. 'I mean, why would the thief bother to take any tack? You'd have thought it wasn't worth the risk of getting caught.'

Mrs Grace came back into the kitchen and drew a chair up to the table. 'Well, it's all official now,' she said. 'Charity's reported stolen and we've even got a crime number – H58.' She looked in disbelief at the scrap of paper in her hand. 'Impossible to take in, isn't it?'

'I'll pour you a cup of tea,' Mr Grace said, rubbing her back comfortingly. 'That might make you feel better.'

'What did the police say?' Josie asked. 'Have any other horses in the area been reported missing?'

'Not so far,' her mother replied. 'At first they told me

319

she'd probably just strayed, but her tack having gone too made them take me seriously. It's odd, though – apparently horses are usually stolen just before an auction, and there aren't any round here that I know of. Not for a few weeks, anyway.'

'I hate thinking about someone creeping round here and taking her off in the middle of the night,' Josie said with a shudder. 'Nothing like this has ever happened to us before.'

'You don't think it could be something to do with having advertised Charity in the paper, do you?' Mr Grace asked his wife. 'Could someone have come round and had a good look at the place, to check it out before coming back later?'

'But the Taylors were the only people who saw her,' Mrs Grace said, running her hands through her hair distractedly. 'They didn't exactly look like horse thieves, did they? And we can easily trace them.'

'We'll have to tell the Taylors what's happened if Charity doesn't turn up soon,' Mr Grace remarked. 'Perhaps we should ring them if there's been no news by the end of the day.'

'This is just horrible!' Josie said, pushing back her chair and pacing up and down the floor. 'If anyone touches a hair on her head, I'll find out who they are and – well, I don't know what I'll do to them!'

'Don't worry, love,' said her father, reaching round to

squeeze her hand. 'I'm sure whoever took her won't hurt her. They're probably only in this for the money. And she's been freeze-branded with a number on her shoulder, hasn't she? We'll be able to identify her for certain if she turns up at a sale.'

'Oh, yes! I completely forgot to tell the police about that,' Mrs Grace said. 'I'm so worried I can't think straight. Still, there's an officer coming round later to ask us questions and take a look at the field and the tackroom. I'll mention it then.'

'I'm going to ring Anna and Ben,' Josie said, going to the door. 'I feel like talking to someone and there's nothing else we can do, is there?'

'Not that I can think of,' said her mother. 'We'll just have to sit here and wait for the police to arrive.'

Josie dialled the Marshalls' number with shaking fingers. It was still quite early in the morning, and Anna sounded half-asleep as she answered the phone. But when Josie told her what had happened, she immediately snapped to attention. 'Stay right where you are!' she commanded, though Josie wasn't planning on going anywhere. 'I'll wake Ben up and we'll be around before you know it.'

Josie put down the receiver and went back through to the kitchen. Her parents were just sitting there in silence. They seemed to be in a state of shock, and she knew exactly how they felt. 'I'm going to have another look round till Ben and Anna get here,' she told them. 'Perhaps I can pick up some clues.'

'Don't touch anything,' her mother warned. 'Just tell the police if you find anything – they're the experts.'

'OK,' Josie said, heading out of the house. She stared at the empty field, trying to re-create what must have happened in her mind. Why would someone run the risk of coming right up to the riding stables? If they were going to steal a horse, why not pick one in an isolated field, miles from anywhere, where they could drive up with a trailer, load the pony in and get away really quickly.

There was no need to look for weak spots in the fence now, but Josie walked along it anyway as far as the gate, keeping her eyes open for any little thing that shouldn't have been there – a patch of grass that had been flattened, perhaps, or a scrap of material or paper. She found nothing. Everything looked just as it usually did, except for the fact that Charity had gone. It was as though she'd been spirited away by magic.

She combed the yard next, her eyes fixed to the ground, and then looked in the loose boxes before turning her attention to the tackroom. Jamming her hands in her pockets to remind herself not to touch anything, she looked at the open door. It had been unlocked, not forced open, and the key was still in the lock. The flowerpot under which it was always hidden was neatly back in its place.

Josie was still staring at the tackroom door when Ben and Anna arrived on their bikes. Anna jumped off and flung hers against the office wall, her eyes wide with concern. 'Josie! Are you OK?' she gasped breathlessly. 'What's happening? Where are the police?'

'They're coming on later,' Josie told her, her mind on other things.

'When did this happen?' Ben asked, following close behind his sister. 'Did you hear anything? Was it a gang?'

'No, it must have happened in the middle of the night,' Josie replied. 'And I don't think it was a gang. Whoever stole Charity took her tack as well.'

'You wouldn't have thought they'd bother, would you?' Ben said, frowning.

'And that's not the only thing,' Josie said, pointing at the tackroom door. 'They unlocked the door with the key from under the flowerpot. How did they know where it was kept?'

'Maybe a lucky guess?' Anna suggested.

'But why waste time fumbling round in the dark, searching for a key, when it would be quicker to simply force the door open?' Josie replied. 'No, I think whoever it was knew exactly where to find that key.'

'So you think the person who's stolen Charity is someone who knows the stables well?' Anna said. 'That's awful!'

'It is, isn't it?' said Josie slowly, thinking the whole

thing over. An image of herself, bending down to take the key from its hiding place, had suddenly flashed into her head. The beginning of an idea was taking shape at the back of her mind but, as it seemed so far-fetched, she dismissed it at once.

'Here come the police,' Ben said. 'You can tell them all about it.'

A panda car drove up and parked in the yard. Two officers got out: a burly middle-aged man and a younger woman, who had been driving.

Josie walked over to meet them, while Ben and Anna hung back. 'Hello, I'm Josie Grace. Thanks for coming so quickly,' she said. 'My parents are in the house.'

'I'm Sergeant Bryant and this is PC Hutchins,' said the man, looking surprised. 'But I think there's been some misunderstanding. Were you expecting us?'

'Yes,' Josie answered. 'My mother rang the police station a little while ago. You've come about our pony, haven't you?'

'No, as a matter of fact, we haven't,' said Sergeant Bryant, looking round the yard as he spoke. 'What's happened to it, then, this pony of yours?'

'Well, she's been stolen,' Josie stammered, looking at the two police officers in surprise. 'Didn't you know? And why are you here, if you haven't come about that?'

'It might be best if we all go indoors so we can talk to

your parents,' Sergeant Bryant said. 'We can explain everything there.'

'But what's happened?' Josie asked in alarm. 'Has there been an accident or something?'

'Don't worry, Josie,' the woman constable told her kindly. 'It's nothing like that. We're making enquiries about a young girl who's been reported missing, that's all, and we think you and your parents might be able to help us.'

Josie stared at her without speaking. That crazy idea in the back of her mind forced its way to the front. 'A young girl?' she repeated faintly.

'That's right,' said Sergeant Bryant. And when he spoke her name, Josie found that she wasn't the least bit surprised. 'Kirsty Fisher,' he said. 'She was here yesterday afternoon, wasn't she?'

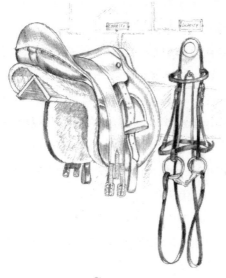

Seven

'So you think that Kirsty Fisher going missing at the
same time as your pony isn't just a coincidence?'
Sergeant Bryant asked Josie. The two police officers
were now sitting round the kitchen table with her
parents and they were all drinking cups of tea as the
Graces answered the officers' questions.

'The two things *have* to be connected!' Josie said,
leaning forward over the table in her eagerness to
convince the sergeant. 'It all adds up! To start off with,
we know Kirsty's crazy about Charity. When we told
her that Charity was going to her new owners next
week she was really upset, and so she must have decided

to try and do something about it.'

Sergeant Bryant looked across at PC Hutchins, who was busy taking notes, and raised his eyebrows. 'And how do you think she took the pony?' he asked, turning back to Josie.

'Kirsty watched me unlock the tackroom door a couple of weeks ago, so she saw where we hide the key,' Josie told him. 'She obviously came back last night, took Charity from the field, saddled her up, and rode her away. That's why we didn't hear anything! Charity is used to Kirsty, and she would have gone quietly with her.'

'But Kirsty hasn't ever caught Charity before,' Mrs Grace objected. 'Do you really think she'd have tried to do it in the middle of the night like that? She's such a shy, quiet little thing.'

'Creepy, more like,' Anna snorted. Mrs Grace gave her a sharp look, and PC Hutchins glanced up from her notebook. 'Sorry,' Anna said, a little shamefaced. 'But it's a really deceitful thing to do to your friends, isn't it?'

'I'm sure if Kirsty has taken Charity, she didn't do it to spite us,' Mrs Grace replied.

'Whatever she has or hasn't done,' Sergeant Bryant added sternly, 'we have to concentrate on finding her as quickly as we can, before anything goes badly wrong.'

'Kirsty *has* caught Charity before, anyway,' Josie said, picking up the thread of the conversation in the silence that followed his words. 'She came with me into the field that day and I showed her how. Come on, Mum, remember how upset she was yesterday! She must have thought this was her last chance to save Charity.'

'Yes, Mrs Fisher said she was beside herself,' PC Hutchins put in, looking back over her notes. 'That's why she was so worried when she saw Kirsty's empty bed this morning.'

'I don't suppose the girl could have just gone round to a friend's house without telling her parents, could she?' Mr Grace asked.

'Well, her mother's rung everyone she can think of, but no one's seen her,' PC Hutchins replied. 'She told us Kirsty doesn't have many friends, anyway. Oh, by the way – I think you need to check your phone. Mrs Fisher says she tried to call you straight away to see if Kirsty was here, but she couldn't get hold of you.'

'That's strange. We used it this morning,' Mr Grace said, frowning as he went out to the hall. Seconds later, he was back. 'Mystery solved,' he announced. 'The receiver was off the hook – it hadn't been put back properly.'

'Oh, that must have been me!' Josie said. 'I was in such a state when I rang you, Anna, I didn't know what I was doing.'

'Now let me just make sure I've got this straight,' Sergeant Bryant said heavily. 'You told Kirsty yesterday afternoon that her favourite pony was going to a new home. She left here very upset at about four o'clock and you haven't seen her since. No one heard or saw anything unusual in the night, but you found the pony gone about seven this morning and reported it to us half an hour or so afterwards. A head collar and the saddle and bridle were also missing and the tackroom door was unlocked. Is that it?'

The Graces nodded and he went on, 'Well, let me know if you remember anything else that seems significant. I'll have to let the station know we might be looking for a girl on horseback – it'll make a difference to the area we search.' He got up from the table. 'We'll just take a look at the field and the tackroom on our way out. I'll get one of our fingerprint lads to come over as soon as possible. You haven't touched anything, have you? Good.'

'They probably haven't got far,' PC Hutchins said reassuringly to Josie, Ben and Anna as she followed the sergeant out with Mr and Mrs Grace. 'And I'm sure we'll find them quickly.'

'I hope so,' Josie said, resting her head in her arms on the kitchen table. She suddenly felt absolutely exhausted.

'Don't worry,' she heard Ben say, and glanced up to see him looking at her sympathetically. 'After all,' he added, 'at least we know Charity hasn't been taken by a real thief.'

'Well, Kirsty seems real enough to me,' Josie answered. 'And now I'm worried about what's happened to her, too. Still, I know what you mean.'

Mrs Grace put her head round the kitchen door. 'I'm just going to ring Kirsty's mother and talk all this over with her,' she said. 'Dad's gone upstairs to have a shower. Why don't you three have some breakfast?'

'Oh, Mum, I couldn't eat a thing,' Josie said. She still had a strange, empty feeling in her stomach, but she wasn't the slightest bit hungry.

'Well, just help yourselves if you feel like it,' her mother said, noticing that Ben was already reaching in the cupboard for a cereal packet.

'I know we mustn't be too hard on Kirsty when she could be lying injured somewhere,' Anna said, after Mrs Grace had gone out. 'But if she has taken Charity, I still think it's a nasty thing to do. Especially when you've always been so kind to her, Josie.'

'I've got a feeling she's trying to help me, in some weird way,' Josie said. 'When I first thought she might have taken Charity, I was really angry. And then I remembered some of the things she's said in the past, about helping me keep her. She thinks it's really unfair that Charity can't stay with us. Perhaps she wanted to stop her from being sold, and didn't think about what would happen next.'

'That's for sure,' Ben said, pouring milk on to a big

bowl of cornflakes. 'Did she imagine your parents would just say, "Oh well, perhaps we won't sell Charity after all, now Kirsty's gone off with her"? And how long is she planning to stay on the run, d'you think?'

'I don't know,' Josie said, looking out of the window at the rain that had begun to fall again. 'I bet she's regretting it already. But where on earth is she?'

'Well, her mother's frantic,' Mrs Grace said, coming back into the kitchen. 'She didn't want to talk to me for too long, in case the police were trying to get through with any news. But she did tell me that Kirsty's asthmatic, which I never realised. Apparently she's taken her inhaler with her, but what if she has a really bad attack and there's no one around? It doesn't bear thinking about!'

'They've just got to find her!' Josie said anxiously, and even Anna began to look seriously worried.

'Why don't we go out on our bikes and help look?' she said. 'We might be able to spot something.'

'Then you really must all have something to eat,' Mrs Grace insisted. 'I don't want to be sending out search parties for you, too.'

The day seemed to pass agonisingly slowly. In the morning, Josie, Ben and Anna went out on their bikes along the lanes round the village. They were passed several times by police cars and saw officers on doorsteps making house-to-house enquiries. There was no trace of a blonde-haired girl on a grey pony, though, and cycling along in the rain made them feel tired and depressed. They couldn't get far across the fields, either, which they all agreed was probably the way that Kirsty would have gone.

'After all, she wouldn't ride along the road, would she?' Ben said. 'She must realise everyone will be out looking for her by now.'

'We might as well go back home,' Josie said disconsolately. 'I don't think we're doing much good out here. Let's see if there's been any news.'

'Any phone calls, Mum?' she asked as they trooped back into School Farm, but Mrs Grace just shook her head.

'Only a couple for Dad, I'm afraid,' she said. 'The fingerprint man came, but he couldn't get any clear prints from the door frame. Now, you'd better get changed out of those wet clothes, love. Lynne's coming up for lunch – I'll ring and tell her to bring some dry things for Ben and Anna.'

Robert Grace had cooked roast chicken for lunch, with vegetarian sausages for Lynne. Apart from Ben, though, no one felt like eating much.

'So why did John Phillips have to ring you up on a Sunday?' Mrs Grace said to her husband, as they all sat round picking at their food.

'My demon headmaster?' Mr Grace replied. 'Oh, just something that's cropped up at school. I'll have to go in for a meeting tomorrow morning, I'm afraid. But it shouldn't take too long.'

Tomorrow morning, Josie thought to herself. *I wonder what will have happened by then?* She could tell her mother was thinking along the same lines.

'I just hope they're under cover, that's all,' Mrs Grace said as she stared out of the kitchen window at the steadily falling drizzle. 'It can't be doing Kirsty's asthma much good to be out in this damp weather.'

'You wouldn't believe it was nearly August today, would you?' Lynne Marshall said, making an effort to be cheerful. 'Still, it's been lovely and sunny up till now.' She began to clear the scarcely touched plates of food.

'Rob and I thought we might go out for another look in the fields this afternoon,' Mrs Grace said, looking round the table. 'Are there any other volunteers? I'm sure the police wouldn't mind some help with the search.'

'I'm going to try and contact Horsewatch over the Internet at home,' Anna said. 'It's a website specially for lost and stolen ponies. D'you want to come, too, Josie?'

'No thanks,' she replied. 'I'd sooner stay here by the phone, just in case there's any news, if that's OK with you.' Suddenly a new anxiety occurred to her. 'Mum!' she said urgently. 'What if Charity finds her way back here on her own, after we've moved? She won't know where we are, will she? We *have* to stay here until she's found – we've just got to!'

'Don't worry, love. I'm sure she'll turn up before Wednesday,' Mrs Grace said, putting an arm round Josie's shoulder. 'There are so many people out looking by now, and I don't think Kirsty will have gone too far away.'

Josie passed a miserable afternoon, wandering round among the half-packed tea chests and boxes that filled the house and listening out for the phone. The only person who rang was Anna, asking if she could come and stay the night at School Farm. Josie said yes at once, glad of some company to take her mind off things. She couldn't believe that Kirsty and Charity would be spending another night out in the open. Surely they should have been found by now? But by the time it was getting dark, and she and Anna were getting ready for bed, there had still been no news.

'It was bad enough trying to get used to the idea of Charity being sold,' Josie said despairingly, 'but this is even worse! I keep imagining all the dreadful things that might be happening.'

'I'm sure Kirsty will take care of her,' Anna said comfortingly. 'She knows how to, doesn't she?'

'She might be able to ride OK, but she hasn't learnt much about looking after a pony,' Josie worried. 'What if she does something stupid, like tying Charity up by her reins so that she hurts her mouth? Or she might let her drink when she's hot and blowing, and then she'll get colic. I can't bear to think about it, Anna!'

'Then don't think about it,' Anna said sensibly, giving Josie a quick hug. 'You'll only get more upset and that won't help anybody. Let's try and go to sleep. By the time it's morning, they'll probably have turned up somewhere, safe and well.'

'Oh, I hope so,' Josie sighed, taking one last look out of her bedroom window at the empty field before drawing the curtains. 'I don't know what I'll do if anything happens to Charity, Anna – I really don't!'

Eight

Try as she might, Josie found it almost impossible to sleep that night. She lay tossing and turning until it was almost light, listening to Anna's quiet breathing from the mattress on the floor next to her bed. Birds had begun to sing the dawn chorus by the time she eventually dropped off, and she didn't wake up until late the next morning. When she opened her bleary eyes, she saw that the mattress was empty. Anna was already down in the kitchen, sitting at the table with her mother and Ben and Mrs Grace. One look at their tense faces told Josie there had been no news of Kirsty or Charity.

'Morning, love,' her mother said, giving Josie a peck on the cheek. 'We still haven't heard anything, I'm afraid. Dad's gone into school for his meeting and I have to go to the police station to give a statement and answer some questions.'

'Questions?' Josie asked, after she'd greeted everyone. She poured herself some orange juice, wishing her heavy, aching head would clear. 'What kind of questions?'

'Oh, the kind of state I thought Kirsty was in when she left here, where she might have gone – that sort of thing,' said Mrs Grace, looking for her car keys on the table.

'I'll be staying here for a while this morning,' Lynne added. 'Just to keep an eye on things and listen out for the phone in case there's any news. Ben's come up to lend a hand, too.'

'Right, better be off,' Mrs Grace said, waving goodbye as she rushed out of the door. 'I'll see you in a couple of hours, I hope. Be good!'

'So, are you lot going out on bikes again today?' Lynne asked, after they'd heard the front door slam. 'I brought Ben and Anna's up in the van, just in case. And at least it's not raining any more.'

'I don't know,' Josie sighed. 'It's useless trying to cover the fields on bikes, and I'm sure that's where we should be looking.'

'If only Tubber was still here,' Ben put in, 'I could have gone out on him. That would have been the best thing. We really need a horse to go across country.'

'It's a pity Hope's so far away,' Lynne said thoughtfully. 'I'm sure Liz wouldn't have minded you taking her away from Friendship House for the day.'

'But Faith is much nearer!' Anna suddenly exclaimed. 'I've just had a brainwave! We could give Jill and her mother a ring and tell them what's happened. I'm sure they wouldn't mind lending Faith to us – not in these circumstances! Don't you think, Josie?'

'Maybe,' Josie said, not wanting to land herself in one of Anna's impetuous schemes without thinking it through. 'It *would* make it easier to look for Kirsty, that's for sure. But I don't know if Faith could manage a long ride. And how would the Atterburys get her here? They don't live that close by.'

'They've got a trailer, haven't they?' Anna said, all fired up and eager. 'They might bring her over for us. Oh, come on, you guys. It's worth a try!'

'I suppose it wouldn't hurt to give them a ring,' Josie said. 'They can always say no. What do you think, Lynne?'

'The main thing I'm concerned about is not giving your mother any more reason to worry,' Lynne Marshall said, running a hand through her spiky blonde hair and making the silver bracelets on her wrist jangle together. Ben and Anna had inherited their father's dark colouring, passed down from his Spanish mother, and no one would ever have guessed they were related to Lynne.

'What if you have an accident or something, Josie?' she went on. 'You'd probably be the one riding Faith, wouldn't you?'

'I'm not sure. We haven't really decided about that,' Josie said, but Ben and Anna were already nodding in agreement.

'Charity's your pony,' Anna said. 'And I'm sure Kirsty would much rather see you than either of us, if you did find her.'

'We'd have to decide on a route first,' Josie said, beginning to catch some of Anna's enthusiasm. 'Then you'd know where I was. We could work out where Kirsty would be most likely to have gone, and I'll just cover as much ground as I can, depending on how Faith gets on. Oh, Anna – this could be the best idea you've ever had!'

'Look, Josie, I just have to be extra careful because your mum's not here,' Lynne said. 'I know she lets you go out riding on your own, but if anything happens, I'd be the one responsible.' She rooted in her huge leather shoulder bag and brought out a mobile phone. 'Here, take this with you,' she said. 'We'll stay back at base, and you can ring us if you find anything or you need help.'

'Oh, Mum, that's fantastic!' Anna said, flinging her arms round her.

'Now, don't get carried away,' Lynne laughed, disentangling herself. 'You've still got to ring the Atterburys, remember? And if they say no, you've got to accept their decision.'

'OK,' Josie answered, rushing out to the hall to look for the address book and start phoning. *Oh, please say yes*, she prayed as she dialled the Atterburys' number. *This is such a good plan. It has to work!*

Jill answered the phone. She had already heard from friends who lived in Northgate that Kirsty and Charity were missing, and she was only too pleased to help in any way she could. 'Of course you can take Faith!' she told Josie. 'It's a brilliant idea, and it's lovely to think of her looking for Charity. After all, she's kind of like her aunty, isn't she? I'll have to check with Mum first, though. We'll ring you back in five minutes.'

It seemed like an hour before the phone rang again and Josie heard Mrs Atterbury's voice on the other end of the line. 'We'll be over in about half an hour,' she said. 'Jill's going to help me load Faith into the trailer and we'll come as quickly as we can.'

'Oh, thank you!' Josie said for the third time. 'It's so kind of you, it really is!'

'Don't think anything of it,' Mrs Atterbury replied kindly. 'We're just pleased to be able to help. It's awful to think of that poor girl out on her own somewhere.'

'Yes!' Josie called to the others, hurrying back into the kitchen. 'Faith will be here in half an hour or so!'

'Then have some breakfast,' Lynne said, pushing a bowl and a packet of cereal across the table to her. 'We don't want you fainting with hunger.'

'What is it with mothers and this thing they have about breakfast?' Josie grumbled good-naturedly. She suddenly felt wide awake and much too excited to eat anything.

'Here they are!' Anna called a little while later from the path outside School Farm, as an estate car towing a horse trailer pulled slowly into the Graces' yard.

'Right, I think that's everything,' Lynne said, pulling up the drawstring of a small rucksack and handing it to Josie in the hall. 'The phone's in there, plus a torch I managed to find in one of those boxes in the kitchen. And there's a bag of pony nuts, peppermints, glucose tablets and a drink. You probably won't need any of it, but it's just as well to be prepared.'

'Thanks, Lynne,' Josie said, giving her a hug. 'You've been great!'

She rushed out into the yard, to see Mrs Atterbury beginning to unfasten the side ramp at the front of the trailer. Jill soon emerged, grinning from ear to ear and leading Faith slowly down the ramp. Josie felt a pang when she saw the elderly bay mare back in the yard where she'd spent so much of her life. She rushed over to greet the Atterburys and give Faith a cuddle.

'So how's my sweetheart?' she said, laying her head against the pony's smooth neck and feeling Faith nuzzle her hair. 'She's looking even better than the last time I saw her,' she added to Jill, patting Faith's glossy coat. 'Do you think she's up for this, though?'

'You'll have to see how it goes,' Jill said, 'but I don't see why not. My friend Bev took her out quite a lot last week, so I think she's quite fit.'

'I'm just so grateful to both of you,' Josie said again as Mrs Atterbury came over to join them. 'At least now we feel as though we're doing something.'

'I told you – we're glad to help,' Jill's mother replied. 'And you and Faith must be the perfect team to go out looking for Charity.'

'Come on, then,' Anna said, beginning to unbuckle Faith's travelling boots. 'Time you got a move on.'

Soon Faith was tacked up and Josie was fastening her riding helmet. Lynne and Mrs Atterbury talked quietly together by the trailer while Ben, Anna and Jill stood around the mounting block. 'Do you really think this is going to do any good?' Josie asked them, suddenly suffering a last-minute attack of doubts, now that she was finally about to set off. 'I mean, think of all the police out searching already. If they haven't found them, do you think I've got much chance?'

'Yes,' Ben said firmly, holding on to the offside stirrup as Josie pulled herself up into the saddle. 'You've got one big advantage – you know Kirsty. Try and put yourself in her shoes. Where would you have gone, if you were her? That's what we've tried to work out, isn't it?'

The three of them had thought back over all the

344

times Kirsty had gone out hacking, and which routes she had taken. 'The spinney it is, then,' Josie said, shortening her reins. There was a little wood at the top of a hill on one of their favourite rides. It was full of dens and natural shelters, formed by the thickly growing trees, and they'd decided there was a good chance Kirsty might have gone there. 'If there's no sign of them, I'll follow Mum's path along the river and search the fields that way,' Josie went on. 'Anyway, I'll keep in touch by phone.'

'I feel quite jealous now,' Anna said enviously, rubbing Faith's nose. 'It must feel great to be doing something constructive instead of just sitting here, waiting.'

'Yes, it does,' Josie admitted, surprised how much her spirits had risen. 'It's lovely to be riding Faith again, for one thing. If we were just out for a hack, it would be perfect.'

'Well, keep that for next time,' Jill added. 'Be careful, though, won't you? We can't imagine life without Faith now.'

'Don't worry,' Josie called as she rode out of the yard. 'We'll be back safe and sound!' *And maybe Charity will be with us*, she couldn't help adding to herself.

'Come on, now, Faith,' Josie said as they trotted up the hill to the spinney. 'We've got a job to do!' Kirsty had often ridden Charity this way before. Mrs Grace would take her pupils up the hill, through the wood and then down to the river and back across the fields. It made a perfect hour-long hack.

Josie shivered as she peered into the trees on either side of the narrow path, wondering how Kirsty had spent her second night out in the open. *Please let me find them*, she prayed to herself. *And please let them be safe and well.*

'Kirsty! Charity!' she called softly, wondering whether Kirsty wanted to be found by now, or whether she'd try to run if she saw someone coming. There was no reply: only a flurry of wings as a couple of startled pigeons flew up from the undergrowth. Josie could tell there was no one in the wood but herself.

She reined Faith to a halt in the lane beyond the wood, and reached round for the mobile phone in the rucksack on her back. 'No sign of her in the spinney,' she told Lynne. 'I'll try down by the river.'

'How's Faith doing?' Lynne asked. 'Jill wants to know how she is.'

'Oh, fine,' Josie said affectionately, giving the pony's withers a scratch. 'It's funny, but I think she can tell something's up. She seems to know we're not out here just for fun.' It was true – Faith had been walking along alertly, her head held high and her ears flicking back and forth. Perhaps some of the urgency Josie felt was being transmitted to her.

'You'd like to go down by the river, wouldn't you, Faith?' Josie said as they set off again, this time along the bridle path. She looked around constantly, straining to catch a glimpse of anything unusual, but was always disappointed. Except for a couple of police cars that passed her in the lane, everything was quiet. There had been several officers in the village and yet more with tracker dogs searching the fields immediately around it, but no one seemed to be looking out this way.

Josie rode Faith down through the water meadow until they reached the river, and then tried to turn her left, following the route Mrs Grace usually took with her pupils. To her surprise, though, Faith wouldn't move. She planted her feet firmly on the ground and stood there, throwing her head up in the air and swishing her tail as Josie pulled on the left rein.

'Faith!' Josie said, astonished. 'What are you doing?' She simply couldn't understand it. Faith had never been a naughty pony – she'd always done as she was told. What on earth was she behaving like this for? She kicked more firmly with her right leg, but Faith still wouldn't move. She threw up her head again and then took off to the right, so suddenly that Josie nearly fell off, trotting quickly along the river path in the other direction.

Josie's first instinct was to try and make Faith turn back the way she'd first asked her to go, but something about the pony's sense of purpose made her think again.

There was an urgency in her pace that reminded Josie of Basil when he had caught the scent of a rabbit.

'Oh well,' she said to Faith, 'you've got as much chance of finding them as I have, I suppose.' She was puzzled, though – this stretch of the river took them past the boathouse and, as far as she knew, Kirsty had never come this way.

And yet ... the boathouse! Wouldn't that be the perfect place to come if you needed somewhere to hide? It was secluded, for one thing – hardly anyone knew where it was or walked along that stretch of the river. The building was half falling down, but it would offer some shelter from the rain and wind and no one could see into it from the river. The more Josie thought, the more convinced she became that the boathouse was definitely worth a look.

'Oh, well done, Faith!' she said, stroking her satiny neck. 'You are a clever old thing!' The pony blew down her nose, trotted even faster and, before Josie knew it, they were cantering along the path. She laughed, and let Faith have her head.

Before long, the boathouse had come into sight, and Josie felt her heart lurch as she caught sight of its rotting timbers. Could Kirsty and Charity really be hiding there? It was such a forbidding, desolate place. Faith slowed to a bumpy trot and then a walk. Josie gave her a pat as they approached, to comfort herself with the feel of the pony's warm, smooth skin as much as anything.

There were no clues to be seen from the outside. Josie slipped her feet out of the stirrups and lightly jumped down. Quickly, she took off Faith's bridle, slipped on the head collar and tied her to a fence post by the side of the path. 'I won't be long,' she said quietly. Then she stealthily approached the building for a closer look. The door was propped half-open, revealing a glimpse of the dark rooms inside. Josie shivered, not exactly eager to venture in, and decided to take a proper look round the outside to see if there was any sign of life.

Faith seemed to be watching Josie anxiously as she crept round to the ruined side of the building. Being careful where she put her feet, she made her way cautiously towards the open courtyard. And there, tied to a window frame in the far corner, was Charity.

Nine

'Charity!' Josie shouted, quite forgetting to be quiet and rushing over to fling her arms round the pony's neck. 'You're here! I've found you!' She smothered her with kisses, while Charity pushed her head into Josie's shoulder and nickered in welcome. Drawing back, Josie looked her quickly over to see what kind of state she was in. Her coat was dirty, but her eyes were bright and she seemed to be in fairly good shape. She was wearing a head collar, and her saddle and bridle were tucked in a sheltered corner near by.

'Oh, thank goodness,' Josie sighed, laying her head against Charity's neck. The two of them stood quietly together for a moment, then Josie took off the rucksack and began to search for the pony nuts. 'Here you are, girl. This'll keep you going for a bit,' she said, holding a handful out flat on her palm. 'We'll soon have you home!' Charity blew down her nose and crunched them up eagerly.

'Now for Kirsty,' Josie said, turning to look at the other half of the boathouse. 'She must be in there somewhere!'

Leaving Charity tied to the wall, she went back round to the front and peered through the open doorway. 'Kirsty!' she called softly. 'I know you're here. It's me, Josie! Don't be afraid.'

But there was no reply. Summoning up her courage, Josie walked over the uneven threshold, round the half-open door and into the room. She'd never been particularly frightened when she'd come here with Anna and Ben, but this time she was all on her own, and she had no idea what she'd find. Kirsty might be hurt, and she would certainly be scared and upset.

Josie stared round the room, but she could tell at a glance it was empty. There were no possible hiding places. 'Kirsty,' she called again nervously, walking on towards the doorway into the back room. 'Don't worry! I've come to help you.'

This door was shut. There was nothing Josie would sooner have done than simply walk away from it and take Charity home, but she knew she had to go on. Kirsty might be on the other side of the door, and she might be in trouble. Telling herself to be brave, Josie pushed the door open, her heart thumping. This room, too, was bare. There was no sign of life – only the bench and the rotting lifejacket underneath it met her gaze. Beside the lifejacket, however, was a strange-looking blue plastic object. Josie walked over and picked it up, trying to work out what on earth it could be. And then she remembered where she'd seen something similar. A boy at her school had once had an asthma attack after gym, and he'd used one of these to help him breathe. It was an inhaler. Kirsty's inhaler – it had to be! So where was she?

Josie stared out of the window above the bench, hardly daring to imagine what she might find. She caught a flurry of movement out of the corner of one eye – a wisp of blonde hair and a flash of pale skin. Her heart began to pound wildly as she rushed towards the door leading out to the verandah. Kirsty wouldn't have gone out there, would she? It was so unsafe! Surely she couldn't be so stupid!

But she had. Josie couldn't believe her eyes as she looked through the big hole in the doorframe where once there had been glass. There was Kirsty, huddled against the wooden railings of the verandah and staring back at her with terrified eyes.

'Don't worry, Kirsty!' Josie called in a shaking voice. 'It's only me. I won't hurt you!'

'Don't come out here!' Kirsty cried. 'Leave me alone!' She was obviously frightened out of her wits.

Josie tried to think of what she could say to reassure her. She cleared her throat and licked her dry lips. 'But I can't leave you here, Kirsty,' she said soothingly. 'Why don't we go home together? Faith's here – I've tied her up outside. You can ride Charity back, if you like.'

Kirsty didn't reply. Slowly, Josie began to push the door further open. 'No one's cross with you,' she went on. 'We're all just very worried. Your mum's desperate to know where you are.'

Kirsty's lower lip began to tremble, and Josie could see she was close to tears. *Poor thing*, she thought to herself. *She's backed herself into a corner and she doesn't know how to get out of it*. 'You've looked after Charity very well,' she said gently. 'But now it's time to take her home.'

'I didn't mean to upset anyone,' Kirsty gasped, the tears beginning to spill over on to her cheeks. 'I did it for you, Josie! I thought you'd be pleased with me.'

'It doesn't matter now,' Josie said. She gave the door a final push and prepared to step out on to the verandah – but when she looked down at it, her blood froze. The whole thing was even more unstable than she'd first thought. There were huge gaps in the rotten floorboards and the rickety structure was swaying alarmingly. If she put her weight on it too, the verandah would almost certainly collapse. Kirsty would have to get off it on her own.

'Come over to me, Kirsty,' she said. 'But you'll have to move very slowly. Do you understand? Take it gently – no sudden movements.'

Kirsty looked around as though she had absolutely no idea where she was. She must have rushed out to the verandah without thinking, in her anxiety to hide. When she saw the danger she was in, her eyes widened at once and she dropped to a sitting position.

'It's all right,' Josie said as calmly as she could, though the sight of the verandah shaking as Kirsty moved terrified her. 'You can shuffle over on your bottom, if you like. Just come to me.' And she stretched out her arms.

'Josie! I'm frightened,' Kirsty said in a quavering voice. There was a tight, wheezing sound coming from her chest as she spoke, and she seemed to be having trouble breathing.

'Don't worry, Kirsty. You'll be fine,' Josie replied, trying not to show her own fear. 'Come on – it's not far!'

Kirsty just shook her head, though. She had gone as white as a sheet, and her eyes were fixed and staring. 'Can't – breathe!' she said painfully, her arms wrapped round her chest.

Josie's mind raced. Then she remembered what she was still holding tightly in her sweating hand. 'Look, I've got your inhaler,' she said. 'I'll throw it across to you. When it lands, don't grab it – just reach for it very slowly. OK?'

Kirsty nodded, her eyes still locked on to Josie's. 'Here it comes,' Josie said, her heart in her mouth. Carefully, she took aim and lobbed the inhaler so that it landed about half a metre from Kirsty's hand. Just a little too short.

'Reach for it slowly, remember,' Josie said, trying not to show her concern. 'No sudden movements.'

Kirsty nodded and shuffled forward. The verandah lurched. She stretched out a trembling hand and took her gaze away from Josie just long enough to grab the inhaler and put it into her mouth. The look of panic left her eyes and her shoulders relaxed as she breathed the medication in.

'That's better, isn't it?' Josie said, forcing herself to smile. 'Now let's get you off this verandah. Stay sitting down, and come towards me. That's the way!' *As soon as she's inside, I can ring for help*, she decided to herself. She felt that if she took her eyes off Kirsty for a second, the terrified girl would lose her head completely.

Inch by agonising inch, Kirsty struggled closer. Josie's nails were digging into her palms and her jaw was aching with the effort of smiling. And then suddenly, the inhaler slipped out of Kirsty's grasp.

'No!' she cried, leaning quickly forward to grab for it. With a terrible, blood-curdling crash, the rotten wood on which she was sitting gave way, and she plunged through the floor.

'Josie! Help me!' she screamed, desperately clinging on to the edge of the gaping hole. Her head and shoulders were visible, and her arms were scrabbling at the splintering wood, but the rest of her must have been hanging in mid-air above the swirling river.

'I'm coming!' Josie cried. There was no time to think. Quickly, she threw off the rucksack and, dropping to her knees, stretched full length on her stomach across the unstable verandah floor. 'Take my hand!' she shouted urgently.

'I can't!' Kirsty shouted, desperately trying to reach Josie's outstretched fingers. 'I'm slipping!'

Another section of wood began to crack as Kirsty struggled to hold on. Despite all her desperate efforts, however, she began to slide further down. And after seconds which seemed to last hours, she finally lost her grip and vanished from sight.

There was a scream, a splash – and then, nothing.

Josie could tell the whole verandah was about to give way at any moment. Quickly, she wriggled back on her stomach to the door as several more floorboards fell

away, and dived inside the boathouse. She rushed over
to the window. At first, she couldn't see anything in the
river below, but then she suddenly caught sight of
Kirsty's blonde hair swirling out in a cloud on the water.
She had managed to catch hold of an upright post with
a mooring ring attached to it.

'Help!' Kirsty screamed. There was a very strong
current in the river at this point, and she was having to
fight to hold on to the ring.

'Hang on!' Josie shouted. She picked up the lifejacket
to throw it out of the window, but the crumbling
material fell to pieces in her hands. Her heart thumping,
she rushed out of the boathouse and flung herself down
the bank to reach the river's edge. She waded into the
water, hardly noticing how cold it was. 'I'm coming!'
she shouted again to Kirsty as she struggled out towards
her.

But Josie found it almost impossible to make any
headway at all. The current was against her, and every
step forward was a huge effort. Trying to swim was no
better, and she felt herself powerless against the force
of the river. She was now out of her depth and quickly
becoming exhausted. Kirsty wasn't very far out, but
there seemed no way she could reach her. At this rate,
they would both drown.

And then, suddenly, Josie heard another splash.
Turning round, she saw a flash of white and realised, to

her amazement, that Charity was swimming towards her. The pony's eyes were rolling as she struggled to keep her head above water, while, beneath the surface, she threw out her long legs steadily.

'Charity!' Josie exclaimed. She couldn't believe that her wonderful pony had managed to free herself and come out to rescue them, but here she was. And in the nick of time, too. Josie sobbed with relief as Charity swam nearer and she felt her solid, reassuring presence next to her in the river. She flung out one arm and grasped a handful of her mane, feeling the current force her back against Charity's strong neck. And then she caught sight of the nylon lead rope, trailing out from her head collar. If they could just swim out a little

further, maybe she could throw it to Kirsty.

'Kirsty! Charity's here!' she called over. 'She's come to help us.' She saw to her alarm that Kirsty was tiring, too. She only just managed to turn her head in their direction.

'Come on, Charity!' Josie urged. 'You can do it.' The pony's breath was coming in great gasps as she struggled with all her strength against the surging water. Slowly but surely, though, they were moving forward. Seconds later, Josie judged they were near enough for the rope to be within Kirsty's grasp.

'Catch this!' she shouted loudly, and hurled the end of the lead rope towards her. It floated tantalisingly close by, but Kirsty was obviously terrified of letting go of the post and being carried off by the current.

'Take it!' Josie screamed, hanging on to Charity's head collar to keep herself afloat. 'It's your only chance!'

With one last look at Charity, Kirsty seemed to summon up all her courage. Still holding on to the ring, she managed to grab the rope with one hand. Then, closing her eyes and gritting her teeth, she let go of the post altogether, launched herself into the water and grasped the rope with both hands.

'Yes!' Josie shouted. 'Now hold on – we'll get you back.'

Charity wheeled around, her legs thrashing, and swam strongly towards the riverbank. She seemed to know exactly what to do. It was much easier going back this way, for the current was behind them. Anxiously, Josie looked back. Kirsty's head kept sinking under the water, but she was still hanging on to the strong nylon rope with all her might.

Soon Josie could feel solid ground beneath her feet and, a few seconds later, she was able to put her arms round Kirsty and lift up her head. Coughing and spluttering, they staggered out of the water together and collapsed on the riverbank.

'Charity saved me,' Kirsty gasped, when she was able to speak.

'Yes,' Josie answered as she got her breath back. Her heart overflowed with love and pride as she looked at the exhausted pony standing on the bank next to them. 'Sweet Charity. She saved us both.'

Ten

'Will you be OK if I go to the boathouse?' Josie asked Kirsty, as they tried to recover, sitting on the grass. 'I left my rucksack there, and the telephone's inside it.'

Kirsty nodded, so Josie staggered to her feet and went off to ring for help. Charity was obviously tired – she could see that as she went past – but she was up on her feet. And at least now they weren't in any immediate danger.

Josie retrieved the rucksack from the floor of the back room where she'd tossed it aside what seemed like hours earlier, and dug out the phone. Should she ring the police straight away, or School Farm? Feeling a

361

sudden need to talk to her parents, she decided to phone home. 'Mum! I've found Charity, and Kirsty too,' she said breathlessly, so relieved to hear her mother's voice on the line that her legs suddenly weakened underneath her.

'How are they? Is everything OK? Where are you?' Mrs Grace replied urgently.

Josie slid into a sitting position against the wall. 'We're at the boathouse,' she said. 'We're all right, but I think Kirsty needs to see a doctor quite quickly. She's lost her inhaler and I'm worried she's going to have an asthma attack. We're both wet through.'

'Wet through?' Mrs Grace repeated. 'What on earth have you been doing?'

'I'll explain later,' Josie replied wearily. 'Please, Mum, can you get help as soon as possible?'

'Of course,' Mrs Grace replied seriously. 'Just stay where you are. Got that? Don't move!'

Josie made her way back to where Kirsty was sitting on the riverbank. She flopped back down beside her and rummaged in the rucksack for the glucose tablets and flask. 'Help yourself,' she said, offering them to Kirsty. 'I've rung the stables. Someone will be coming to get us soon.'

'My mother's going to be really angry with me,' Kirsty said anxiously. She took a couple of glucose tablets and washed them down with several mouthfuls from the flask, before passing it back to Josie. 'I'm sorry that I've caused everyone so much trouble.'

'Oh, it's all right,' Josie replied. 'I bet your mother will be so pleased to see you she won't be angry at all. But why did you do it, Kirsty? You couldn't have stayed out here forever.'

'I know,' Kirsty sighed. 'I just couldn't let Charity be taken away from you and sold to some stranger. I thought if we hid for a while, your parents might change their minds and let you keep her.'

'But they don't want to sell Charity any more than I do!' Josie said. 'We've just got to – there's no way round it. And you stealing her wasn't ever going to make any difference.'

'I wasn't stealing her!' Kirsty cried, looking horrified at the suggestion. 'I was keeping her for you, Josie. I thought you'd be pleased with me!'

'Oh, Kirsty,' Josie said, 'that's not the way to go about things. Look at the trouble you got into! I'd never have come to the boathouse if it hadn't been for Faith, and you might not have been found for days.'

'What do you mean?' Kirsty asked curiously. 'What did Faith have to do with it?'

'Well, somehow she knew where you and Charity were,' Josie replied. 'I only came out here because she wanted to come this way. It's such a dangerous place. What if you'd fallen into the water when no one was around? And we probably both would have drowned if it hadn't been for Charity.'

'They've been amazing,' Kirsty said, looking over to where the two ponies were standing, peacefully grazing on the long grass at the edge of the path. Charity had caught sight of Faith, tied to the fence post, and trotted up to greet her with several nuzzles and playful nips.

'I don't understand how Charity managed to get out to us in the river, though,' Kirsty went on. 'I'm sure she was tied up properly. I used that special knot you showed me once.'

'A quick release knot?' Josie asked, smiling. 'Well, those are Charity's speciality. She pulls the loose end of the rope with her teeth, and the knot's undone in three seconds flat.'

'I've never met a pony like her,' Kirsty said. 'Your parents just can't sell her now, Josie! Not after she saved us.'

Josie lay back on the grass and closed her eyes, too tired to waste any more time trying to explain. Dimly she became aware of the sound of car engines, gradually growing louder. Sitting up, she and Kirsty saw two police cars bumping their way towards them over the uneven ground along the riverbank. When the path narrowed, they were forced to stop. The passenger door of the first car was flung open, and a woman came running over the grass. 'Kirsty!' she shouted, tears streaming down her face. It was Mrs Fisher, and Josie could see at once that Kirsty had nothing to worry about. She wasn't about to get a telling-off.

'You were so brave!' Anna said admiringly. She was sitting on the end of the sofa at Josie's feet, listening to the whole story all over again. Lynne and Ben had gone home, but Anna couldn't tear herself away. 'Wasn't it incredible that Faith knew where they were?' she added. 'And that Charity went into the river after you?'

Josie nodded. 'I wouldn't be here now if it wasn't for her,' she said.

'Charity seems to be fine,' Mr Grace announced, coming into the sitting room with some cartons of juice and a plate of sandwiches. 'Mum's given her a hot bran mash, and she's tucking in.'

Kirsty had been taken to hospital with her mother for a thorough check over. Mary Grace had come in the second police car with Ben and Anna, so Josie was taken back home by car with her mother, wrapped in a rug. The twins had ridden the ponies back to School Farm, where the Atterburys were waiting to take Faith home in the trailer. Charity was now recovering in her loose box.

'I suppose we'd better tell the Taylors she's here,' Josie said, leaning back against the cushions. 'They're meant to be picking her up tomorrow, aren't they?' She didn't want to think about how painful that was going to be. Still, at least now she knew Charity was safe and well.

'Well,' Mr Grace said, sitting on the edge of the sofa, 'we've actually put the Taylors on hold for the moment.'

'On hold?' Josie repeated, looking at her father curiously. 'What do you mean?'

'I think I've found somewhere that might suit Charity better,' Mr Grace replied. 'Nothing's definite yet, but I've asked the Taylors to give us a little more time before they come for her.'

'But you're moving the day after tomorrow, aren't you?' Anna said. 'There isn't much time left!'

'And what is this place?' Josie asked. 'I thought we'd agreed the Taylors could give her the best home we were going to get.'

'Nearly the best home,' her father said mysteriously, getting up to leave the room. 'But not quite.'

'Dad!' Josie said indignantly. 'Aren't you going to tell me any more than that?'

'There's not much more I can say at the moment,' Mr Grace replied. 'Don't worry about anything, love – I'll let you know the minute it's all sorted out.'

Josie and Anna exchanged looks. 'Well, something's going on, that's for sure!' Josie said. 'Dad's still wearing a suit, for one thing, and I wonder why he had to go to that meeting this morning?'

'Curiouser and curiouser,' Anna said. 'I hate it when parents know something and you don't. Maybe you can try and get the information out of your mum.'

'Yes, maybe,' Josie replied. But when she cornered Mrs Grace in the kitchen after Anna had gone home, her mother was just as tight-lipped.

'This is your father's idea,' she said. 'He hasn't told me the full story either. Just keeps saying we've got to trust him and we'll find out everything tomorrow.'

'But tomorrow we're moving!' Josie wailed. 'This is all so last-minute!'

'You're telling me!' her mother replied. 'All this business with Kirsty has really set me back. I'm never going to get all the packing finished!'

'Have you heard how Kirsty is?' Josie asked.

'Yes, I rang the hospital last night, when you'd gone to bed,' Mrs Grace replied. 'They were just keeping her in overnight to be on the safe side, but she doesn't seem to have come to any harm.'

'Good,' Josie said. 'I know Anna thinks I'm mad, but I still can't help feeling a bit sorry for her. I wonder if the new owners would let her come and ride Charity sometimes?'

'Well, that would be up to them,' her mother replied. 'Whoever it is that ends up having Charity.'

'So, have you got anywhere with solving the mystery?'

Anna said as soon as she saw Josie the next day. She'd come up to share the last afternoon they would spend together at School Farm, and found Josie in Charity's loose box.

'No, I haven't,' Josie replied crossly. 'Mum says Dad hasn't told her everything, but I'm sure she knows more than I do. Why won't they tell me what's going on? I've got a right to know, after all.' She was trying to soothe her feelings by giving Charity a full groom but, so far, it wasn't working.

'Why don't we plait Charity's mane and tail?' Anna suggested. 'That's the fiddly sort of job that'll take your mind off things, and she looks so lovely when it's done. I'll do the mane – you know I'm hopeless with her tail.'

'All right,' Josie said, rather gracelessly. 'Might as well, I suppose. It'll keep us out of the house. Dad's disappeared somewhere, as usual, and Mum keeps unpacking boxes and then packing them again. It's a nightmare.'

For a while, they worked together quietly, not talking much. 'I can't believe Charity's going to be sent off tomorrow, and we don't even know where,' Anna said eventually. 'After everything that's happened!'

'You're beginning to sound like Kirsty,' Josie said. 'I told her, what Charity did yesterday doesn't make any difference to the fact that we haven't got enough money to keep her.'

'It's so sad,' Anna sighed as she snapped an elastic band round one sleek white plait. 'D'you know, this morning I rang the estate agent and found out who owns that field behind the house. It belongs to a local farmer. I phoned him at lunchtime but he says someone else has asked him to keep a space for a pony in the field, so he wouldn't have room for Charity anyway.'

'Well, it was nice of you to try,' Josie said resignedly. 'We couldn't have afforded it, though. I'm afraid it's too late to try and change things, Anna.'

Charity spent her last night at School Farm in the loose box, so the Graces didn't have to worry about catching her in the morning. Josie was up and dressed the next day before either of her parents. There was a terrible sinking feeling in the pit of her stomach as she watched her father eat his way through a mountain of toast, then wash the plate and pack it with the others in the tea chest. He seemed to be quite unconcerned. When Josie caught his eye, he even smiled at her. How could he?

'Oh, the post should have arrived by now,' he said, looking at his watch. 'Just think, it's the last delivery we'll have here. Josie, be a love and go and check the mailbox, will you?'

'OK,' she replied, glad of something to do. Basil followed her as she wandered out of the house, through the yard and down the drive. All the commotion was making him nervous, and he obviously felt he couldn't let anyone out of his sight for a second, in case he was left behind. She opened the rusty letterbox flap and took out a horse feed catalogue for her mother and a letter for her father.

'That's the one!' he said when she brought it back, tearing the envelope open. 'Great! I've been waiting for this.' And he read the letter with a look of great satisfaction that made Josie feel even more irritated.

'Just a couple of phone calls to make before we're cut off,' he said when he'd finished, rubbing his hands and hurrying out of the kitchen. 'Mary! Where are you? I need a word!'

Fifteen minutes later, he was back. 'Right, Josie,' he said. 'If you and your mother could just load Charity into the trailer, we can take her off to her new home. We'd better bring her tack, too.'

'Dad!' Josie burst out. 'You've *got* to tell me where you're taking her. Why are you being so secretive?'

'Don't worry, love,' he replied. 'You'll know everything soon. I want you to come with me. I'd rather not have to unload Charity on my own, and Mum has to stay here for the removal men.'

'Oh,' Josie said, taken aback. She didn't know if she was quite up to being there when Charity was handed over – it had been hard enough seeing Emily Taylor riding her. But, on the other hand, it seemed as if it was going to be the only way she was going to find out more about this new home.

'Go on, love,' her mother said, appearing in the kitchen with the vacuum cleaner in one hand and a black dustbin bag in the other. 'It's not far, and Dad needs you with him.'

'OK,' Josie said mechanically. So this was it. She'd just have to prepare herself for the worst.

She put on Charity's travelling boots and her tail guard, then led her out of her loose box for the last time and up the ramp into the trailer. 'Say goodbye to School Farm, Charity,' Robert Grace said cheerfully, fastening the bolts behind her. Josie shot him a suspicious look, but there was obviously no point asking any more questions. She would have to wait to find out.

They drove through the town of Littlehaven and kept going on the main road out of it. 'We'll be coming to Lime Tree Lodge in a minute,' Josie remarked, feeling somehow consoled by the thought. Maybe Charity wouldn't be too far away, and she could go and visit her sometimes.

'Yes, we will, and as it happens I just have to call in there,' Mr Grace replied. Soon he was turning off the main road and driving through the big iron gates. But he carried on past the cottage and started up the long drive that led to the housing estate. He pulled in opposite the gate to the field that backed on to Lime Tree Lodge.

'Why have you stopped here?' Josie asked, as her father turned off the engine.

'So we can settle Charity in her new home,' he said. 'What are you sitting there for, Josie? I told you, I can't manage on my own.'

'But – but I can't believe it!' Josie stammered. 'This is *our* new home! What are you saying? Come on, Dad, put me out of my misery!'

'I'm saying,' he answered, grinning from ear to ear, 'that you can keep her!'

Josie launched herself across the seats to give her father a big hug. 'But I still don't understand!' she said, drawing back for a second.

'Well,' said Mr Grace, disentangling himself from Josie's grip. 'I rang the Taylors this morning to let them know that our circumstances have changed. And to apologise. They were really nice about it, though.'

'But how have our circumstances changed?' Josie said. She couldn't believe what she was hearing. Such wonderful, incredible, fantastic news would take time to sink in.

'Because your father is now Head of the English and Drama Department at Littlehaven High,' Mr Grace answered, looking very pleased with himself. 'That's what my letter confirmed this morning. I didn't want to say anything until I knew for certain. The post suddenly became vacant because my colleague who's been doing it for years announced he was going back to New Zealand. The Head wanted to appoint a replacement before September, so I had an interview on Monday. I got the job, and quite a lot more money to go with it!'

'Oh, Dad!' Josie said, hugging him even more ferociously. 'That's fantastic! Thank you so, so much. Our new home is going to be just perfect now Charity can share it with us!' And then she couldn't say any more, because all the excitement and fear and suspense of the last few months and days was dissolving in a great wave of happiness.

'Come on, love,' her father said gently. 'Let's get this pony into the field before she thinks we've forgotten about her.'

'OK!' Josie replied, swallowing her tears of joy and relief. 'My own sweet Charity. Now nothing's going to take her away from me!'

DOG IN THE DUNGEON
Animal Ark Hauntings 1

Lucy Daniels

Mandy and James will do anything to help an animal in distress. And sometimes even ghostly animals appear to need their help . . .

Skelton Castle has always had a faithful deerhound to protect its family and grounds. But Aminta, the last of the line, died a short while ago. So when Mandy and James explore the creepy castle the last thing they expect to see is a deerhound – especially one which looks uncannily like Aminta . . . Could it possibly be her? And what does she want with Mandy and James?

h HODDER   *Another Hodder Children's book*

CAT IN THE CRYPT
Animal Ark Hauntings 2

Lucy Daniels

Mandy and James will do anything to help an animal in distress. And sometimes even ghostly animals appear to need their help . . .

Mandy is haunted by dreams of a mysterious cat. Could it be because she is worried about Bathsheba, the vicarage tabby who has run away? Or does the strange, stone-coloured cat of her dreams have something to tell her?

Another Hodder Children's book

STALLION IN THE STORM
Animal Ark Hauntings 3

Lucy Daniels

Mandy and James will do anything to help an animal in distress. And sometimes even ghostly animals appear to need their help . . .

Mandy and James can hardly wait to accompany her dad to Folan's Racing Stables. But they find that Folan's is in trouble. Some of the jockeys believe it's because the stables are haunted by Tibor, one of their stallions, who died in a race. Can Mandy and James discover the truth – and help Tibor make his peace?

ANIMAL ARK *by Lucy Daniels*

1	KITTENS IN THE KITCHEN	£3.99	❐
2	PONY IN THE PORCH	£3.99	❐
3	PUPPIES IN THE PANTRY	£3.99	❐
4	GOAT IN THE GARDEN	£3.99	❐
5	HEDGEHOGS IN THE HALL	£3.99	❐
6	BADGER IN THE BASEMENT	£3.99	❐
7	CUB IN THE CUPBOARD	£3.99	❐
8	PIGLET IN A PLAYPEN	£3.99	❐
9	OWL IN THE OFFICE	£3.99	❐
10	LAMB IN THE LAUNDRY	£3.99	❐
11	BUNNIES IN THE BATHROOM	£3.99	❐
12	DONKEY ON THE DOORSTEP	£3.99	❐
13	HAMSTER IN A HAMPER	£3.99	❐
14	GOOSE ON THE LOOSE	£3.99	❐
15	CALF IN THE COTTAGE	£3.99	❐
16	KOALA IN A CRISIS	£3.99	❐
17	WOMBAT IN THE WILD	£3.99	❐
18	ROO ON THE ROCK	£3.99	❐
19	SQUIRRELS IN THE SCHOOL	£3.99	❐
20	GUINEA-PIG IN THE GARAGE	£3.99	❐
21	FAWN IN THE FOREST	£3.99	❐
22	SHETLAND IN THE SHED	£3.99	❐
23	SWAN IN THE SWIM	£3.99	❐
24	LION BY THE LAKE	£3.99	❐
25	ELEPHANTS IN THE EAST	£3.99	❐
26	MONKEYS ON THE MOUNTAIN	£3.99	❐
27	DOG AT THE DOOR	£3.99	❐
28	FOALS IN THE FIELD	£3.99	❐
29	SHEEP AT THE SHOW	£3.99	❐
30	RACOONS ON THE ROOF	£3.99	❐
31	DOLPHIN IN THE DEEP	£3.99	❐
32	BEARS IN THE BARN	£3.99	❐
33	OTTER IN THE OUTHOUSE	£3.99	❐
34	WHALE IN THE WAVES	£3.99	❐
35	HOUND AT THE HOSPITAL	£3.99	❐
36	RABBITS ON THE RUN	£3.99	❐
37	HORSE IN THE HOUSE	£3.99	❐
38	PANDA IN THE PARK	£3.99	❐
39	TIGER ON THE TRACK	£3.99	❐
40	GORILLA IN THE GLADE	£3.99	❐
41	TABBY IN THE TUB	£3.99	❐
	SHEEPDOG IN THE SNOW	£3.99	❐
	KITTEN IN THE COLD	£3.99	❐
	FOX IN THE FROST	£3.99	❐
	HAMSTER IN THE HOLLY	£3.99	❐
	PONIES AT THE POINT	£3.99	❐
	SEAL ON THE SHORE	£3.99	❐
	ANIMAL ARK FAVOURITES	£3.99	❐
	PIGS AT THE PICNIC	£3.99	❐
	DOG IN THE DUNGEON	£3.99	❐
	CAT IN THE CRYPT	£3.99	❐
	STALLION IN THE STORM	£3.99	❐

All Hodder Children's books are available at your local bookshop, or can be ordered direct from the publisher. Just tick the titles you would like and complete the details below. Prices and availability are subject to change without prior notice.

Please enclose a cheque or postal order made payable to *Bookpoint Ltd*, and send to: Hodder Children's Books, 39 Milton Park, Abingdon, OXON OX14 4TD, UK. Email Address: orders@bookpoint.co.uk

If you would prefer to pay by credit card, our call centre team would be delighted to take your order by telephone. Our direct line *01235 400414* (lines open 9.00 am–6.00 pm Monday to Saturday, 24 hour message answering service). Alternatively you can send a fax on *01235 400454*.

TITLE	FIRST NAME	SURNAME

ADDRESS

DAYTIME TEL:	POST CODE

If you would prefer to pay by credit card, please complete: Please debit my Visa/Access/Diner's Card/American Express (delete as applicable) card no:

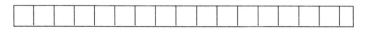

Signature ....
Expiry Date: ....

If you would NOT like to receive further information on our products please tick the box. ❐